Praise for
Kay Hooper

"Kay Hooper writes a wonderful blend of wit, whimsy, and sensuality . . . She is a master of her art."

—Linda Howard

"A multi-talented author whose stories always pack a tremendous punch." —Iris Johansen

"Kay Hooper's dialogue rings true; her characters are more three-dimensional than those usually found in this genre." —*The Atlanta Journal-Constitution*

"Kay Hooper is a master at painting the most vivid pictures with words!" —*The Best Reviews*

"Not to be missed." —*All About Romance*

Kay Hooper

The Haviland Touch

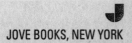
JOVE BOOKS, NEW YORK

THE BERKLEY PUBLISHING GROUP
Published by the Penguin Group
Penguin Group (USA) Inc.
375 Hudson Street, New York, New York 10014, USA
Penguin Group (Canada), 90 Eglinton Avenue East, Suite 700, Toronto, Ontario M4P 2Y3, Canada
(a division of Pearson Penguin Canada Inc.)
Penguin Books Ltd., 80 Strand, London WC2R 0RL, England
Penguin Group Ireland, 25 St. Stephen's Green, Dublin 2, Ireland (a division of Penguin Books Ltd.)
Penguin Group (Australia), 250 Camberwell Road, Camberwell, Victoria 3124, Australia
(a division of Pearson Australia Group Pty. Ltd.)
Penguin Books India Pvt. Ltd., 11 Community Centre, Panchsheel Park, New Delhi—110 017, India
Penguin Group (NZ), Cnr. Airborne and Rosedale Roads, Albany, Auckland 1310, New Zealand
(a division of Pearson New Zealand Ltd.)
Penguin Books (South Africa) (Pty.) Ltd., 24 Sturdee Avenue, Rosebank, Johannesburg 2196, South Africa

Penguin Books Ltd., Registered Offices: 80 Strand, London WC2R 0RL, England

This is a work of fiction. Names, characters, places, and incidents either are the product of the author's imagination or are used fictitiously, and any resemblance to actual persons, living or dead, business establishments, events, or locales is entirely coincidental. The publisher does not have any control over and does not assume any responsibility for author or third-party websites or their content.

THE HAVILAND TOUCH

A Jove Book / published by arrangement with the author.

PRINTING HISTORY
Published in 1991 by Silhouette Books
Included in *The Real Thing* published by Berkley Sensation November 2004
Jove mass market edition / December 2005

Copyright © 1991 by Kay Hooper.

Cover design by Rita Frangie.
Cover photo: "Couple Wearing Sunglasses, Running Down Street [B&W]" by Antonio Mo/Taxi/Getty Images.

ISBN: 0-515-14040-6

JOVE®
Jove Books are published by The Berkley Publishing Group,
a division of Penguin Group (USA) Inc.,
375 Hudson Street, New York, New York 10014.
JOVE is a registered trademark of Penguin Group (USA) Inc.
The "J" design is a trademark belonging to Penguin Group (USA) Inc.

PRINTED IN THE UNITED STATES OF AMERICA

10 9 8 7 6 5 4 3 2 1

The Haviland Touch

chapter one

THE MAN BEHIND the massive antique desk reached one elegant but curiously powerful hand into the chamois bag his visitor had just set before him and pulled out a heavy, ornate necklace. The instant light caught them, a half-dozen green stones threw shards of color in a glittering show of emerald fire.

"I told you it was something, didn't I? Thirty thousand, Haviland, and not a penny less."

Without commenting aloud, Drew Haviland produced a jeweler's lens and studied the necklace intently under the bright light of his desk lamp. The six large teardrop emeralds came under his scrutiny, as well as the numerous smaller diamonds and the craftsmanship of the gold work. Finally he raised his head, slipped the lens back into his pocket and looked at the other man. He was smiling slightly.

"Thirty thousand, Hanson?"

Hanson knew that smile, and his own was a bit uneasy. "You can't say it isn't worth it."

"Let me ask you," Drew said pleasantly. "Is it worth a decade or so in jail?"

"I *told* you it wasn't stolen, and it isn't," Hanson protested quickly.

The silence lengthened, and Drew's usually amused blue eyes were curiously flat as he stared across the desk at the other man. Finally he said in a very soft voice, "These are the Wyatt emeralds, Hanson."

A look of surprise crossed Hanson's face, swiftly followed by comprehension. "Hell," he muttered, "I'd forgotten that you'd probably know them."

"Yes, I know them."

Something about that level voice made Hanson rush on quickly, even nervously. "But not stolen, I swear. The—the lady came to me. She said she needed the money and couldn't sell the necklace on the open market. I didn't ask why."

Drew gazed at the chamois bag resting in the center of his neat blotter and asked mildly, "How much did you give her for it, Hanson?"

"That's not a fair question," Hanson muttered. He might have said more, but when those vivid, usually amused blue eyes lifted to meet his he decided not to bother. Several years' experience in dealing with the urbane and aristocratic Haviland had taught him that underneath that smooth exterior was an iron will, a rare but explosive temper and the kind of sheer physical strength it wasn't wise to provoke. Sighing, Hanson said, "Ten thousand."

"I'll give you fifteen."

"What? But—"

"That's five thousand for your trouble. And since your trouble consisted of hardly more than a few minutes' work, you shouldn't feel cheated."

"I could find another buyer."

"No, you couldn't." Drew smiled. "I'd see to that."

Hanson eyed him resentfully. "You would, too, damn you."

"Certainly I would. Is it a deal?"

"What choice do I have?"

Half an hour later, Drew stood at a large window of his study and stared out into the night. The room behind him was empty, the visitor having departed with fifteen thousand dollars in cash, and the chamois bag containing a costly necklace resting on the desk blotter. Drew hadn't looked at the necklace again after his first methodical examination, but if asked he could have described it in minute detail.

The Wyatt emeralds.

When had he first seen them? Eleven years ago? No, twelve. He couldn't even pretend to himself that he'd forgotten. It had been twelve years ago. The first time he had seen her. She had been a heartbreaker even then,

Miss Spencer Wyatt, barely sixteen years old and already a belle of Washington, D.C., society. Her mother's death the year before had pushed her early into the position of her father's hostess, and she had claimed that responsibility with a grace and poise far beyond her years.

Drew could still remember, with disturbing clarity, the sight of her at one end of the long dining table. The promise of great beauty had shone in her flawless complexion and delicate bone structure, in the wide-spaced gray eyes that held intelligence and humor as well as an unusual sweetness. Her shining raven hair had been swept up in a sophisticated style, she'd worn very little makeup, albeit expertly applied, and the green of her dress had complemented the emeralds perfectly. Her figure had been trim but girlishly plump; within the next two years the puppy fat had vanished, leaving seductively womanly curves on a petite and slender frame.

Washington society regarded her as a woman long before the law agreed, and considering her father's preoccupation with his own affairs, as well as his doting fondness of her, she might have been expected to run wild with a kind of freedom few teenagers in her position enjoyed. But she hadn't. She had clearly enjoyed the parties and other social events, yet had been at the top of her class in the private school she attended and had steadfastly refused to go out with any man other than her father alone until she turned eighteen.

Allan Wyatt was no one's idea of a stern father and,

in fact, openly and proudly said that Spencer ran her own life. He would have granted her far more freedom than she accepted, particularly since he was by nature an indulgent man and openly adored his only child. Spencer hadn't taken advantage, at least not in that way. Drew had believed then that her poised social mask had hidden an innate shyness; she had sometimes seemed a little nervous and wary in his company.

Innocence, he had thought. For all her surface confidence and polish, she had been a very young woman who'd had a fairly sheltered upbringing, and more than once Drew had seen a look almost of dismay in her eyes whenever some eager swain had showered her with compliments or tried to get her alone. She had seemed more comfortable when those around her adhered to at least the surface courtesy that convention demanded, as if she felt safer when the rules were plainly marked.

Staring out the window and blind to the night landscape of the gracious Washington suburb where he kept a house, Drew moved slightly, restlessly, a frown crossing his face as the memories refused to leave him alone.

Would it have all been different, he wondered, if he had not chosen to play by those rules? If he had followed his instincts? He'd wanted her from the first time he had set eyes on her, but she'd been too young then and he had known it. Two years of watching her, of feeding the hunger inside him with prosaic dinner-table conversations and sedate dances while he waited with what patience he could muster for her to grow up.

Apparently he waited too long. He could still remember, too vividly, his bitterness and anger, and pushed it aside with an effort. Ten years was a long time, he reminded himself. He was over that now, had been over it for years. He hadn't wasted a thought on Spencer Wyatt.

Drew turned away from the window and returned to his desk, sitting down in the chair and staring at the chamois bag on the blotter. Why had she sold the necklace? It had been in her family for generations, the famous Wyatt emeralds, and had been, he remembered reluctantly, a personal favorite of hers. With all the Wyatt jewelry hers after her mother's death, she'd had her pick of a number of exquisite pieces, but the emeralds had been most often around her slender throat.

It wasn't his business, of course. If she wanted to sell every jewel she owned, it was entirely up to her. But why not sell it on the open market? She could have gotten fifty thousand easily, and likely more. Selling privately to someone like Hanson made the whole thing look . . . secretive and desperate.

Drew told himself again that it was none of his concern, but he reached for his phone anyway. He made several calls but managed to get only a few sketchy bits of information in answer to his discreet inquiries, none of which indicated that the Wyatts might be having financial problems. Not that it meant anything; it was quite possible for a prominent family to be a whisper away from broke without any of their friends or acquaintances being aware of it. Many an old and proud family had drained the last of their resources just trying to keep up appearances.

The Wyatts could have been in that situation but, if so, certainly showed no signs of it. In fact, six months ago while Drew had been in Europe and just before Allan Wyatt's stroke, Allan had bought his daughter a hideously expensive sports car—the latest in a long line of extravagant gifts.

Of course, Wyatt's illness meant medical expenses, probably enormous ones, but his finances had always been, on the surface at least, rock solid. Spencer had gone to the most expensive schools, worn the finest clothes and had owned a half-dozen thoroughbred hunters as well as two racehorses. The elder Wyatt had spent money lavishly on her, probably without much wheedling on her part since it wasn't necessary, and had himself been known as a man with expensive tastes. He wasn't a collector, like Drew, but he had more than once paid fantastic sums for a piece of artwork or some other trinket that had taken his fancy.

The more Drew thought about it, the more his curiosity grew. That was all it was, just the hell-bent curiosity that had gotten him into trouble in the past. He told himself that. Then he picked up the Wyatt emeralds and left his study.

Half an hour later he parked his car in the curving driveway of an elegant old Georgian mansion and approached the heavily paneled front doors. It was after nine o'clock in the evening and he had no certainty that she was even at home. He'd been out of the country for the better part of the past six months, since her father's stroke, and hadn't seen her at all in nearly a year. She could have been heavily involved with someone or still making the nightly rounds of glittering D.C. parties for all he knew.

He pushed the doorbell and waited. A couple of minutes later the door was opened by a formally attired butler who briefly lost his customary impassivity when he recognized the visitor.

"Mr. Haviland . . ."

"Hello, Tucker." Drew stepped inside the foyer, unwilling to wait and find out if he'd be invited in. "Is Miss Wyatt at home?"

"I believe so, sir." Tucker was back on balance, his elderly face bland once again. He had followed Allan Wyatt all over the world in their younger days, acting as a general factotum in an age when wealthy men had personal servants no matter what uncivilized corner of the globe their wandering footsteps crossed, and Drew had always thought that he could have told some incredible stories about those adventurous times if he'd wanted to.

But Tucker, who had been with Wyatt since the late nineteen thirties, was very much of the old school. He offered the kind of loyalty that came from an earlier age, the kind no amount of money could buy, and whatever he thought of his employer of more than fifty years he kept to himself. He also kept most other emotions to himself, but Drew heard the faint note of restraint in his otherwise toneless voice.

"But she may not be—receiving visitors?" he asked, deliberately mocking.

Tucker's expression didn't change. "If you would care to wait, sir, I'll inquire."

"I'll wait in the library." Drew hadn't set foot in this house for ten years, but turned unerringly toward the short hallway that led to the book-lined room at the rear of the house. He paused and looked back, however, before he left the foyer. "Tucker . . . I heard about Allan's illness. How is he?"

The butler, one foot on the bottom tread of the curving staircase, looked at him impassively. "Dying, sir," he said without inflection, and continued up the stairs.

Drew went on to the library, frowning a little, what he had noticed in the foyer and now along the hallway just touching the edge of his awareness because he was thinking of Allan Wyatt. He had barely seen Allan in the past ten years, but during the two years before that they had been close. They had in common a love of art and antiquities, and though forty years separated them in age they had found a great deal to talk about. While Drew was an amateur archaeologist with an instinctive feel for what was genuine, Allan had been trained in his youth by some of the most famous explorers and archaeologists in history, and he had enjoyed talking about those colorful days.

9

Drew had felt a great deal of respect for Allan, seeing in the older man one of the last of a dying breed. He'd been a true adventurer in his time, wandering all over the world in search of relics, and if his family's wealth had made his travels easier than they might have been, that took nothing away from his courage. Those days prior to and following the Second World War had been dangerous ones for any traveler.

He'd survived. He had survived the reckless adventuring of his youth and a war in which he'd been decorated for valor. He had settled down in his forties to marry and raise a child, becoming a well-known and respected figure around his nation's capital both for his past exploits and for his sheer charm. His young wife had died early. And now, at seventy-five, he was dying.

Drew went into the library, thinking about that. Allan Wyatt was truly the last of his kind. There might be others once humanity pushed out into space, but for now there was no real frontier left to explore.

He stood looking around the room, noticing a few things even as he remembered what he had seen in the foyer and hallway, adding it all together. Drawn across the spacious room to the old oak desk because of the working lamp glowing there, Drew stood looking down at the cluttered surface without really paying attention for a minute or so. Then his gaze sharpened, and he leaned forward to intently study the pages of several open books.

When the door opened a few minutes later he was standing behind the desk, engrossed in reading pages of notes carefully printed on a legal pad.

"What are you doing here?"

Her voice was uniquely hers, low and a bit husky, still with that thread of sweetness in it that Drew knew better than to believe in now. He straightened, looking at her as she slowly moved across the room toward him. It was the first time in more than ten years they had met alone, face-to-face. For a moment, as she reached the other side of the desk and came into the bright glow of the lamp, what he felt most of all was anger, because she was still beautiful, damn her, and he still wanted her.

Only a few inches over five feet tall, Spencer Wyatt was petite, almost fragile in appearance, with small bones and delicate features. She was more slender than he remembered from the last time he'd seen her a year or so before, and the big, smoke-gray eyes seemed more opaque, almost completely unreadable. Her generous mouth was held firmly steady in a look of control, but her chin was up, Wyatt pride and confidence in the gesture he found disturbingly familiar. In that moment Drew was conscious of an almost savage urge to do something—anything—that would cause her to lose her unfailing composure.

"What are you doing here?" she repeated.

Quite deliberately, Drew looked her over with insolent thoroughness from the raven hair bound in an elegant chignon to the plain, high-heeled black pumps she wore. He allowed his gaze to linger on the firm mounds her breasts made beneath the green sweater, then trail slowly down to her narrow waist, and to the curved hips that were snugly encased in black slacks. He saw her small hands bunch suddenly into white-knuckled fists, and when he looked back at her face—angry heat rose in her cheeks, eyes glittering, bottom lip a bit unsteady now and her chin several degrees lower than before—he felt a jolt of almost brutal pleasure.

So her haughty poise could be disturbed, after all. He wondered what was underneath it, wondered what she would look like with the self-possessed mask at her feet in splinters. Would Wyatt pride keep her chin up and her voice soft even then? Or would the spoiled, calculating, ambitious bitch he believed was there finally show her treacherous face?

Perhaps that was what he needed to see, Drew thought. One glimpse of the Medusa, to cure him of her once and for all.

Leaving that thought where it lay, he reached into his pocket and pulled out the chamois bag, then tossed it to land on her side of the desk. Still a little flushed, she stepped forward stiffly and picked up the bag. Her fingers quivered just a bit as she opened it and drew the necklace partway out.

Without looking up at him she said evenly, "Where did you get this?"

"I bought it. From the man you sold it to." His own voice sounded normal, he thought, even casual.

Spencer pushed the necklace back into the bag and then tossed it to his side of the desk carelessly. "I hope you got it at a good price."

She was back on balance again, meeting his gaze with a direct, unreadable stare. A faint smile curved her lips, and her chin was back at its accustomed imperious angle. "An excellent price—considering that it's worth about three times what I paid."

"Then you got a bargain."

"Why did you sell it, Spencer? And why to Hanson?"

"None of your business."

Drew picked up the bag and returned it to his pocket, then said, "I could ask Allan."

Something flickered in her eyes, some emotion that was restrained too quickly for him to be able to read it, but her expression didn't change and her voice remained calm. "He's sleeping right now. He sleeps most of the time. And I don't want you to upset him."

"Upset him? You mean if I tell him you sold the Wyatt emeralds secretly, he'd be upset?" Drew smiled, and wondered fleetingly how it looked to her, because it felt strangely unnatural. "He doesn't know, does he?"

"The necklace was mine to sell."

Very softly, Drew said, "Like the paintings that used to hang in the foyer and hallway, the ones you've replaced with prints? Like the Ming vase that was once on the mantel over there? And the ivory lions that should be on that shelf by the door? Were all those yours to sell, Spencer?"

13

She was a little pale now, but he couldn't tell if it was anger or something else. And she remained silent, staring at him as though frozen.

Drew laughed. "You finally did it, didn't you? Reece Cabot divorced you without a penny in settlement, so you came crawling home to daddy—and in a few short years you managed to go through a fortune it took the Wyatt family centuries to build. But that wasn't enough for you, was it? You couldn't wait to inherit what was left from Allan; you're selling everything off piecemeal before he's even in the ground."

Spencer heard him as if from a great distance, heard him saying things that were even more devastating because they were uttered in his cool, unemotional voice. She had always felt inadequate in his presence, miserably aware that while her gloss of elegance was only that, only a pretense to hide the shyness and uncertainty inside, his was innate and the genuine article. He was never rattled, never at a loss, never unsure of himself.

She had watched him cross crowded rooms and had seen other men give way to him as if by instinct, and she had seen women look at him in unconscious fascination because they recognized what Spencer had understood from the first time she had seen him. That he was different from most men, set apart from them somehow, like a thoroughbred stallion in a herd of mustangs.

He had awed her then, left her tongue-tied and nervous. Now those old feelings swept over her again, battering at her hard-won assurance until she wanted to find a dark corner somewhere and crawl into it. He had looked at her in a way he never had before, bringing tears of both pain and humiliation to her eyes. She'd felt as if he had stripped her naked and clinically assessed her body—and was contemptuous of the conclusions he had arrived at.

She had known what he must have thought of her all these years, but his distant politeness during their occasional public encounters in the past hadn't prepared her for that shattering appraisal or for this chilling attack.

How he must despise her!

"Nothing to say, Spencer?" His voice was smooth and yet, at the same time, indifferently cruel. "Not a word in your defense? Not even an attempt to shift the blame? That isn't like you, sweet. You always used to perform such a wonderfully innocent act of surprise and dismay whenever Allan gave you some expensive new trinket. But I suppose you've used up all your curtain calls over the years."

Shift the blame . . . With an effort she continued to meet his scornful gaze squarely. All she had left was pride, and she clung to that desperately because she couldn't let him destroy her. There was nothing she could say to change his opinion, his idea of what she was; that obviously was too deeply rooted to be affected by words. Accustomed most of her life to playing a part, Spencer numbly accepted the one he handed her simply because she was too exhausted to fight.

"What do you want, Drew?" she asked flatly.

"I want to hear you admit it. You have been selling off Allan's things, haven't you?"

"Yes." She was willing to say anything, if only he'd go away and leave her to find some kind of peace.

"He doesn't know."

It wasn't a question, but Spencer shook her head slightly, anyway. No, her father didn't know. Her father had no idea how bad things had gotten in the past months, and she had no intention of allowing him to find out.

"Do you have any jewelry left, or were the emeralds the last to go?"

If he was after his pound of flesh, she thought tiredly, he was certainly determined to get it all. "The last." It wasn't hard to make her voice cold; she felt frozen inside.

He laughed again, a sound that seemed honestly, if derisively, amused. "Every well has a bottom—what happens when you hit yours? Another besotted idiot like Cabot?"

Spencer lifted her chin another fraction of an inch and called on all the acting ability he had so mockingly referred to before. "Whatever it takes," she said deliberately.

He stared at her for a long moment, his classically handsome face completely expressionless, and then reached down and lifted a bulging file folder from the desk, holding it up between them. "But first this, I think," he said in a soft tone. "Do you plan to sell Allan's notes to the highest bidder, is that it? Just throw his life's ambition to the wolves and watch someone else finally locate the Hapsburg Cross?"

As if his slow movement and soft voice had hypnotized her, Spencer's gaze drifted to the folder and the lifetime's notes it contained. Notes on a holy relic that most historians and archaeologists denied the existence of, asserting that it was only myth. For fifty years those same experts had referred to the Hapsburg Cross as Wyatt's Holy Grail or, more commonly, Wyatt's Folly.

He had talked about it for all of her life, and searched for it all of his. In recent years he had called it merely a hobby, perhaps discouraged by the fruitless search, but he hadn't given up and Spencer knew it. Sifting through books, journals, diaries, poring over maps, endlessly speculating and piecing together the tiny bits of information he regarded as accurate, he had collected an impressive amount of data.

To think she would sell that . . . She wasn't capable of telling that lie, and answered involuntarily, "No, I won't sell the notes. I'm going to find the cross."

Drew laughed. He laughed as if the very idea of Spencer doing anything of the kind was utterly and completely ridiculous, and the contempt in that sound hurt her worse than anything else he had said. Already daunted by the task she had set herself and wretchedly aware of her lack of any formal training, his derision could have been enough to make her give up before she'd even tried. Could have been—but wasn't.

Spencer looked at him and found within herself a determination stronger than anything she had ever felt before. Now she had two overwhelming reasons to find the cross: to put it in her father's hands before he died, and to see the man in front of her shaken off his imperturbable balance just once.

"I'm glad you find it so amusing," she said icily. "I hope you're still laughing when you have to deal with me to add the cross to your splendid collection." Now why, she wondered with a pang of sudden dismay, had she said that? It was bound to make him think—

"Of course," Drew said in a tone of understanding, no longer laughing. "The things you've been selling can't begin to compare to the Hapsburg Cross. With that in your greedy little hands you could ask for millions— and get it."

He would never believe the truth, Spencer knew that. Never believe that all she wanted was to see her father's face when the dream of his life was put into his hands. Never believe that all she could give the father she adored in the last days of his life was the triumph of knowing that he had been right, and that his work had uncovered not a myth but a priceless relic.

Drew wouldn't believe that, no matter what she said. So Spencer clung to her pride and let him believe what he wanted, wishing only that his opinion didn't hurt so much.

"You'll never find it," he said flatly. "You don't know a damned thing about archaeology."

"I had the best teacher in the world—my father. He's

forgotten more about archaeology than most of today's experts ever learn. And I have his notes."

For the first time, Drew showed some emotion other than scorn: incredulity. He looked at her as if she had lost her mind. "You think that's going to make it easy? These notes aren't step-by-step instructions, Spencer, and they don't contain a nice, neat little treasure map for your convenience."

She wouldn't allow herself to be withered under his ridicule, even though it cost her to continue to meet his eyes. "I know that. But the notes give me a place to start, and I—"

"A place to start? You mean Austria?" Drew put the file back on the desk, shaking his head. A pitying smile curved his lips. "That's a fine place to start. In fact, it's where legitimate archaeologists began searching a hundred years ago. Since the Hapsburgs supposedly owned the cross—and lived there—it only makes sense. Common sense, honey, of which you appear to have less than your share."

Though she badly wanted to convince him she wasn't the fool he thought her, she wasn't about to tell him that her father's notes narrowed the field considerably more—and to a place in Austria where no search for the cross had ever been conducted. No matter what Drew thought of her, the last thing on earth she would have done was give *him* a place to start.

Her father used to say that whatever formal training Drew lacked was more than made up for by an intuitive, almost instinctive sense of understanding. He had "the touch," an unerring ability to detect the genuine over the false, and a singular gift for finding artifacts, relics and ancient works of art that other more educated eyes had missed.

Until now, Spencer hadn't considered that someone else could beat her to the cross; since the experts maintained it didn't even exist, no one except her father had tried to find it in the past thirty years or so. But Drew, she realized with a sinking feeling of panic, could well decide to try his hand at the search. Given his obvious enmity toward her, he might even decide to do so just to teach her a lesson.

One of his elegant, powerful hands was resting on the file now, and she looked at it fixedly as she tried to regain control of her panic. Even if he had looked in the file, she assured herself desperately, he'd hardly had time to see the clues it had taken her months of intense study to find. From what he'd said, it was clear he believed she was planning to jaunt off to Austria without the least idea of any specific location.

That realization eased her anxiety, and she returned her gaze to his face. "I'm going to find the cross," she said, refusing to give him the satisfaction of listening to her try to defend herself. Since he so obviously thought her a stupid, greedy little gold digger, then so be it.

"You don't have a hope in hell."

Spencer managed to force a smile that she hoped was a mocking one. "Then you can gloat later, can't you?"

He stared at her for a long moment, then shook his head with a touch of impatience. "I'll deny myself that pleasure. Even if I decide not to go after the cross, I'd hate to see Allan's work lost—and you're bound to lose it between here and Austria. You'd better sell the notes to me."

He didn't even think she was bright enough to copy everything and leave the originals safely here, Spencer realized. She had no conscious intention of throwing down the gauntlet, but because he'd had the upper hand from the first moment she'd walked into the room and her own control was strained almost to the breaking point, her emotions got the better of her and she wasn't very surprised to hear the icy certainty in her own voice when she said softly, "Not if you were the last man left alive."

He stiffened, vivid eyes suddenly hard and curiously bleak, and his mouth a grim line. Spencer felt no pleasure from having successfully struck back at him, though she was vaguely surprised that she'd been able to. What she felt most of all was a bone-deep weariness, a raw pain like an open wound at the conviction that she had turned this man into an enemy, and an overwhelming knowledge that nothing in her life had prepared her to cope with any of this.

Drew removed his hand from the file and came around the desk toward her. She managed not to flinch away from him, and even turned to face him as he reached her, fighting the still-familiar apprehensive urge to back away. Too close. He was too close, forcing her to look up in order to meet his eyes. She felt smothered, backed into a corner by some primitive threat she couldn't even name and had no idea how to protect herself from. She had always felt that way whenever he was close to her—nervous, wary and terrifyingly inadequate.

Halting no more than an arm's length away, he reached for her hands and held them in his, turning them briefly as he stared down at her soft palms and slender fingers. Her nails were long and perfectly manicured, polished in glossy red. The pale gold flesh of her hands was smooth and unmarked by scars.

"You haven't done a day's work in your life," Drew said, his deep voice not cool now but curiously taut. "Even if you knew exactly where the cross was, do you really think it's just lying out in the open for you to pick up in your delicate hands?"

"I'm not stupid, whatever you think," she said, trying without success to draw her hands away. His touch was warm against her chilled skin, the slight roughness of his palms mute evidence that he had worked with his hands despite his elegant appearance. But it wasn't that which unnerved her. It was the strength she could feel in him, the almost tangible aura of sheer physical power.

He seemed larger than she remembered, his shoulders broader, his entire body more impressive and overwhelmingly masculine. She had the confused idea that she'd never really looked at him before, or that some part of himself always hidden beneath the cultivated exterior was closer to the surface now. She felt surrounded by him, trapped.

"What I think?" He seemed to lean down toward her, his features stony, eyes glittering. "I think you're a greedy, ruthless little fool. I think you broke that sick man upstairs, just like you'll break any man insane enough to love you."

chapter two

SHE WAS TRYING again to pull away from him, desperate to escape the knives of his words. She could feel the last of her control deserting her, rushing away just like the strength in her legs, and she knew she was going to afford him immense satisfaction by bursting into tears any minute now.

Then Drew released her hands, but before she could back away he was grasping both her shoulders and looking her up and down the way he had earlier, stripping her naked with insolent eyes and coolly weighing her charms.

"And it doesn't show at all," he said almost to himself. "That's the most dishonest thing about you, sweet, that beautiful, enticing package. It could easily blind a man until he'd believe he had struck gold instead of greed. But I know the truth, don't I?"

"Stop. Don't say any more." Every word she forced out hurt her tight throat. "Please, Drew—"

"Please, Drew," he repeated in a musing tone, his eyes on her face now and narrowed consideringly. "I like the sound of that. The surroundings could be better, though. A bedroom, I think, with you flat on your back between the sheets saying 'Please, Drew.' "

She made a smothered sound like the muted whimper of an animal in pain, both small hands lifting to push against his chest. Her mask was cracking, but he still couldn't read the depths of her darkened eyes. For all he could tell she was just furious.

He was furious, at himself as well as her. He *knew* she was a heartless bitch, and everything she'd said in this room only confirmed what he knew—but he still wanted her. The hunger he felt was so intense it had been gnawing at his control from the moment he'd looked up and seen her. Fighting that, he had needled and mocked her, trying savagely to make her reveal her true colors so that he could *see* the truth and be cured of this bitter craving for her.

But it hadn't worked. And once he had held her hands in his, the response of his body to just touching her had pushed aside everything except his painful struggle against it. He had forgotten her ludicrous plan to find the Hapsburg Cross and her frosty refusal to even consider selling him Allan's notes.

"Let go of me," she said huskily, pushing against his chest. "Get out of this house."

He laughed, the sound harsh in his ears. "You forgot to say please. And you, of all people, should know you're more apt to get what you want if you say please. I like hearing you plead with me, Spencer. It almost makes up for feeling like a fool when you jilted me."

She went still, gazing up at him with enormous smoky eyes he couldn't read. "That was ten years ago," she said, her voice still husky. "I'm sorry for what happened between us, but—"

"Between us? Nothing happened *between* us. You didn't even have the guts to face me once you'd made up your grasping little mind to run off with Cabot. I suppose I should have been grateful that you at least sent my ring back to me since it was a family heirloom, but I find it hard to forgive you for leaving Allan to break the news to me."

She flinched visibly, and he almost shook her because her look of pain and regret was so real he almost believed it. "I was only eighteen," she said with a tinge of despair in her voice. "I was afraid to face either of you."

"Afraid, hell. You just took the easy way out, honey, and left the mess for daddy to deal with. But you made a bad mistake, didn't you? Cabot might have been besotted, but his family's pure steel, and it didn't take them long to toss you out on your pretty bottom without a dime. I've often wondered—didn't you know then that I was the better catch? Or were you just convinced that he'd be easier to handle?"

Spencer stared up at him mutely, unable to deny that because it was partly true. Not that she'd wanted to handle Reece, but he had appeared simpler and less complicated than Drew, all his emotions on the surface—and his love had seemed so *real*. She had felt sure of herself with him, at least then, in the beginning. Reece's intense, passionate emotions had convinced her that to be loved so totally was far better and less painful than to love a man she didn't understand and was half afraid of.

Drew smiled cynically at her silence. "You should have married me, you know. I might have divorced you as quickly as Cabot did, but I probably would have paid for the privilege of being rid of you."

Under the hands gripping her shoulders, he felt her slump a little, and saw bloodless lips quiver in a starkly white face. Unblinking gray eyes were as blind as fog and held the same desolate chill.

"Lucky for you I did marry someone else," she whispered, her hands sliding away from his chest to hang loosely at her sides. "Think of all the money you saved."

The oddest sensation came over Drew as he stared down at her. It was a feeling he'd known before, countless times, but always and only when some object had been placed in his hands, its age or authentication in dispute. In every case he had felt the way he did now, as if a bell went off inside him, and the clear or discordant note of it told him what he needed to know. Yes, it's the real thing. Or no, it's a fake.

Now that bell was loud inside him, almost jangling, the harshly dissonant sensation too strong to ignore, and his recognition and understanding of it was completely involuntary. *She isn't what I think. Somehow, I've got it wrong.*

He had learned to trust his instincts when it came to objects, but he had never depended on that when it came to people. In fact, he couldn't remember ever experiencing the reaction to anything but inanimate objects. And he didn't trust it now. His mind and his emotions told him what she was, and he'd believed too long to let go of the certainty easily. His instinct for detecting the genuine, no more infallible than any other ability, had been deceived by her, that was all.

She was good, he acknowledged, staring down at that pale, beautiful face. She was so good that for a moment he had felt as if he'd kicked something defenseless and vulnerable. And she'd done it so easily, like turning on a switch that worked his emotions. It made him furious that he had let her get to him, if only for a moment. He wouldn't make that mistake again, he promised himself savagely.

He wouldn't let her make a fool of him twice.

But she had infected him years ago, her sweet, false smile lodging itself like a painful dart in some place deeper than his flesh, and for years he had let himself believe her betrayal had cured him of the hunger for her. Now he knew it wasn't true, knew that she'd have the ultimate triumph of destroying him unless he could rid himself of the poison of wanting her.

"I can't go back and change anything," she was saying now, her voice little more than a murmur.

"Very affecting," he drawled. "You should take to the stage if all else fails."

She shook her head a little, as if in bewilderment, then said tiredly, "Think what you like. If you've said what you came here to, I wish you'd leave. It's late. It's too late for any of this to matter."

"There's just one more thing," Drew told her, his hands tightening on her shoulders as he began pulling her toward him.

In the blankness of her eyes panic stirred, and her body tensed as she saw or sensed his intentions. "No—"

"I made the mistake of treating you like the innocent virgin you were supposed to be ten years ago," he said tautly, "and all I got for it was a slap in the face. You're treacherous and selfish and predatory, Spencer, but I didn't know that then and you got under my skin."

She felt like some small creature frozen in dread as it gazed at the hawk diving toward it, all her instincts shrieking for her to run, to get away, yet she was held immobile by something greater than terror. His hands were on her back now, relentless, and she gasped when he suddenly jerked her against him. His body was hard, and even through their clothing she could feel a heat that was almost feverish emanating from him. It seemed to seep into her flesh, her muscles, melting her resistance so that her body molded itself to his with instant, stunning compliance.

She was shaking her head unconsciously, and felt one of his hands slide up her back until his long fingers tangled in her hair. His hand was rough and abrupt, scattering the pins restraining her thick hair so that it tumbled loosely around her shoulders, and then holding her head steady. He was staring at her fiercely, narrowed blue eyes burning so hot that she felt scorched by them, one hand pressing her lower body tightly to his until the unmistakable hardness of his arousal shocked her senses.

"I know what you are now," he muttered. "But it doesn't matter. Your tricks don't work on me anymore, and this time I'm calling the shots. You were promised to me years ago and I intend to collect the debt."

"What?" She could barely get the word out, so stunned by the ferocity she could see and feel in him that she could hardly think. If his cool sophistication had daunted her years ago, this strangely intense and implacable determination she saw burning in his eyes made her feel utterly helpless.

His laugh was short and harsh. "Oh, I don't want a wife, sweet, so don't think you've found another poor bastard you can try to bleed dry. All I want is you in my bed—for a while."

"No—" Her instant, whispered denial was cut off

when his fingers tightened in her hair, drawing her head farther back. It wasn't painful, but she felt another queer shock when she realized that he could hurt her very easily. He was almost a foot taller and twice her weight, his arms steely around her—and he was angry, he was so angry.

"Yes," he said with flat certainty, his head beginning to lower toward hers.

Spencer closed her eyes as his hard features filled her field of vision and made her dizzy. She was quivering in his grasp like a trapped animal, her mind crying out silently against this. Both her arms were pinned to her sides, and she knew she wouldn't have been able to escape him even if they'd been free, because he was too strong to fight.

Then his mouth closed over hers, hard and hot, and it was like an electric jolt of pure raw sensuality. She had never in her life felt anything like this, and it was all the more shocking because she could feel it now with him. Everything else, all the confused, painful emotions, were submerged beneath waves and waves of sharp, heated pleasure. She couldn't fight the sensations any more than she could fight him, her mouth opening helplessly beneath the pressure of his. A convulsive shiver rippled through her when his tongue probed deeply, and she was suddenly very conscious of her breasts flattening against the hard planes of his chest as her body sank limply against him.

He had been gentle with her before, his kisses soft

and his embraces light—careful, she realized now, of her inexperience and youth; at the time, she had seen detachment rather than restraint, and since he hadn't seemed to care deeply about her it had made her own unexpressed yearning feel somehow wrong.

Now there was no doubt of his desire, and even though Spencer knew that at least part of that passion was meant to punish her, she couldn't help but respond. When his hold on her shifted slightly, both her arms lifted as if by instinct to slide inside his suit jacket and around his lean waist.

He kissed her as if he were taking what belonged to him and demanding even more, the force of his hunger unrelenting and overwhelming. But he didn't hurt her. She was, on some dim level of awareness, surprised by that, because he could have hurt her so easily and because he seemed bent on doing just that.

Then, suddenly, Drew lifted his head, and his voice was little more than a hoarse rasp when he said, "Look at me."

Spencer forced her eyes to open, feeling dizzy and breathless. Her lips were throbbing, her whole body was throbbing, and she realized vaguely that she'd fall if he wasn't holding her so tightly against him.

"I could take you right now," he said. "I could pull you down to the floor, here, and in five minutes you'd be begging me to take you. I'm looking forward to that, sweet. I'll enjoy every minute of watching you go so crazy with wanting me that nothing else matters. When the time comes, you'll know what it feels like to be in thrall to someone else."

She couldn't even accuse him of arrogance or vanity in his certainty; her response had been instant and complete, and they both knew she couldn't fight it.

The heat inside her ebbed, leaving her chilled, and her arms dropped limply to her sides when he put his hands on her shoulders and set her brusquely away from him. She felt the edge of the desk behind her, and leaned against it because her legs were shaking so badly. He was looking at her, she thought, the way a cat would look at a mouse it intended to play with before killing.

"Don't run this time, Spencer," he warned almost lightly. "I'd only come after you."

She wanted to cry out. *It was only your pride I hurt, not your heart—why are you doing this?* But she was no longer so sure of that. What she felt in him was too intense to have its roots in wounded pride; hate came only when the cut went much deeper.

Unable to say a word, she watched him turn away from her and cross the room to the door. He was entirely himself again, the force that had washed over her numbingly now buried underneath his elegant, smoothly polished surface. Almost as if it had never existed. He didn't say good-bye or even look back at her; he simply left the room, closing the door behind him.

After a moment Spencer pushed herself away from the desk and went around it to the chair. She sat down, looking blindly at the clutter of books, maps and notes covering the blotter.

How did the saying go? That the road to hell was paved with good intentions? Her intentions had been good ten years ago. Selfish, perhaps, and in the end stupid, but not deliberately cruel, and motivated by the blind fears and confusions of an eighteen-year-old. She had been obsessed by Drew as only the very young can be, her emotions a painful tangle of love, fear, uncertainty, passionate hunger and a miserable sense of her own inadequacies.

Only seven years older than she, he had been far more mature, and people accorded him a respect that a much older man might have envied. British by birth but American by inclination, he had grown up all over the world. His father had been known for wanderlust, packing up his wife and son at least once a year for another move, often to the opposite side of the globe, so that Drew's schooling had been incredibly eclectic.

It occurred to Spencer now that the wanderer's life might also have been lonely, though Drew had never shown a sign of feeling deprived in any way. Still, it must have been at the very least disconcerting for a boy to be plucked out of a school in France and dropped into one in Hong Kong, or to start the year in Spain only to finish up in Italy. A close family life could have eased those strains, but from all Spencer had heard that hadn't been the case for Drew.

Despite the elder Haviland's penchant for taking his

family along wherever he went, he was reputed to have been a reserved and even withdrawn man. A wealthy speculator with the Midas touch, he had built up his personal fortune to a level the old and aristocratic family hadn't seen in centuries. By all accounts, his wife had been a beautiful and languid woman, apparently content to follow her husband and with no ambition to assert herself in any way that ran contrary to his wishes.

At eighteen, Drew had left his parents somewhere in the Orient and had come to the States to enroll at Princeton; Spencer had no idea if he had done so for more emotional reasons than simply to remain in one place long enough to complete his education. In any case, he had stayed in America for the next four years, studying business as well as art, and becoming an honor student. Two months before his graduation, both his parents had been killed when their private plane crashed near London.

As far as Spencer could remember, he had never mentioned either his parents or anything about his childhood to her. She had found out what little she knew on her own, asking other people and reading newspaper and magazine accounts of the family. She hadn't asked Drew because she hadn't wanted to pry.

Pry! The man she had promised to marry, and she'd been so nervous around him that she hadn't felt comfortable asking about his family.

Her feelings about him then had been so confused. She had always felt too much, her emotions surging wildly from one extreme to the next all during her earliest childhood and into adolescence; it was as if there was a storm inside her, one she couldn't control. Then her mother had died, and at fifteen Spencer had faced the stark truth that the people one loved sometimes went away.

Like all of life's bitter truths, it changed her, but what might have been a maturing process became instead a kind of subterfuge that, once begun, turned into a prison. She had been wrenched from the self-preoccupations of adolescence, forced for the first time in her life to provide strength for someone else. Her father had been shattered, and it had been left to her to make all the arrangements that so swiftly and relentlessly follow a death. Burying her own wild grief, she had assumed a mask of quiet confidence and had set about trying to fill the place her mother had left in the family.

Spencer didn't regret that, but she knew now what it had cost her. She had pretended to be something she wasn't, hiding, even from her father, her lonely fears and insecurities. Because her mother's death had left such a gaping hole in her life, she always felt that she came up lacking in trying to be the poised, assured, gracious woman her mother had been.

And then Drew had stepped into her life, just at the moment her self-doubt was greatest. The first emotion she could remember feeling toward him was something very like wonder; at an age to worship blindly, she had taken one look into his amused blue eyes and tumbled headlong into love. He had seemed so . . . perfect. Tall, blond, classically handsome, his deep, slow voice holding the slight lilt of the cosmopolitan and his smile charming, he had appeared to Spencer like a god.

A girl could worship a god at sixteen. She could even, two years later, promise to marry one. But by then had come the confused questions and anxieties that had churned endlessly beneath her mask. What did he feel? Why did he want *her*? He said he loved her, but his voice was calm and matter-of-fact, with no hint of the frantic emotions she felt. And what was it she felt? Love, yes, but nervousness, too, and when he was close she felt uneasily threatened in some way that she didn't understand.

In the end, she had run—as much away from Drew as toward Reece. With an adolescent's panicked confusion, she had thought that Recce's intense, passionate, all-consuming adoration would make her happier than Drew's restrained love.

Hindsight, as they say, is perfect. Spencer hadn't been emotionally mature enough to recognize that Reece's love had been as completely ephemeral as it had been violent. Like a child with a new toy, he had been devoted only until familiarity bred boredom and another new toy gleamed brightly with promise on the horizon.

She wondered now, with a sharp pang, if she would have found Drew's love to be everything she had wanted. Looking back, she could remember how he had watched her, how his voice had changed slightly when he talked to her, and how he had touched her often even if those touches had seemed impersonal. Not a detached man, she realized now, but a very private man whose emotions, though controlled, went deep.

Tonight he had lost control. Some part of her recognized that. She was older now, and if she was still uncertain of herself she had at least learned to see other people with more clarity. She didn't know why he had decided to come here tonight, why her selling of the emeralds had acted as a catalyst to finally release his bitterness and anger. All she knew was that his promise of physical possession had been no idle threat.

He wasn't a cruel man; she couldn't believe that of him even now. But he was angry and had—from his viewpoint, anyway—reason to believe she was a greedy, heartless bitch.

She hadn't been able to defend herself against that belief, partly because she was just too tired. The past few months, since her father's stroke, had been mentally and emotionally exhausting. The shock of his illness had been bad enough, but then to find out that he was uninsured and that they were heavily in debt had been almost more than she could handle.

It had been a nightmare, and one she had struggled through with a crushing feeling of hopelessness. Still, she had managed to at least hold back the floodwaters of defeat. She had learned to negotiate with creditors, from the bank that held the stiff mortgage on this house to the IRS—which had granted her a moratorium on back taxes. Forced to get a job doing the only thing she felt reasonably adept at in order to pay for the private nurse her father required, she had been slowly selling off everything she could for living expenses and to whittle away at the mountain of debt.

Her own things had gone first. Her car, the horses she owned, her jewelry. Her trust fund provided some income. She couldn't touch the principal—a bitter frustration—but the interest brought in at least enough to stall creditors while she struggled to pay them off.

She wasn't sure, even now, where all the money had gone. Her father was no businessman, but there had at one time been income from real estate property and stocks that were gone now. She couldn't even ask her father what had happened to it all, because she didn't want him to worry. His memory had been affected by the stroke, and if he had ever realized he was on the edge of financial ruin he didn't remember it now.

Spencer honestly didn't know what she would do when she reached the end of her dwindling resources. Virtually everything of value was gone, the house was not only heavily mortgaged but also had a tax lien against it, and despite the lesser expense of being at home with a private nurse, her father's medical bills were staggering.

And with all that weighing her down, she was determined to travel alone to Europe, for the first time in her life, and find a holy relic that had eluded experts for centuries.

"Miss Spencer?"

She looked up with a start, her racing heart slowing as she saw Tucker standing in the doorway. If he had knocked she'd been too lost in thought to hear it. "Oh—Tucker." She forced her mind away from the useless and numbing thoughts. "Is there something wrong?"

He crossed the room soundlessly, his face as usual impassive, and placed a chamois bag on the desk. "Mr. Haviland left this, miss. He said to give it to you. I would have brought it in sooner, but the nurse required my help."

"Is Dad all right?" Spencer asked automatically, her disbelieving gaze fixed on the bag.

"Yes," Tucker replied. "He insisted on changing his bed jacket, miss, as he does every night before you visit him."

It was her habit to spend an hour or so sitting by her father's bed each evening, talking to him cheerfully or reading to him, and the visits had become a ritual. But Spencer wasn't thinking about that right now. She was staring at the bag holding the emeralds she had sold.

Why had Drew left them? As a mocking gesture, made in the confident expectation that she would instantly sell them again? It had broken her heart to sell them once. . . . She drew a breath and lifted her gaze to Tucker's.

"I want the emeralds returned to Mr. Haviland first thing in the morning," she said evenly.

"Any message, miss?" Tucker inquired.

Her mouth twisted. " 'Go to hell' might be appropriate, but, no. No message."

Tucker picked up the bag, but hesitated. In his normal colorless voice, he said, "He could help you. With everything. It won't be easy, finding the cross."

Spencer had no secrets from Tucker, and he'd been an absolute godsend these past months. She had never viewed him as a servant, seeing him more as her father's friend and her own. If there was a rock of solid support and quiet understanding in her life, it was Tucker. He continued to run the house and to take care of her father as he'd always done, as well as quietly make her life as easy as he could. And though he was, and always had been, invariably formal in speech and behavior, he never hesitated to offer his opinion or advice when she asked. Or sometimes even when she didn't.

She half nodded in acknowledgment of what he'd said, and replied, "I know he could find the cross, but . . . I can't ask him to help me. Not him. Even if he'd agree to do it, which I doubt very much, I can't ask him. And I don't want him to know how bad things are."

"He noticed the missing paintings."

"Yes." She forced a rueful smile. "He had his own ideas about those, but it doesn't matter. All that matters is that I find the cross. Dad's friend in Austria has talked to the authorities, and even though they don't believe I can do it, I have permission to bring the cross back here for Dad to see."

From what Drew had said, Spencer knew that he thought she was ignorant of international law and expected to be able to call the cross her own if she found it; why else would he make that remark about her selling it? Or else, she realized dismally, he thought her totally dishonest and believed she'd try to smuggle the relic out of Austria. But Spencer didn't consider the cross the answer to her financial problems, only a last gift to her father. And her biggest anxiety . . .

She looked at Tucker with unconsciously pleading eyes. "Dad will wait for me, won't he? He'll hang on long enough for me to find it and bring it back here?"

Tucker hesitated, then said quietly, "The doctors give him a few more months, but he's stronger now. Your plan to find the cross has given him a reason to fight."

It was all she could hope for—no guarantee, but at least a chance.

Spencer nodded and watched the old man turn back toward the door. Just before he left the room, she said, "Tucker? Have I thanked you?"

He looked back at her, the hint of a smile softening his stolid features. "Yes, miss," he said quietly.

She gazed at the closed door long after he'd gone, her own faint smile slowly dying. She was booked on a flight to Paris only a few days from now, and after that her journey would take her by train to Austria. She would arrive there virtually without money, driven to hurry because her father's health was precarious, and knowing no one there except an old friend of her father's who wouldn't even be in the area she had to search.

And if all that wasn't enough, now there was Drew. She had no doubt that he would make good on his promise to take her, a prospect that was both humiliating and painful but also something a longing part of her desperately wanted, if only . . . But she had thrown away his love once, and this was hardly a second chance for that. He meant to use her, to—what had he said?— hold her in thrall to him. And despite her knowledge of his motives, her ability to resist him sexually was nil. She'd gone to pieces when he kissed her, instantly mindless with pleasure and need, totally unable to resist what she had craved for so long.

And he knew. He knew she couldn't fight him. She wasn't smart enough to outthink him, or quick enough to outmaneuver him, or fast enough to outrun him. Her pride wouldn't let her surrender, yet her body already had, and she lacked his force, his will, his hatred. . . .

Spencer hated feeling inadequate. It was like her own personal nemesis, a sick, shamed feeling that dogged her steps constantly. She always seemed to be at the mercy of that painful emotion, and suddenly, knowing how easy it would be for Drew to destroy her, something snapped. All her weariness coalesced into a single, wildly fierce realization.

She was tired of it. Tired of feeling powerless and inept and somehow lacking. Tired of being afraid. And tired of being *tired.* All she could do was her best, and if that fell short of her own standards or someone else's, then so be it. She wasn't her mother. Elegance and assurance couldn't be borrowed or fashioned out of thin air—they had to be earned. She had her own strengths, and those would become apparent with time.

And if she couldn't fight Drew physically, she could at least struggle to have something left when he was through with her.

With that decided, Spencer felt strangely calm. No more pretense. She straightened in the chair, aware only then that she'd been slumping. One hand lifted to her hair, and she mentally pushed aside the unbidden image of Drew's hand there even as she wondered what Tucker had thought when he'd seen her. Probably, she realized, he had a very good idea of at least part of what had happened in this room, but he would, as usual, keep his thoughts to himself.

She got up and went around the desk, bending to collect the scattered hairpins. She left them among the cutter on the blotter, deciding not to try to put her hair back up. It was getting late and she wanted to sit with her father for a while before she went to bed. Tomorrow would be a long day, since her job began early in the morning; she was trying to put in as many hours as possible before she left.

She turned off the lights in the library and left the room, and for the first time she didn't notice the missing paintings in the foyer as she went steadily up the curving staircase.

*　　*　　*

"ARE YOU SURE he's ready?" Mike Bartlet asked the next morning as Spencer was leading her third mount of the day out into the big ring. "You've done wonders with him, but after that hellish fall he took, any jump higher than a foot makes him crazy with fear."

Spencer stroked the glossy chestnut neck of the young horse and smiled at his owner reassuringly. "He'll be fine. I want to take him over the jumps this week, and then we'll let him stay in his paddock until I get back. With no pressure and no show crowd to get on his nerves, he's already gotten a lot of his confidence back."

Bartlet smiled at her. It was almost impossible not to, because her smoky eyes and slow smiles were so direct and honest. She was such a little thing he'd initially objected to her handling his big, rawboned hunters, but the owner of this farm, where he boarded his horses, swore she had a special talent for gentling the ones that were bad tempered or that had picked up nasty tricks and habits. After several months of watching her work, Bartlet definitely agreed. She certainly knew what she was doing and the horses clearly loved her. Whether it was her soft, sweet voice or gentle touch, they responded to her in a way he'd never seen before.

A middle-aged man with a weather-beaten face and gruff manners, Bartlet found himself speaking softly around Spencer Wyatt. She had that effect, he'd noticed, on a lot of people. There was something very fragile about her despite the physical strength and endurance she showed with the horses, and people in her presence wanted to do things for her. Especially men. She could hardly lift a saddle without one of the grooms rushing over to help her, and even though she gently and firmly insisted on doing her own work, they kept right on trying.

She worked on a commission basis, being paid for each horse she handled. This farm was a large one with scores of boarders year-round, most of them hunters and many of them temperamental, and Spencer was easily the most popular trainer who worked here. She had a great deal of quiet confidence, and she was always even-tempered and friendly.

Bartlet liked her very much. And he worried about her. Though she never said much about herself and certainly never complained, he had the feeling that she was having a difficult time right now. Sometimes she arrived here with a look of strain around her fine eyes, and even though she seemed to forget her troubles while she worked with the horses, it bothered him.

Life should be good, he thought, for someone like Spencer. She was such a gentle lady. Sometimes he tried to make her laugh, just to hear the sweet sound and see her eyes light up.

"You be careful," Bartlet said now, unable to help himself.

She looked a little surprised, but nodded, and as he

gave her a leg up into the saddle Bartlet reflected that she seemed to have no idea why people—especially men of all ages—wanted to watch over and protect her. He stood watching as she rode the big hunter in an easy trot around the ring, then went back through the gate to get out of her way and watch from outside the ring.

Spencer eased the hunter into his workout, allowing his muscles to warm and loosen in slow gaits and a series of limbering turns. She spoke to him softly, watching his ears flick backward. At first he hadn't wanted to pay attention to her, but after weeks of rides he now responded as quickly to her voice as he did to her knees and hands. Unlike many of her mounts, he had no vices; a crashing fall in his first show had simply resulted in a bad case of terror. It had taken her days to get him anywhere near a jump, but her idea of turning him out into the jumping ring every night for a week, alone and riderless, so that the fences could become familiar and unthreatening sights, had worked.

Now he trotted and cantered past imposing jumps with no sign of fright, weaving in and out among them obedient to her guiding touch, his gaits smooth. When she calmly put him to a very low and simple jump, his ears pricked up and he took it in stride.

Praising him with her voice and a stroking hand, Spencer felt a sense of heady accomplishment. She loved horses, and handling them was the one thing she knew she did well. From the time her father had set her atop her first pony twenty-five years earlier, it had been a love affair. Until a few months ago she had never considered riding as work, but her position at this farm was one she valued over and above the necessary earnings; she could be herself here, with no need to pretend. Her abilities were genuine, and her confidence in them secure.

For the next half hour she rode the powerful chestnut, gradually putting him to higher jumps—though she had mentally set a limit of four feet. The only jump he seemed wary of was one resembling the one he'd fallen at, an obstacle built to resemble a red brick wall. Its height was set at three and a half feet, the top foot of that made up of lightweight "bricks" that would dislodge easily when bumped. Spencer had no doubt that the gelding could take the jump—it was his confidence that was in question. She was determined to try it, however, and lined him up with the fence steadily.

She felt his stride falter just a bit, a minute hesitation, saw his right ear flick back as she crooned softly, and then he gathered himself and easily cleared the fence.

Delighted, Spencer praised him, beginning to check his stride because the next fence was a bit higher and she wanted him to take it completely balanced. That was when she glanced aside, wanting to see Mike Bartlet's face at his horse's success.

Drew was standing beside him.

Spencer was never sure what happened then, although she blamed herself for it. Perhaps she tensed and jabbed at the gelding's sensitive mouth, or lost her balanced seat, or perhaps, with the peculiar ESP of horses, he sensed her sudden disturbance. In any case, the chestnut's stride broke awkwardly and he couldn't stabilize himself in time to attempt the jump looming in front of them. He tried to stop or shy away or both, and Spencer was unprepared for the sudden violent movements.

She went over his head and crashed into the fence.

chapter three

THE JUMP, LIKE all the others in the ring, had been designed with an eye to falling riders and horses. From the ground to a height of just over two feet the barrier was merely a line of neatly trimmed potted hedges, and above them two red-striped poles rested on pegs so that they'd be easily dislodged. If she had to fall, Spencer thought somewhat dizzily, this was one of the least dangerous jumps at which to do it.

However, she'd come off an unusually large horse moving at a fast gait, and even if bushes were relatively soft and wooden poles designed to give way when struck, the jarring contact with the ground was more than enough to knock the breath out of her. She had released the reins as she started to fall, partly because they were in a training ring where the chestnut would be confined and partly because she had a poor opinion of riders who dragged at the mouths of their horses by throwing the whole weight of their falling bodies against the reins.

It wasn't the first time she'd fallen, and it wouldn't be the last; she had learned as a child how to fall with the least risk to herself. Her jumping helmet protected her head, and though she was vaguely aware that one of the poles had left its mark on the small of her back, she was also reasonably sure that she hadn't broken or seriously bruised anything. She didn't move right away, knowing from experience that it was best to just remain still for a few moments and recover her breath and equilibrium.

She had turned a somersault in the air, landing flat on her back on the far side of the jump with her head toward it, and found herself gazing up at a cloudless blue sky—and then a very worried chestnut face. A slightly breathless laugh escaped her, and she thought for perhaps the thousandth time that the animal experts could say what they liked about people's tendency to accord horses human emotions but anyone who knew a particular horse well was convinced they felt emotions just like people. And any horse who felt a bond with his chosen rider tended to get visibly upset when he lost that rider. Spencer had known horses to express emotions that varied from sheepish embarrassment to panicked anxiety when they and their riders, from whatever cause, parted company.

The chestnut, Beau, was dismayed and anxious about her. She would have tried to reassure him, but the involuntary laugh had taken what little breath she could claim and she wasn't quite ready to try moving yet. Though it felt like hours, only moments had passed, and as she felt Beau's warm, grass-sweet breath and looked up into his worried brown eyes, she heard quick steps approaching. The horse was pushed back roughly, and Drew knelt beside her.

"Is she all right?" Mike Bartlet asked hoarsely as his face appeared on her other side.

Drew's long, powerful fingers, surprisingly gentle now, were methodically examining her arms and legs for injuries. Spencer gazed up at him and thought that he looked a little pale, but his voice was cool and steady when he replied to Mike.

"Nothing broken. I think she just had the wind knocked out of her."

"I'm fine," she managed, albeit in a breathless voice, as she struggled to sit up.

"Easy," Drew ordered, slipping an arm around her shoulders for support.

Spencer was glad for his assistance, because the motion of raising up made her head swim for a moment. "I'm fine," she repeated in a stronger voice, and then couldn't help but laugh. Beau, pushed back by Drew when the men reached her, kept trying to get his head down to her and was frustrated because Mike was holding the reins and trying to keep the horse away from her.

"Stay put," Drew said in a sharp voice, but she ignored that and got to her feet anyway. He rose with her, an arm still around her until he was sure she was steady.

Though she was honestly grateful for his aid, Spencer didn't waste any time moving away from him; she couldn't forget what had happened between them last night. So she stepped toward the horse, reaching out to stroke the velvety nose gently.

"It's all right, Beau, it was my fault," she murmured, taking the reins from Mike's relaxed grasp. "I threw you off balance, didn't I, boy?" She looked aside to Mike. "He didn't hit the fence, did he?"

Mike shook his head. "No, he went around. Spencer, are you sure you're all right? The way you hit that fence—"

Trying to reassure him, she said solemnly, "A forward one and a half out of the saddle. I'd give it a seven-point-six. At least two points off for not keeping my feet together."

He gave a short bark of a laugh, unwillingly amused. "And your arms were windmilling, too. Lousy form."

Spencer grinned at him. "Next time I'll try the forward pike position. Will you give me a leg up, please?"

"Hey, you don't have to—"

"Prove anything. I know. It's Beau I'm thinking about, Mike. I need to take him over a few jumps and then finish with this one, or he'll think it was his fault I came off." She kept her gaze determinedly on Mike. Drew wasn't saying a thing, and even though she was strongly aware of his presence just behind her, the last thing she wanted was to have her self-confidence threatened by his undoubted mockery.

Mike shook his head, but stepped up to give her a leg into the saddle. Spencer landed lightly and found her stirrups, gathering the reins as she settled into place.

"Put the bars back where they were," she said, still avoiding any glance at Drew. She waited for Mike's resigned nod, then turned the horse away from the jump.

She admitted honestly to herself that she was still shaken by the fall, and the stinging sensation across the small of her back told her there'd be a bruise there within hours, but Spencer also knew she had three more horses to ride today—and she quite literally couldn't afford to take time off just because she'd had a tumble. But it would have been much easier, she acknowledged silently, if Drew hadn't been watching. She knew he was, she could feel it, and it took all her concentration to block out the sensation of his eyes on her.

He owned horses, but kept none here, and she had the unnerving feeling he'd come here today only because someone—perhaps Tucker, she thought—had told him she was here. Was this how he meant to conduct his cat-and-mouse game? Showing up unexpectedly to remind her of his intentions? How could she cope with that tactic? And how could she keep her mind on her work when her eyes and her thoughts were continually drawn toward him?

She was too *aware* of him. Even though he was

dressed to blend in here—a black leather jacket over a pale blue shirt and dark slacks—to her he still seemed to stand out vividly from everything around him. Despite ten years and everything that had happened to that eighteen-year-old girl, she still saw him as a man who was larger than life.

Spencer had to put it all out of her mind, at least for the moment. She rode the chestnut around the ring a couple of times to relax him, noting that Mike had replaced the bars of the jump as she'd asked and that both men had left the ring. Concentrating only on the horse beneath her and the jumps ahead, she put Beau to three low fences in succession, praising him softly when he took them in stride. Two more higher fences were jumped cleanly, and then she turned him smoothly to the jump where she'd fallen.

This time he was balanced perfectly, and his stride never faltered as he cleared the striped poles with a foot to spare.

She rode him around the ring a few more times, slowing him gradually. He was in superb condition and hadn't broken a sweat, but she wanted him completely relaxed when she dismounted. When she finally turned him toward the gate, he was moving in the easy, almost shambling walk of a naturally gifted hunter.

Drew opened the gate for her. Without looking at him, she said, "Where's Mike?"

"He had to leave to make an appointment," Drew said, cool and calm as usual. "He asked me to tell you that Traveler was running a light fever this morning, and the vet said to leave him stabled for the day."

Which meant she had two mounts left to ride today. Spencer nodded in acknowledgment and rode Beau toward one of the dozen spacious barns. She dismounted just inside the wide hallway, and cross-tied the horse to be unsaddled and groomed. Stable hands did that sort of work for some of the trainers, but Spencer preferred to do all the handling herself in order to build a stronger bond with her mounts.

She knew that Drew had followed her into the hall, and that he was leaning against the jamb of an open stable door as he watched her, but she still refused to look at him. She was afraid to look at him. She felt wary and threatened. Here at this farm, surrounded by horses and the people who worked with them, she was normally relaxed and confident; she counted on this place and her job for a much-needed note of success and triumph in her life. If she lost that, she wasn't sure she could recover from it.

He could take it away so easily. With his mockery, his deliberate, cutting smiles, his contempt. Despite her decision after he had gone last night to simply do the best she could and stop pretending, she hadn't expected Drew to come here at all, much less so soon, and his presence disturbed her deeply.

"Bartlet said you'd been training for months now," Drew said suddenly as she carried her saddle past him to the tack room.

Spencer put the saddle on its stand and picked up a utility tray of brushes, waiting until she walked past him again to say simply, "That's right."

"Why?"

She pulled off her hard hat and riding gloves, setting both aside, then selected a brush and began grooming the big chestnut, vaguely aware that her entire back was now throbbing dully as a result of her fall. Ignoring the protesting twinges of bruised muscles, she brushed Beau in long, sweeping strokes and kept her attention fixed on the horse. "Why am I training? Because it's the only thing I'm good at. What are you doing here, Drew?"

"I came to return the emeralds," he said.

Spencer moved around to the other side of the horse so that the animal was between them; she couldn't look over his back and she was glad of that. "Not to me, you didn't. I sold them, you bought them—they're yours." A flicker of motion in the corner of her eye told her Drew had moved as well, obviously to watch her as they talked.

"A gesture of defiance, sweet?" he asked.

She paused in her work, one hand resting on Beau's relaxed shoulder and the other gripping the brush. She heard less mockery than there might have been in his voice, but the milder tone hardly made his question any better. And she couldn't help but wonder if this, too, was a part of his plan. Did he enjoy needling her? Did he derive some kind of satisfaction from her defensive denials even though he didn't believe a word she said?

Spencer's hesitation was brief. There was no way to convince him he was wrong about her, but she had decided last night never again to accept a role someone else wrapped around her and she clung to that determination even though she knew it left her terribly vulnerable where he was concerned. She began brushing the horse again, and said, "Not at all. The necklace doesn't belong to me anymore. Period." Her voice remained calm, and her grooming of the horse was firm and thorough.

"Not even as a gift?" More mockery this time.

"No." *Not from you.* "Now, if you don't mind, I have work to do."

There was a long silence, and then his voice came very softly. "Don't dismiss me, Spencer."

An alarm bell in her mind jangled warningly at the anger she heard, and she felt a dim surprise at how close to the surface his temper seemed to be. That was new, hardly part of the man she remembered, and it made her even more wary of him. She had the odd notion that from the moment he had touched her last night he had been just a bit out of control—as if some dam had cracked and the pressure of stormy floodwaters was widening the fissure. A fractured dam was dangerous.

So was a man who was a bit out of control.

Again she stopped grooming the horse, and this time she turned to face Drew. She met his flinty gaze steadily, and kept her voice calm, consciously trying to avoid anything that would sound like a challenge or provocation of any kind. "I'm sorry if I sounded autocratic. I didn't mean to. It's just that I have more than a day's work ahead of me. Work I'm paid to do."

"And you need the money," he said.

Spencer could detect no softening of his impassive features, but she hadn't expected to. "Yes," she said. "I need the money. I've run out of things to sell." Wishing she'd stopped herself before that last faintly bitter comment, she returned to grooming Beau.

Drew was silent while she continued with her work, and it wasn't until she set the brushes aside and started to untie the horse that he finally spoke. "How bad is it?"

There was no way she was going to tell him that, so she ignored the question totally. "You'd better stand back," she warned smoothly as she turned Beau toward the stable. "My next pupil isn't a gentleman."

She didn't look to see if Drew heeded the advice, but stabled the chestnut and then went on down the barn's wide hall to a stall at the far end. The horse she led out into the hall a moment later was a contrast to the placid Beau in almost every way. Formally named Intrepid Shadow on the papers listing his lengthy pedigree but fondly referred to as That Bloody Devil by all who knew him, the big stallion was pitch-black, rattlesnake mean, and hated everything that breathed with the exception of Spencer—whom he merely disliked.

He tried to bite her when she snapped the lead rope onto his halter but, inured to his ways, she evaded the wicked teeth and kept a wary eye on him as she led him out into the hall. As usual, he made a spirited attempt to bolt, rearing with a squeal of rage and lashing out with both forelegs, but she was ready for that as well and never lost control of him.

Spencer had learned a long time ago that in handling horses she could never hope to use physical strength in mastering half a ton of bundled nerves and muscle; what she depended on was quickness, skill and an intuitive understanding of how the equine mind worked. Devil was an angry creature, pure and simple, and to try either to contain that rage or to beat it into submission would have been a bad mistake. She did neither. She simply stayed out of his way when he lashed out, handled him quietly and firmly and clung like a burr to his back once she was in the saddle.

By the time she had the big black horse cross-tied with relative safety in the hall, he had settled down a bit, but still presented the almost rigid, wild-eyed appearance of an animal on the fine edge of exploding. Drew had taken Spencer's advice, and was standing some feet away as he watched her begin grooming the horse.

"Are you out of your mind?" he asked, keeping his voice unusually soft. "That horse is a killer."

"Oh, you know him." She kept her own voice quiet, and her hands were steady as she brushed the glossy ebony neck. "It was never proven that he killed that trainer."

"Do you doubt it?"

"No," she replied somewhat wryly, very alert to

Devil's tense stillness even as she appeared as relaxed as possible. "I don't doubt it."

"He should have been put down."

Spencer began humming softly, interrupting the soothing sound only to speak to Drew. "Maybe. His bloodline's priceless, and so far none of his foals have inherited his temper. Do you mind not talking for a little while? If I don't settle him down, he's going to erupt."

Drew forced himself to be silent, even though he badly wanted to swear good and loud. If Spencer had looked fragile beside the rawboned chestnut, the black made her look like a child—and a delicate one at that. One blow from the wicked animal could easily kill her, and it wouldn't take a fraction of a second for the horse to lash out.

She was humming, a soft, crooning sound that the stallion responded to with nervous flicks of his ears, her hands steady and relaxed as she groomed him. Drew wanted to yank her away, but he didn't dare move a step closer, because he knew that the horse hated men above all else and couldn't bear to have one near him. The white-rimmed eyes were fixed on the nearest man— Drew—now, and contained an almost palpable fury.

So Drew remained motionless, filled with the icy awareness that he was too far away to reach Spencer if anything were to happen. It was a helpless feeling, and he didn't like it. He didn't like anything he'd been feeling since arriving here a couple of hours before. First

Bartlet, then Spencer's sudden fall and now this dangerous horse . . .

Drew knew Mike Bartlet by reputation—and he was reputed to be nobody's fool when it came to people. A hardheaded businessman who despised pretense and who could spot a phony across a crowded room, he had talked about Spencer in glowing terms. And not just regarding her expertise with his horses. Clearly, Bartlet had adopted her emotionally; he fretted over her apparent habit of skipping meals, her tendency to work long hours, her willingness to take on horses that other trainers wouldn't get near, and the strain he thought he saw in her eyes.

Drew had listened, increasingly disturbed by this picture of a woman he didn't know. He told himself that Bartlet had been deceived by Spencer, but the assurance held a hollow note. She was *here* after all, doing a relatively dirty and sweaty kind of work that demanded physical strength and endurance, considerable skill and endless patience. Hardly the sort of job for a spoiled, greedy hothouse flower reluctant to damage so much as a fingernail—especially since Drew knew damned well her earnings here weren't a fraction of the allowance Allan had given her for years.

It didn't jibe, didn't fit his idea of her.

Then she had fallen, her slight body appearing terrifyingly fragile as it had catapulted from the big horse and crashed through the fence, and Drew didn't like to remember the sick feeling in his chest when he had watched that. The relief of finding out she was all right had been supplanted by surprise, because she had reacted to the fall with instant humor and self-blame, wasting no time in easing Bartlet's worry, soothing the horse and climbing back into the saddle.

Now she was just a few feet away, handling a deadly stallion that ninety-nine out of a hundred trainers wouldn't have taken on for any price, and she was doing such a good job that the animal was relaxing visibly, calming, becoming manageable. She even made it look easy, and Drew knew it wasn't.

Ten years ago, jilted without warning and left to make what sense he could, Drew had believed he'd figured her out. It had seemed to fit then, his idea of her. And if his conviction had been born in hurt and bitterness, it had still been based on the facts as he had seen them. Now . . . now he wasn't so sure. And he hated that uncertainty.

If he *was* wrong about her, there had to be things he didn't know—about her and about her motives in running away to marry another man. There had to be a *reason* she'd done it, and if not greed, then what? Love? Had she discovered that she'd loved Reece Cabot? The marriage hadn't lasted long, and several members of the Cabot family had heavily implied to friends and acquaintances that Reece had misjudged Spencer, foolish boy, and that they'd handled the problem for him.

A lie to save family pride? Had it been Spencer who

had sought a divorce, bailing out of a bad situation and asking for nothing but her freedom?

Drew wasn't accustomed to feeling uncertain, and it had a gnawing effect on his temper. Wary of letting Spencer get to him and yet driven to find out for sure if he was right about her, he found himself examining every nuance of her voice and every fleeting expression he saw in her face.

He had needled her deliberately; she had reacted without either defensive venom or coldness. Her eyes were still unreadable, but he could see the strain as well as Bartlet had. And today there was none of the chin-in-the-air haughtiness that had the power to anger him so. She was subdued but not sulky, impersonal but not chilly. He thought she was wary of him even though there was no visible sign of it, and if she was disturbed by his expressed intention of taking what had been promised to him there was no indication of that, either.

As he watched her gradually calm the big black horse, Drew admitted to himself that he was the one who was disturbed—by her because she didn't seem to be what he had believed her to be, and by his own emotions and motives because both were tangled and unsure. The only thing he was absolutely certain of was that he wanted her, and that he intended to have her.

Even if she was a greedy little bitch.

* * *

THE MAN LOOKED like any other of the dozen or so owners who happened to be at the farm that day. He was casually dressed, and wandered from training ring to training ring intently watching the horses being worked. Everyone who saw him merely assumed that he belonged there, so his presence wasn't challenged.

Spencer probably wouldn't have noticed anything unusual about the watcher even if she'd seen him. She had focused her entire attention on Devil in an attempt to block out her unnerving awareness of Drew, and didn't notice the man or his covert interest. Drew was watching her too intently to realize that the two of them were under observation. If he had noticed the man at all, he would have been suspicious; with ten years spent in pursuit of antiquities in some very rough areas of the world, Drew had developed a keen sense of potential danger and could usually sense watching eyes.

This time, however, he sensed no threat.

The man continued to watch them unobtrusively, moving within the general area so that he didn't remain in any one place too long. From the shadowy interior of a barn hall, he saw Spencer ride the black stallion into one of the training rings, his gaze straying to Drew, who stood at the fence watching her. He studied Drew for long minutes, then checked his watch and eased away toward the parking area.

He used the phone in his car to place a call, and as soon as the connection was made said, "There may be a problem."

"What is it?"

"She has a visitor today—and I don't think he came here to see the horses."

"So? With her looks, it'd be a little strange if she *didn't* have men coming to see her."

The man in the car grimaced slightly. "There's no love lost between these two, believe me. I've seen blood enemies that were friendlier."

"What's your point?"

"My point is that her visitor is Drew Haviland."

There was a long silence, then a soft oath.

The man in the car nodded to himself. "Yeah. From what I've heard, he isn't a man to make a fool of himself over a woman, but he's gone a hell of a lot farther than Austria to pick up a nice new bauble for his collection."

"You think he knows about the cross?"

"Look, all I can tell you is what I've seen. He showed up late last night at the Wyatt house, and when he left I wouldn't have wanted to get in his way. Something had him ticked off plenty. He's been here for hours. He and the girl aren't saying much to each other, but he's watching her like a hawk. So you tell me."

"I don't know—but I don't think we can take any chances. It would have been easier and safer to let her find the cross for us and bring it back here, but if Haviland knows she's going after it he could complicate things."

"That's an understatement," the man in the car muttered. "You know his rep as well as I do—if he gets a good look at Wyatt's papers, you might as well kiss the cross good-bye. Even worse, if she won't let him see them and he decides to tag along after her, we won't be able to get close enough to grab the cross."

"You sound a bit intimidated, Clay."

The mockery had no effect on Clay, who merely said, "I count myself handy in a fight, but you aren't paying me enough to take on Haviland. I had it from somebody who knows—the man can handle himself and gets a bit touchy when you try to take things away from him."

"That's assuming he gets his hands on the cross before we do."

"You changing the plan?"

"I don't want to take any chances. We need Wyatt's papers. Can you get in and get them?"

"Piece of cake, I told you that before. But even if we can figure out where the cross is, getting it out of Europe is going to be hell. The girl has permission to bring it back here, but we certainly don't."

"You worry too much, Clay. We'll get the cross out. It'll take more time and effort, but we'll get it."

"What about the girl? When the papers come up missing, she'll know someone else is interested in the cross."

"Spencer Wyatt," his employer said contemptuously, "is no threat to us no matter what she knows. And Haviland won't be as long as we get to Austria ahead of him. Just get the papers, Clay. Tonight."

"Yeah, all right," Clay responded, then added, "but I think I'll make it look like a common robbery just to be a little safer."

"Suit yourself. Can you watch those two the rest of the afternoon?"

Clay frowned a little as he stared through the windshield. "Depends. The way Haviland's watching her, I doubt he's even seen me—but I could get real visible if he took a look around. I'll have to play it by ear."

"Stay there if you can. If not, come back here. She'll go straight home after she's finished for the day, won't she?"

"Always does. And she doesn't go out at night. Crying shame, if you ask me."

"I didn't ask you."

"Right."

"Check in later."

"Right," Clay repeated, and broke the connection. He sat in his car a few minutes longer, frowning, feeling a growing uneasiness. He didn't like wild cards, and from all he'd heard Drew Haviland was definitely that. And though his boss might have a poor opinion of Spencer Wyatt, Clay had his doubts about that, too. He'd watched the lady handle people and horses over the past weeks, and he thought there just might be both smarts and steel underneath her delicate exterior.

He was beginning to wish he'd never hired on for this job.

*　　*　　*

"IT'S PAST TWO," Drew said when Spencer had finally stabled a much more relaxed Devil. "Don't you eat lunch?"

Spencer automatically glanced at her watch, but she was already heading toward another stall when she answered. "I'm not hungry."

Drew took two long strides and caught her arm, pulling her around to face him. "According to Bartlet you've been here since seven this morning, and I haven't seen you take a break during the past five hours."

Very conscious of his grip on her arm, of the way he towered over her despite the high heels of her riding boots, and of her own weariness, Spencer found it very difficult to keep her voice steady and calm. But she tried. She did try. "I haven't taken a break because I haven't needed one."

"Are you lying out of habit, or do you just want me to feel sorry for you?" he snapped.

She jerked free of his grasp, wanting to back away from him but holding her ground. Ignoring the taunt, she said, "I have one more horse to ride today. Will you please let me do my job?"

"Answer my question," he ordered flatly, both his hands catching and holding her shoulders with a force that stopped just short of pain.

She could feel her control slipping. All during the hours he'd been there she had felt it diminish, seeping away from her relentlessly, until now it was not more than a thin veneer. He'd said very little, but she had felt his eyes on her, heard in her mind all the unspoken mockery and had waited with a kind of numb apprehension for him to start cutting at her.

Waiting for it had been worse, she thought, than coping with it would have been. The tension of being certain that he was going to start needling her any moment had destroyed her tenuous peace. She'd found no comfort in working with the horses today, no sense of achievement or triumph. She just felt sore all over from her fall earlier, unusually tired, and her nerves were so raw she was very afraid she'd burst into tears any moment.

But not in front of him. Please, God, not in front of him.

In a carefully steady voice that betrayed more than she knew, she said, "I'm not lying, Drew. I'm not hungry, and I don't want to take a break. I just want to get Corsair out of his stall and saddle him up and take him over the jumps. Please let go of me so I can do that."

A frown drew his brows together, and his eyes probed her face so sharply that she almost felt them cut her. "The horse can wait," he said, his tone a little rough. "You may not want to admit it, but you'd have a hard time lifting a saddle right now."

Spencer didn't hear concern in that statement; she heard criticism, and it easily pierced what was left of her self-control. "Don't," she murmured, hating the thready sound of her voice but unable to steady it.

"You're entitled to your revenge—at least from your point of view—but not this, please."

"What are you talking about?" Drew demanded, his frown deepening.

"I need this. The horses, the people here . . . Don't ruin it for me." Spencer had the most peculiar feeling of distance, as if she were floating away from him. Light-headed. That was it, she decided vaguely. It had come over her all of a sudden and she was puzzled by the sensation. She also didn't understand why she couldn't stop talking, but her mouth seemed to have a mind of its own. "I have to have this, or I couldn't do the rest. It isn't much, you can let me have this, can't you? You don't have to destroy everything, I didn't do that to you . . ."

"Spencer, did you eat breakfast?"

She frowned up at him. "I wasn't hungry. Let go of me now. I have to get Corsair—"

Drew said something extremely violent under his breath, then put a hard arm around her and led her out of the barn. He was moving her along so rapidly that Spencer felt even more dizzy, and it wasn't until he put her in the passenger seat of a racy-looking sports car that she managed to protest.

"I can't leave now. I have to—"

"Be quiet," Drew said roughly, folding his length easily behind the wheel and starting the engine with a roar.

She thought maybe she'd better be quiet, because he

looked very angry. For twelve years she had thought him an utterly calm, even unemotional man, and she wondered now how she could have believed that. Surely there'd been signs, indications that his unruffled surface was misleading? Why hadn't she seen that? Had Reece's bright, temperamental glitter blinded her to *everything*?

She was still thinking about that, her mind locked methodically in a single puzzling track, when Drew parked the car in the lot of a small restaurant. He got out and came around to open her door, then took her arm firmly when she rather carefully got out.

"I'm not dressed," she protested as he led her toward the entrance.

"Of course you're dressed." His voice was calm again, but curiously controlled, as if the composure was deceptive.

"I mean I'm not dressed right," she tried to explain. "You have to dress right, so people think you belong. I'm wearing riding clothes, not—" She broke off abruptly, finally hearing the little voice in her head that was telling her to shut up before she made a total fool of herself.

She didn't say another word while an attentive hostess conducted them to a booth in the back of the nearly deserted restaurant, and she didn't realize that Drew had ordered for both of them until a glass of milk was placed in front of her. She frowned at it.

"Drink it," he said quietly.

Spencer had never been very good at following autocratic orders—probably because of her father's indulgence—but every instinct now told her it would be safer to do as Drew ordered. She picked up the glass and began sipping the milk, watching him steadily. The light-headedness she'd been aware of faded by the time she finished the milk, and she slowly realized that skipping meals had finally caught up with her. No breakfast this morning, and she'd only picked at her dinner last night—no wonder she'd felt so peculiar.

He probably thought she was making a ploy for his sympathy. The way he was watching her, she couldn't be sure. Her gaze skittered away from his and fixed itself on the polished tabletop as she tried to fight the hot surge of embarrassment.

"Better?" he asked, still quiet.

She nodded. "Thanks. Sorry I made a fool of myself."

"You didn't. But you did say a few things you're going to have to explain."

Spencer glanced up at him fleetingly, then looked away again. "I don't think—"

"Not now," he interrupted. "After we've eaten."

She didn't have the energy to protest. Instead, she sat silently until the food arrived, then began eating. She couldn't have said later what she ate, and she still didn't feel at all hungry, but ate simply because her body and Drew thought she needed food. And she did feel better for it. He ate as well, watching her from time to time, but said nothing until they finished the meal.

Their waitress came to take the plates and offer dessert—which both Spencer and Drew refused—and coffee. They accepted the coffee, and Spencer was once more conscious of her worn and somewhat dusty riding clothes as she watched the pretty blond waitress smile at Drew. To be tall and blond like him, that's what she had wanted all those years ago. To have blue eyes instead of her indeterminate gray—

She cut the thoughts off sharply, determined to teach herself to stop thinking like that. Especially around Drew. "Now," he said as the waitress reluctantly went away with her coffeepot, "I think we have a few things to discuss."

Spencer shook her head a little. "Whatever I said back there at the farm isn't important. You were right. I needed a break and something to eat. I didn't know what I was saying."

He ignored that. "You said that you had to have this—meaning your work at the farm—or you couldn't do the rest. What did you mean by that, Spencer?"

She'd promised herself she wouldn't lie to him, wouldn't pretend to be anything she wasn't, but she didn't want him to know how bad things were. "Just— coping. Dad's illness. Having to take care of things. That's all."

"Financial problems?"

"Nothing I can't handle," she said stubbornly.

His eyes narrowed slightly, but instead of persisting he said, "You said you supposed I was entitled to my revenge. And the bit about me ruining your work, destroying everything? What did you mean?"

Spencer managed a shrug. "You made it pretty plain last night that you're out to . . . even the score. I just—I'm asking you not to mock me or belittle my work." Her gaze dropped to her coffee cup. "I know you probably think it's hilarious, to say nothing of trivial, but I—I enjoy working with horses, and I'm good at it. It's the only time I feel . . . Well, never mind."

"I never said it was hilarious or trivial."

She shrugged again. "When you showed up this morning, I expected you to say something like that."

"Because I want revenge?"

"It wasn't difficult to figure out. I can't—I can't fight you with words, Drew, you use them too well. I found that out last night."

chapter four

"SO I STRUCK a nerve or two," he said.

"Weren't you trying to do just that?" When he remained silent, she looked up at him suddenly. "Maybe I deserved it, maybe I deserved everything you said to me."

"Don't you know if you deserved it?" he asked with a trace of mockery in his voice.

Spencer wondered what she really thought about that, but shook her head a little and said, "It doesn't matter. The only thing that matters to me right now is finding the cross, and if you intend to interfere with that—"

"Wait a minute," he interrupted, frowning. "You aren't seriously planning to try to find the cross?"

"I know you thought it was a terrific joke," she said evenly, "but I wasn't kidding. My father believed the cross existed when no one else did, and I am *not* going to let him die without knowing he was right."

"You don't know that he was right about it. And even granting its existence, experts *have* looked for the thing without luck. For God's sake, Spencer, think a minute. Even if you had a hope in hell of finding the cross—which you don't—just how do you propose to get it out of Austria? In case you don't know, it would be considered a national treasure."

She laughed softly, but it wasn't a sound of amusement. "I guess I'm not as stupid as you think I am. I have permission from the authorities in Austria to bring the cross back here for Dad to see. They'll arrange transport as soon as I can find the cross, and provide a courier to keep me honest. No matter what you believe, I don't intend to try to keep the thing for myself."

If anything, Drew's frown had deepened, and his gaze was very sharp. "What did you tell the authorities?"

Spencer wondered why it mattered, but shrugged and answered anyway. "I told them I'd gone over Dad's papers, and I thought I had a good chance of finding the cross. An old friend of Dad's works for the government over there, and he vouched for me. Like you, they don't believe I can do it, but they're willing to stand ready just in case."

After a moment Drew said, "According to your itinerary, you leave Monday morning."

She remembered then that the itinerary had been jotted down on the topmost sheet of the legal pad on her father's desk, and remembered Drew studying it when she'd come into the study last night. From what he'd said then, she had decided that he hadn't seen anything important, but she wondered now if he'd seen all he needed to. He would know where she was going.

She tried to concentrate. Did he hate her enough that he would go after the cross himself, or somehow take it away from her if she found it, just for spite? If he found the cross it would certainly gild his already world-renowned reputation, and that success might appeal even more to him than the cross itself. And besting her would be revenge of a sort.

"Spencer?"

She didn't know what kind of game he was intent on playing. He had voiced a promise to take her, to make her surrender to him completely, yet today he seemed—what? Less forceful somehow, less definite in his intentions. He had even been kind in a sense, bringing her here and making certain she ate something. But had his motives changed, or was he simply playing a more subtle and ultimately more destructive game of cat and mouse?

"Yes," she said finally. "I leave Monday."

"And your contact in Austria knows that?"

What was he getting at? "Of course he knows."

"That may not have been a smart move, Spencer." For once, he seemed totally serious and not at all mocking. "The experts might have laughed at Allan, but I know a dozen collectors who've just been waiting for someone to find the cross, and more than one of them wouldn't hesitate to kill in order to get it."

It was a new idea to her, and she wondered if he was just trying to scare her enough that she wouldn't search for the cross. Still . . . this was far more his area of expertise, and perhaps it was a sincere warning. She just didn't know.

Managing a light tone, she said, "Even if those collectors somehow heard that I was going after the cross, I doubt they'd have any more faith in my ability to find it than you do."

After a long moment he said, "That does rankle, doesn't it?"

"Your opinion of my abilities?" Spencer pushed her empty coffee cup away and leaned back, wondering if her smile looked as strained as it felt. "If it gives you any sense of triumph to hear it, yes. I don't suppose anyone likes being considered a stupid and talentless fool."

Drew seemed to hesitate, then reached across the table suddenly and grasped one of her hands. "Why do you want to find the cross, Spencer?" he asked flatly.

She tried to pull her hand away, but abandoned the attempt when his grip tightened. The touch of him was instantly disturbing, and she answered his question automatically as she tried to cope with the response of her body to even so casual a contact with him. "For Dad.

It's the only thing I can give him before he dies, and I have to. . . . Please let go of me." The expression in his eyes bothered her. It was almost distant, as if he were listening to some far-off sound.

Somewhat to her surprise he did release her hand, and when his eyes focused on her face again they were almost angry.

"Damn you," he said softly.

Spencer nervously brushed at a strand of hair on her forehead that had come loose from the neat braid, and then laced her fingers tightly together in her lap. Why did she feel suddenly more threatened than ever? It was as if he was somehow closer than he'd been before, looming, and she couldn't hide from him. Damn her? Damn *him* for making her feel so vulnerable.

Holding her voice steady, she said, "I should be getting back to the farm. The horses are fed at six, and I need to work with Corsair before then."

"You should quit for the day." It wasn't an order, but a flat statement, and before she could say anything he went on in the same level tone. "Today's Friday. If you seriously intend to go to Europe on Monday, you need to rest, Spencer. Be sensible."

He was right, and that didn't make the knowledge any more palatable. She half nodded and slid from the booth. "Will you take me back to that farm, please? I need to get my car."

Drew didn't seem surprised by her acquiescence. If anything, he was matter-of-fact as he joined her. "Fine.

Then I'll follow you back to the house. I'd like to see Allan."

"No!" She got a grip on herself, knowing her voice had been too sharp, the refusal too adamant; she was still wary of provoking him. "He—doesn't see anyone," she murmured, watching Drew toss a few bills onto the table.

Drew didn't say anything in response to that until they were in his car on the way back to the farm a few moments later, and when he did speak his voice was calm. "A lie to keep me away from him, Spencer?"

"I'm not a liar," she said, wondering if he would ever believe that. "Dad doesn't see anyone. He doesn't want anyone to see *him,* don't you understand? He's very thin and—and weak, and the stroke affected his speech. He'd hate it if you saw him. Especially you. He thought a lot of you."

After glancing at her briefly, Drew said, "Did you tell him I came to the house last night?"

"No."

"Does he know you're going after the cross?"

Spencer hesitated. "He knows."

Drew glanced at her again. "But?"

"But nothing. He knows, that's all." She wasn't about to tell Drew that a couple of weeks earlier her father had gotten it into his head that she would have help in her search for the cross, and that the help would be Drew. That was one reason he was confident she could find it. With Drew helping her, he'd said, she was sure to find the cross. After the first moment of shock, she had just assumed that her father's mind had drifted into the past, because it sometimes did that. Still, she'd been more unnerved than she might otherwise have been when Drew had shown up at the house last night.

"You can't go alone," Drew said.

She started slightly. "What? Of course I can. I've been to Europe before."

"That isn't the point. Spencer, weren't you listening when I talked about those collectors? If word gets out— and it will, it always does—that there's even a chance the cross could be located, things could get very nasty for you."

"I can take care of myself," she said stubbornly, even though she wasn't at all sure of that.

"Can you handle a gun?"

The flat question made a chill run down her spine. "If you're trying to scare me—"

His glance this time was impatient and something else, something she couldn't identify. "I hope to God it's working. You should be scared. That cross is worth millions—people have been murdered for a hell of a lot less."

Spencer didn't want to think about that; after all, what could she do except be cautious? But what he was saying caught her interest in another way. Curious, she said, "That sounds like the voice of experience. Surely you haven't had to deal with violent people in building your own collection?"

"Once or twice," he replied, definitely impatient now. "Spencer—"

"I can't imagine you in violent situations," she said. "You were always so cool and calm. I mean, I knew you went to some pretty out-of-the-way places looking for antiquities, but I never thought of you carrying a gun. Have you?"

"Yes, I've carried a gun. Quite often. And before you ask, I've had to use it a few times."

Spencer stared determinedly through the windshield, just stopping herself from wincing at the sharpness of his voice. "Sorry I asked. I know your life's none of my business."

Cool and calm, Drew thought, wondering what had happened to those qualities. He sighed roughly. "No, I'm sorry. I didn't mean to bite your head off. But my past isn't important. Your immediate future is the point right now. You have to take this seriously, Spencer. Some of the people who collect antiquities are very dangerous. They'll stop at nothing to get what they want. You'll be a long way from home, in an unfamiliar situation, and you don't know the players. You could get hurt."

"If you're trying to demolish my confidence," she said a bit shakily, "congratulations on doing a good job."

Drew swore under his breath and abruptly pulled the car off the road just yards from the farm's driveway. He killed the engine and turned to face her, his expression a little tight. "We do seem to read the worst into each other's motives, don't we?"

The car was small, and with his entire attention focused on her it felt even smaller to Spencer. She was already unnerved by what he had said and done last night; his mercurial moods today had served only to confuse her further. She couldn't *not* suspect his motives. Very conscious that only the gear console separated them in the enclosed space of the car, she shrugged defensively and looked at him with wary eyes.

"Dammit, Spencer, I know what I'm talking about when it comes to collectors. Can you accept that?"

"Yes, I can accept it. I can even accept that you're probably right and I'm in over my head." She drew a short breath. "But that doesn't change a thing. I am going after the cross, and nothing you could say to me would make any difference. So why don't *you* accept that?"

"Because you're doomed to fail. You should spend Allan's last days with him, not haring off on a wild-goose chase."

She stared at him for a frozen moment, then said softly, "Thanks a lot. Add guilt to the rest. You really do know where to stick the knife, don't you?"

Drew looked at her white face, still seeing the flash of anguish that had briefly darkened her eyes, and for the first time didn't question his reading of her emotions. She was haunted by the fear that her father would die while she was far away in a foreign country searching for a myth.

"God, I'm sorry," he muttered, reaching over the

console to grasp her shoulders. "I didn't mean—Spencer, I wasn't trying to hurt you."

"Sure." She shifted a little as if to dislodge his hands, then said in the same stiff voice, "If you'll let go of me, I'll get out here. You don't have to drive to the barns."

The past twenty-four hours had been unsettling ones for Drew. Stepping back into Spencer Wyatt's life had opened a Pandora's box of gnawing, unresolved emotions, and he hadn't been able to find a calm balance among them. Last night he had believed that simply taking what belonged to him—her—and making her surrender to him completely would satisfy him, but today he had faced the knowledge that it wouldn't be that simple.

He was angry, worried and frustrated, and talking was doing nothing except exacerbate the situation. Their mistrust made them both believe the worst no matter what was said.

"Dammit, Spencer . . ." Hating the withdrawn look in her eyes and the masklike stillness of her face, he pulled her toward him suddenly and covered her mouth with his.

Spencer wanted to fight him. She wanted to remain stiff and unresponsive, for the sake of her pride if nothing else. But she couldn't. At the first touch of his warm, hard mouth, a dizzying wave of pleasure washed over her with stunning force, and the hands that had lifted to push against his chest lingered instead to clutch the edges of his open jacket. She barely felt the steel teeth of the zipper bite into her fingers.

All her thoughts were submerged, drowned by physical and emotional sensations so powerful they bordered on pain. It was as if he had opened a door to the part of her she had shut away long ago, releasing the wild storm of feelings she'd never been able to control. And couldn't now. Nothing mattered but him and what he made her feel, nothing at all. Every nerve and instinct her body could claim came alive, and the empty ache inside her was a hunger so vast it was like madness. Was madness.

She wondered later where it would have ended if there hadn't been an interruption. But the loud blaring of a car horn jerked them apart as a convertible filled with teenage boys roared past, and Spencer found herself staring dazedly through the windshield at the retreating car and the laughing faces turned back toward them.

Drew said something violent, his voice hoarse, then started the engine with a slightly jerky motion. He didn't say another word until he pulled the car into the lot near the barns and stopped, and when he did speak his voice was still a bit strained. "At least there's one thing we don't fight about."

Spencer reached for the door handle and had one foot out of the car when he caught her wrist.

"Admit it, Spencer."

Her breathing and heartbeat were just beginning to settle down to something approaching normal and she felt feverish from head to toe, and she did *not* want to say anything at all because she knew her voice would be treacherously unsteady. But she also knew he was determined for her to say what he wanted to hear. Without looking at him, she merely said, "Yes."

"It's just a matter of time. You know that."

"Yes," she repeated softly.

His fingers tightened around her wrist, then suddenly released her. She got out of his car and closed the door, then walked steadily to the barn where she'd left her hard hat and gloves. She didn't look back, even when she heard the sports car roar away with an angry sound.

Once inside the cool, shadowy barn hall, she leaned back against a closed stable door and shut her eyes. For the first time she understood why she had felt nervous and threatened around him all those years ago. It was because her deepest instincts had known then what her mind only now accepted as truth—and understanding made it no less frightening.

She was lost when he touched her, instantly his with no will to save herself. From the first time she had looked into his eyes she had been tied to him, had belonged to him on some deep, almost primitive level of herself. Perhaps it had happened because she had been so young, had fallen in love so desperately, or perhaps it had happened simply because it was meant to. For whatever reason, she had known she was his. It was a knowledge deeper than instinct or reason, a certainty that was ancient and without question. So simple. And so terrifying.

She had known it even ten years ago, even though his restraint had kept her from losing control then. With him her instinct was to give whatever he asked, more than he asked, to relinquish even her own identity and let him take that as well. Her mind had rebelled ten years ago, too immature to understand except subconsciously that to give all that she was to him would destroy her unless he gave of himself as freely.

She hadn't believed he could—or would—do that. So cool and calm, so controlled, he had seemed untouchable to her, and the subconscious terror of being lost forever within his detachment had driven her to run from him. And she had run to another man, a man who had demanded nothing of her except that she be the focus of his tempestuous captivation.

She couldn't run again. Spencer knew that, knew the uselessness of it. Because this time he meant to have her. He was risking nothing, not even his pride, and that lack of any vulnerability would make him relentless. She knew he could be relentless now, and she knew she couldn't fight him.

As he had said, it was just a matter of time.

WHEN TUCKER WOKE her up very early Saturday morning with the news that the house had been robbed in the night, Spencer's first emotion was wry amusement. Robbed? There was nothing of value left, only copies of priceless things, and wouldn't the burglar be staggered to discover that?

"What did he take?" she asked Tucker as they walked down the hallway toward the stairs.

In a precise tone, Tucker replied, "Everything he could carry, I would say. Including the contents of your father's safe."

Spencer stopped at the head of the stairs and looked at him, her faint amusement vanishing. "You mean the papers? The set of copies I made of all Dad's papers?"

"Yes."

She began to feel just a little chilled. "How was the safe opened?"

"Professionally," Tucker replied without expression.

"And the security system?"

"None of the alarms were triggered, but the system's still active. I don't know how he got in."

Though it had been expensive to install, the security system of the house cost little to maintain and Spencer hadn't been forced to shut it down. Her father had once told her that no security system was foolproof, that if a burglar wanted to get in badly enough he would, but that both insurance companies and home owners slept better with the illusion that valuables were protected. Even though she had little to protect these days, Spencer had slept better thinking that at least a burglar would have to work at it to get into the house.

Now she knew what her father had meant about illusions.

But even that disturbed her less than the fact that the papers had been taken. Burglars who took artworks and emptied out the silver drawer seldom bothered with papers that were quite obviously without intrinsic value. Stock certificates or bonds were one thing—but handwritten notes, drawings and maps were something else again.

Spencer couldn't help but remember what Drew had warned her about, and a few moments later as she stood with Tucker in her father's study, a fatalistic certainty crept over her. The safe, on the wall at right angles to the desk, was cunningly and quite well hidden behind the face of a working clock. It was open, obviously empty, and nothing had been damaged through carelessness or inexperience. As Tucker had said, a professional job all the way.

Almost to herself, she murmured, "He didn't even try to open the trick safe behind the painting."

"No," Tucker agreed.

In a bit of sleight of hand meant hopefully to fool anyone looking for valuables, her father had installed a far more obvious or "trick" safe behind a hinged painting above his desk. The theory was that a thief would quickly discover that safe, find it empty and conclude that nothing of value was hidden in the room. But their night visitor had indicated contempt for the trick: the painting was pulled out away from the safe and no attempt to open it had been made.

Of course, he might have opened and then closed the

safe—but Spencer didn't think so. Everything else he had opened remained open: the other safe, desk drawers, the silver drawer in the pantry and the few curio and collectible cabinets that had held mostly worthless figurines. No, he had wanted them to know that he saw through the trick.

Spencer was very glad he'd found nothing of value, and even more glad that the originals of her father's papers were safely in a bank vault and that a second set of copies she'd made was upstairs in her bedroom. But she was very much afraid that whoever had broken into the house last night had been after only one thing. The papers. The cross.

Softly she said, "If he was professional enough to bypass the security system, find the safe and get into it without fuss, don't you think he would have known that the silver was plated, and the figurines and prints were worthless?"

Almost as quietly, Tucker answered, "I would think so."

"Then he was after Dad's papers, and the rest was just to cover up his real target." Spencer shivered a little, for the first time seriously wondering if she would risk more than simple failure in going after the cross. "Somebody could be a step ahead of me."

"Someone dangerous. Miss Spencer, some collectors are ruthless in acquiring what they desire. You have no experience with that kind of person—"

"Tucker." She half turned to stare at him. "Don't you

start, please. I've already heard enough from Drew. This theft doesn't change anything except that I have to move faster." Very deliberately, she added, "If I fail, I fail. But I won't spend the rest of my life regretting that I never even tried."

After a moment Tucker said, "The cross isn't worth dying for. Your father would never forgive himself if that happened."

"It won't happen."

"I know you, Miss Spencer. I know how much this means to you. I believe you'll find the cross, where it's lain hidden all these years or in the hands of someone who got there first. But I also believe that it won't be easy, and it will be dangerous. I don't want you to forget that you mean more to your father than anything else in the world. He'd be the first to consign that cross to hell to spare you pain."

It was a long speech for Tucker, and it left Spencer without very much she could say. So she merely nodded and said, "I know that, believe me. Don't worry—I'll be careful." Since his face was expressionless as usual, she wasn't sure if he had any faith in that promise, but he half nodded before speaking again.

"I haven't called the police yet."

"Don't. Not until I've gone. I can't afford to be tied up here answering questions all day. And don't mention the papers to them, just the other stuff. I doubt they'll be much interested anyway, since we didn't lose anything of value."

Characteristically, Tucker picked up on the important part of what she'd said. "You'll leave today, then?"

"If I can get a flight to Paris." More money, she was thinking worriedly, and no guarantee that she wouldn't have to wait until Monday for the train to Austria. But what choice did she have? Even though the papers had been stolen, she still had an advantage—she hoped—if she moved quickly enough. It had taken her two months to piece the clues together, and even someone with expert knowledge would have to study all the papers carefully in order to figure it out. Her father had been too close, too familiar with his own work, to see the pattern. With luck it would take anyone else at least a little time to figure it out.

"What about Mr. Haviland?" Tucker asked.

"He isn't a part of this, I told you that."

After a moment Tucker said, "Can you afford pride?"

The quiet question was too pointed to ignore, and Spencer managed a twisted smile. "No. But it isn't just pride. What I did to him was unforgivable, and he has no reason to want to help me now. He has plenty of reason to want to hurt me—I won't let him use the cross as a weapon."

"Would he do that?"

Spencer shrugged a little, because she just wasn't sure, then said, "I'd better go start making phone calls and finish packing. If Dad asks for me, tell him I'll be up later to see him."

"Very well."

Luck was with Spencer, though by this point she wasn't sure if it was good luck or bad. In any case, she was able to book a seat on an early-afternoon flight to Paris. It meant a scramble to finish packing and take care of the other last-minute details that always accompany a trip, but at least the haste had kept her mind occupied and distracted her from thoughts of Drew and worries about who else was after the cross.

It was a little after noon when she went into her father's bedroom. There was less time to say good-bye than she would have liked, especially since his health was so precarious, and the guilt of leaving him for days at least and possibly weeks ate at her.

She slipped into the wingback chair by his bed, nodding to the nurse, who took the opportunity to slip out and take a break. Spencer sat silently for a few moments, looking at her father as he dozed, her heart wrung as always because of the change in him since the stroke.

Physically, Spencer had inherited more from her small-boned and delicate mother than from her father, but she had gotten his black hair and gray eyes. Allan Wyatt had been a big, bluff, hearty man, the strength of his very active youth remaining with him well into his sixties, but now he was a gaunt shadow of the man he had been. His thick hair, only lightly graying before the stroke, was now almost pure white, and flesh had melted from his big frame. The stroke had completely paralyzed his right side, dragging down the corners of his mouth and eye, slurring his speech, and both his concentration and memory were erratic from moment to moment.

He had been more alert during the past weeks, seemingly because Spencer had been making her plans to go after the cross, but his doctors had warned her that there was little chance of a recovery.

His eyes opened suddenly, fixing on her and gradually clearing of most of the fog. "Hi, Princess," he murmured, his deep voice so distorted that only Spencer, Tucker and the nurse would have understood him.

"Hi, Daddy." She smiled at him, reaching for his left hand as his fingers uncurled invitingly. "Did Tucker tell you? I'm leaving for Paris in just a little while."

The gray eyes brightened. "That's what he said. You're—going after the cross."

She nodded. "It's all arranged. A flight to Paris and then a train to Austria."

"Should fly—all the way," he muttered, a slight frown creasing his brow. "Into Vienna. Why train?"

Not wanting him to know that money was one of her biggest problems, she said soothingly, "I'll be able to see more from a train, you know. I've never been to Austria, and it's supposed to be so beautiful. But I promise not to spend too much time sightseeing."

A ghost of a laugh escaped him. "See it while you're there. Never know when—there'll be another chance.

Always—take advantage of your—opportunities, Princess. I remember—the first time I was there. . . ."

Spencer listened with a smile as he talked about a long-ago visit on the eve of a war, just before the borders had been closed. She knew the story well and was short on time, but wouldn't have interrupted him for anything, cherishing every moment she could spend with him now. But when his voice finally trailed off nearly ten minutes later, she knew she had to go.

"Daddy?" She lifted his wasted hand and cradled it against her cheek. "You be good, all right? Listen to Tucker and Mrs. Perry. I'll be home as soon as I can."

His gaze, very foggy now, drifted around the room briefly and then found her face. "Yes," he murmured. "Yes. You—be careful. The cross—isn't what you think. What you see. Something else. Didn't write it down. Tell Drew—they hid it inside. Like the clock . . ." His eyes closed heavily, and his breathing deepened in sleep.

Spencer held his hand for a moment longer, then gently tucked it beneath the blankets. His mind had drifted again, assuming Drew would be with her, but she didn't think he'd been rambling completely. Still, she didn't understand what he'd meant, and couldn't spare the time to think it through. She bent over to kiss her father's gaunt cheek gently, then left the room.

And it wasn't until she was sitting on the uncomfortable airplane seat and staring out the window at a grayish Atlantic far below that she wondered if her father had tried to tell her something that would turn out to be terribly important. It was just a feeling she had, vague and uneasy, a niggling sense of having missed something somewhere along the way.

What? What was it?

She was too tired to grapple with it just now. She was very conscious of the growing distance between her and her father. And between her and Drew. What would he think when he found out she'd gone? What would he do? She didn't know. But she wished he was with her now. She hated herself for that, but wished it all the same. She felt very much alone.

DREW SPENT ALL of Saturday morning on the phone. It wasn't an ideal day in which to seek the kind of information he was after, but that hardly deterred him. He called in favors, bribed, wheedled and badgered. Some might have said that what he was doing was wrong—some, in fact, *did* say it—but that didn't stop him, either, and he didn't take no for an answer. He had found out long ago that with enough nerve, connections, persistence and money, it was possible to get almost any kind of information at any hour of the day or night.

Discretion went by the board. This time he wasn't probing carefully for hints, but digging for facts. And he got them. By noon he knew that Allan Wyatt had made a series of bad investments just before his stroke, had sold real estate at bargain prices and heavily mortgaged his house in an effort to recoup his losses, and had spent that money just as unwisely. He owed a staggering amount in back taxes, uninsured medical bills and various credit accounts.

And it had all fallen on Spencer's shoulders.

She had sold her car—buying a cheap rattletrap for transportation to and from the farm—her horses and her jewelry. The family silver was gone and she'd tried every means possible to break her trust fund, without success. Allan's car and collectibles had gone more slowly, the reluctance to sell them obvious. Much of the antique furnishings of the house had been sold piece by piece, quietly to private dealers. And there were other economies.

Drew got the whole story, more grim as each fact was revealed, and he knew his instinct hadn't been at fault. The woman he had believed her to be existed only in his bitter imagination.

That woman would not have accepted the burden of her father's debts with such quiet, uncomplaining grace. She wouldn't have negotiated fairly but shrewdly with creditors, earmarked her own trust fund income for debts, or sought a physically demanding job to pay household expenses. And she certainly wouldn't have withdrawn from the social scene in which she'd been brought up, particularly if marrying a rich man was something she considered an acceptable solution to her financial worries.

Drew had asked her how bad it was, and she had

turned the question aside. Wyatt pride? Maybe. But perhaps, Drew realized, that chin-in-the-air Wyatt pride that so angered him wasn't so much haughtiness as it was sheer bravado. Who was she really? What lay underneath that defiant show of courage? And how could he find the truth when his own words and actions had convinced her that he meant nothing but harm?

chapter five

THE PRIVATE SCHOOLS Spencer had attended had offered a wide range of foreign languages to their students. She had taken Spanish. Unfortunately, she was in France rather than Spain, and the taxi driver she had finally snagged at Orly understood neither English, Spanish, nor sign language.

The communication barrier was heightened by the fact that Spencer wasn't sure where she wanted to go. Practically any eastbound train would have satisfied her, but according to the schedule she had, nothing was heading east until morning, and she'd made no provisions for an overnight stay in Paris. It was late, and even though her system was still functioning on East Coast time, she was worn out from the travel and the hectic day behind her. All she wanted—and all she could afford—was some place with a bed and plain food, and she tried to communicate that to the taxi driver.

She was beginning to wonder if she'd ever be able to leave the airport tonight when a deep male voice spoke a couple of sentences sharply in flawless French. The taxi driver looked past her left shoulder, instantly bent to pick up the bags from the pavement at her feet and trotted around to put them in his trunk.

Spencer turned, conscious of feeling absurdly guilty.

"Running away from me again, Spencer?" Drew asked mildly.

Standing no more than two feet away from her and dressed almost as casually as she in dark slacks, a black leather jacket and a white shirt open at the throat, he seemed to her, even more than usual, larger than life. Appearing suddenly, and here, almost as if some supernatural force had spirited him across an ocean ahead of her. He shouldn't have *been* here; he was supposed to be thousands of miles away, and she wasn't prepared to face him. Not now. Not yet. He had the unnerving trick of knocking her off balance, and she spoke without thinking with far more emotion in her voice than she liked.

"No, I didn't run away from you. I won't do that again." His eyes narrowed swiftly, but Spencer managed to get hold of herself and added, "What did you do, leave D.C. last night?"

"I left just after you did."

"Then how—" Spencer realized even before she

could finish the question, and answered it herself. "The Concorde."

Drew nodded, then stepped toward her as the driver came around to open the car door. "Get in, Spencer."

She found herself doing just that, which appalled her so much that she didn't trust her voice until Drew was sitting beside her and the taxi was fighting its way through the crush of traffic. God, was she going to meekly do *anything* the man ordered her to do? It was a terrifying thought.

"Where," she said at last, "are you taking me?"

"A hotel." He was half turned toward her, looking at her steadily in the erratic illumination of passing cars and streetlights. "We're booked on a flight to Salzburg early tomorrow afternoon, with a connection to Innsbruck. There were no direct flights available."

Silently realizing that he'd apparently had enough time to memorize her itinerary—at least her ultimate destination—no matter how briefly he'd studied it, Spencer took a deep breath and tried to hold her voice steady. "Are you after the gold or the glory?"

It was his turn to take a breath, and his voice sounded as if patience was an effort. "Neither. Look, Spencer, whether you want to admit it or not, you're in over your head—and that's no insult to you. The black market for antiquities is a seller's market all the way, and antiquities are getting scarcer by the day. The players in *this* game break necks as easily as they break laws. The stakes are very high."

With the memory of a thief in the night fresh in her memory, Spencer found it hard to protest. But she didn't want to tell him that she was reasonably sure someone else was after the cross, so she had to at least try to protest. "You talk as if I took out a front-page ad in half the world's newspapers claiming I could find the cross. I haven't been that careless, Drew, or that stupid. And Dad's friend wouldn't have told anyone, I know he wouldn't have."

"What about the government officials who had to be consulted? What about their friends and coworkers? The secretaries who typed the paperwork and *their* friends? Spencer, the chances of someone saying the right thing to the wrong person may not be high, but they exist. And since I know for a fact that antiquities have been lost in the past because unscrupulous collectors had people on their payrolls inside government houses, I don't think it's paranoid to assume at least one wrong person knows you're going after the cross."

Spencer stared at him for a moment, then turned her head and gazed out past the driver at scenery she wouldn't have noticed even if it hadn't been dark. "All right," she said finally. "I'll grant that. You're probably right. I guess it would be naive of me to think otherwise. But it isn't your problem. I haven't asked for your help, or your protection, or—anything else."

"Why not?" He actually sounded a little amused. "I am considered to be pretty good at the game."

She sent him one disbelieving glance, then said

stiffly, "That's a stupid question. I may not be terribly bright, but I have sense enough not to ask a shark for help while I'm treading water."

"Ouch," Drew murmured. "I suppose I deserved that." The words were uttered lightly, but there was something else underneath, something a little grim.

This time the look she gave him was a steady one, slightly puzzled and more than a little wary. She wished she could see his expression more clearly, but wasn't sure that would have helped in any case. "Which game are you playing now, Drew?"

He'd had ample time during the long trip to Paris in which to consider how to convince Spencer that his attitude toward her had changed. After the things he'd said to her, he doubted that she would believe so sudden a transformation, and besides that, he was still uncertain of just what he felt about her. There were still too many questions, and there was too much anger inside him.

As far as he could see, his only course of action lay in helping her to look for the cross. Firstly, because he didn't like to think of her facing possible danger alone, and secondly, because during that search he might find the answers to his questions. Still, he hadn't expected it to be easy.

"I'm not playing a game with you, Spencer," he replied after a moment. "In case you've forgotten, Allan and I were very close. I'd like to see his dream in his hands almost as much as you would. Whatever else there is between us—well, that can wait." He wondered, silently, if it could. Or would.

"You said it was . . . just a matter of time," she said slowly. "You made me admit that."

"It is just a matter of time. But you and I have more of that than Allan does. I think I can help you find the cross. I know I can help if there's trouble."

"And I'm supposed to trust you? That's a lot to ask, don't you think?"

Drew glanced out of the taxi window, but without much interest, as if he simply needed a moment to gather his thoughts. Then, looking back at her, he said, "Maybe so. Offhand, I can't think of a good reason why you should trust me—except that you need help and I'm the best."

Spencer wished she could accuse him of vanity, but she knew that he *was* the best. Not only knowledgeable enough about art objects and antiquities, he was also quite famous for his instincts and intuition. And if that wasn't enough, he spoke a dozen languages fluently, was as familiar with most of the world as she was her back-yard and no doubt knew by sight both the collectors and the black market dealers who could pose a threat.

Her instincts told her she *could* trust him, but she didn't trust her instincts. Not where he was concerned.

"Don't fight me on this," he said softly, watching her so intently that she could feel it.

After a moment Spencer said, "Would it do any good if I did?"

"No. A waste of time and energy." He reached over suddenly and took one of her hands in his, holding it lightly. She thought he was frowning just a bit as he gazed down at her hand, but wasn't sure of that. "A dangerous waste. You can't afford to fight me, Spencer, not while you're looking for the cross. Right now I'm the best ally you could have." '

She knew, only too well, that she didn't really have a choice. It wasn't a defeatist thought, it was a logical one. If she said no, he'd only follow her—or get to Innsbruck before her and simply wait. Better to have him close, where she could keep an eye on him. That's what she told herself.

Besides that, she admitted at least silently that she wanted him here, with her. Not because of the possible danger and not even to help her find the cross, but because . . . She didn't let herself finish the thought. Wouldn't let herself. She tried to draw her hand away, but his long fingers tightened around it.

"I know you're finding it hard to trust me," he said evenly. "I know I've given you reason for that. If it helps, I'll give you my word that I don't want the cross or the credit for finding it. That's all I can do, Spencer."

She wanted to ask, *Can you give me your word you won't hurt me?* But she didn't ask.

She looked down, and in the erratic flashes of passing streetlights the clasp of their hands seemed strangely symbolic of what she was feeling. Her hand, pale in the light, almost unseen in the shadows, was lost in his larger, stronger one, held captive, unresisting. She hoped it was only because she was tired, because she hadn't slept much last night and could never sleep on planes and had never been a good traveler anyway.

She was tired. And she was glad he was here, with her. Never mind why. Why didn't matter, wouldn't matter, until he took what belonged to him and got her out of his system. Then it would matter. When he left her. Then she'd have to face it.

"Spencer?"

In a soft, careful voice, she said, "Finding the cross for Dad means everything to me. Promise—please promise me that you won't interfere with that."

His hand tightened around hers, curiously gentle. "I promise. You have my word I won't do anything to hinder you, Spencer. I'll help all I can."

She nodded in the flickering darkness. "All right." She didn't know if she believed him, but she didn't try again to pull her hand away. She had a faint sense of bridges burning behind her, and it gave her an odd feeling of relief. She was going to do her best to find the cross. And whatever happened between her and Drew, she would do her best to emerge from it, if not whole, then at least with enough of herself left intact to go on.

There were worse things to be than a survivor.

Drew didn't release her hand even when they arrived at the hotel, helping her from the taxi after he'd paid the driver and leading her through the imposing lobby. A bellman trotted after them with Spencer's two bags, and she carried a smaller tote bag on her shoulder in lieu of a purse.

Detouring by the desk only long enough to speak briefly with the clerk—in French, so Spencer had no idea what he'd said to produce the smile on the man's face—Drew led her to the elevators, still holding her hand firmly. He said something to the bellman, which also drew a smile, then looked down at Spencer and explained that he always stayed in this hotel whenever he was in Paris, and that the staff knew him.

The information didn't surprise her.

There was no question that Drew was in charge; he was matter-of-fact about it without arrogance, but she had the feeling he wouldn't give way if she challenged that cool authority. He clearly believed that her acquiescence had given him this role, or else he simply intended to take it.

Oddly, Spencer wasn't tempted to protest—not yet, at any rate. She wasn't called on to make any decisions or choices, not even what floor she wanted a room on, and it was easy to simply accept. For a few minutes she even allowed herself to enjoy the feeling of being taken care of. She hadn't been conscious of wanting that during the past months, because there had been too much to do and too many other worries to think very much about shifting her burdens. Now, when it occurred to her that she was at ease with

Drew's having taken charge, she wondered what that said about her.

Grappling with that unnerving question, she didn't pay much attention to her surroundings until Drew unlocked the door of his suite and led her inside. She pulled her hand gently from his grasp and went to stand near the window as she looked around the spacious sitting room. There were two bedrooms; she watched the bellman take her bags into one of them when Drew told him which one was hers, but said nothing until the man accepted his tip and left them alone in the suite.

"I'm surprised you got two bedrooms," she heard herself say in a slightly wry tone.

Drew shrugged out of his jacket and tossed it over the arm of a chair, smiling a little. "I could say it was all the hotel had available."

"You could. Would it be true?"

"No. I meant what I said, Spencer. The priority right now is the cross."

She half nodded, accepting that even though she couldn't help wondering if he was merely amusing himself by toying with her. "What time is the flight tomorrow?"

"Two. Earliest I could get."

Her watch was still on U.S. time and Spencer didn't bother to look at it. No matter what the local time was, she was tired and needed sleep. She'd cope better with jet lag—to say nothing of coping with

Drew—after a good night's sleep. "I think I'll turn in, then," she murmured.

"Did you eat anything on the plane?"

Before she could stop it, a faint grimace pulled at her lips. "I hate airplane food. I'm not hungry though, so—"

"To hear you talk, you're never hungry. But I am, and you need to eat something. Why don't you get ready for bed while I order a light meal from room service. Then you can sleep late tomorrow and we'll both be ready for the hunt."

What he said made sense, and she shrugged an acceptance as she started toward her bedroom. "Okay, fine. Just don't order snails unless you like them."

"I don't." He seemed amused. "Anything else you'd like me to avoid?"

"Anything with alcohol." She paused in the doorway of her bedroom and offered a faint smile. "I'm allergic. Can't even take cold medicine unless it's alcohol free."

Drew was obviously surprised. "I didn't know that. How do you react to it?"

"Putting it as delicately as possible, I get rid of it. Quickly. The stuff makes me vilely sick."

"I suppose that includes wine in sauces?"

"Yes."

He nodded in understanding and watched her bedroom door close quietly behind her. He was more than a little worried about her. Knowing now what she'd gone through in the past months, he was hardly surprised that the trip from D.C. had left her pale with exhaustion. The emotional strain since her father's stroke had to be intense, had to be wearing away at her reserves of strength and will—and she was still on her feet, still determined to go on with this.

Wyatt pride, bred into her very bones? Or something else, an inner core of steel that kept her going when most would have given up the effort? He didn't know, not yet, but he was beginning to believe that she had more than her share of courage. That her seeming fragility was deceptive he already knew; watching her difficult and demanding work with the horses had told him that. But in a few short months she'd been burdened with overwhelming stresses on a level she could never have been prepared for, and there had to be a breaking point.

Only days ago the thought of her control in splinters had afforded Drew a savage pleasure. Now the very idea was something he didn't like to imagine. He wanted to know what was under the control, wanted to be able to read the emotions in her eyes, but he didn't want her broken. He wasn't sure, now, if he ever had wanted that.

He wanted to take care of her. That awareness had lurked in his mind since he had realized at the farm that she hadn't been taking care of herself, hadn't been eating right or resting enough, and he hadn't stopped to examine his own feelings. Now he pushed the matter aside, still too raw and unsettled emotionally to try to untangle what he felt about her.

He studied the room-service menu briefly and then

called to place the order, double-checking to make certain there was no alcohol in anything. After that he killed time by pacing restlessly, too aware of the sound of the shower in the next room, of her nearness. His desire for her had only increased during the past days, and the protective feelings, his anxiety about her, had done nothing except turn what had been a bitter and almost savage need into something that was far less harsh and yet curiously more relentless, more imperative.

She wouldn't fight him, he knew that. She wanted him. But she didn't *want* to want him. He knew that, too. She would burn in his arms with an astonishing passion he'd had only a taste of, but she wouldn't be his. That certainty, more than anything, was responsible for his hesitation to take her now as he'd promised he would. It wouldn't be enough, just to take her, not if it was something she simply surrendered to because her body couldn't fight his. He wanted more. Not just a physical response but the pride and strength of her, the secrets her control hid so well, the emotions he could only guess at. He wanted it all.

Halting near the door to her bedroom, he stood listening unconsciously to the sound of the shower, his mind conjuring up an image of her with haunting ease. Remembering how she'd felt against him, the soft curves and delicate bones, the warm silk of her hair wrapped around his fingers, the electrifying way her body had molded itself to his, the hunger of her mouth beneath his.

In the shower there would be droplets of water cling-ing to her pale gold skin. Steam all around her. She'd be warm and slippery, her lips wet when he kissed her, her eyes dazed with pleasure as he touched her naked body. . . .

The sound of the shower stopped suddenly and, re-alizing what he was doing, Drew turned jerkily away from the closed door and paced over to the window. "God," he murmured, staring blindly out into the darkness.

Control. She had too much. And he had precious little.

The arrival of the room-service waiter a few minutes later was a welcome distraction, and by the time the food had been set out on the table near Drew's bedroom he had managed to pull on a mask of his own. When Spencer came out of her bedroom, covered from neck to ankles by one of the thick terry robes the hotel thought-fully provided its guests, he was even able to greet her lightly.

"Perfect timing."

"Looks that way," she responded with equal casual-ness, taking her place at the table. She didn't appear quite so exhausted as she had, but with her hair loose around her face she seemed very young and almost heartbreakingly fragile.

Drew had never felt protective urges toward any woman in his life except Spencer, and he had never felt a desire for any woman so intense he wanted to make wild love to her until neither of them could walk without help—except Spencer.

He wondered if he was losing his mind.

Taking his own place across from her, he tried to think of something else, some casual topic that would distract his mind. But in the end it was Spencer who spoke first.

"I suppose you'll want to see Dad's papers." Her head was a little bent as she unfolded her napkin across her lap, and she didn't look at him.

He hesitated, then said, "I think I'd probably be more help to you if I saw them, and I'd like to try and find the clues you found. But it's up to you, Spencer."

She sent him a fleeting glance. "The originals are in a bank vault. I made copies of everything, even of some notes he scribbled on odd sheets of paper."

"Was that a yes or a no?" Drew asked wryly.

"It's a yes." She picked up her fork, meeting his gaze steadily this time. "I'm a little curious to see if you find what I did. After all, maybe I'm wrong. Maybe you'll be able to tell me without any doubt that this is a wild-goose chase."

"You have doubts?" he asked curiously, because she had seemed so sure.

"No. But what do I know, after all? You're the expert. I'm not even a talented amateur."

Drew was silent for a few moments, watching as she began eating, then said quietly, "I've said a few things you're not going to easily forgive, haven't I?"

She looked up, clearly surprised and, for an instant, puzzled. Then her slight frown cleared and she said, "I wasn't being sarcastic, if that's what you think. The truth is that any claim to knowledge I have is shaky at best. I went to college and I earned a degree, but I majored in history, not archaeology. I've listened to Dad, but he wasn't trying to teach me and I wasn't trying to learn."

He half nodded, but said, "Still, I've been pretty rough on you. For what it's worth, I'm sorry."

Spencer absently sipped the milk he'd ordered for her, wishing she could read his expression. Even in the light, she had no idea what he was thinking or feeling. "That sounds like an abrupt change of attitude. What brought it on?"

Drew hadn't meant to bring up the subject, but he was angry at himself for having misjudged her out of his own bitterness, and disliked the idea that he had added to her burdens. Flatly he said, "I spent the morning checking a few of my assumptions. You obviously didn't want me to know, but I found out anyway."

"Found out what?" she asked warily.

"That Allan as good as bankrupted himself before the stroke. And that you've been coping with the results for the last six months."

"That's none of your business," she said, chin lifting.

"You should have told me."

"Why? To give you another chance to call me a liar, or to accuse me of trying to drum up a little sympathy? No, thanks. Besides that, it isn't your concern."

Remembering that first night when he had torn at her mercilessly out of his own caustic anger, Drew could hardly blame her for believing that his reaction would have been disbelief or something worse. In fact, he knew it would have been. The realization left him with nothing to say. He finished eating, more automatically than out of any sense of hunger, and thought that she did the same.

"Do you want to have the papers tonight?" she asked somewhat stiffly as soon as she pushed her plate away.

"I can start on them tonight," he said. "I don't need much sleep."

Spencer got up and went into her room, leaving Drew to rise more slowly. He moved into the sitting area, even more restless than he'd been earlier, conscious of frustration and anxiety. He wasn't handling this well, and he knew it. Just when she seemed to have accepted his help, when she appeared to be almost at ease with him, he'd had to bring up something virtually guaranteed to make her retreat stiffly. He hadn't meant that to happen; more than anything, he'd just wanted to make amends for the way he'd treated her that first night. To try to tell her that he knew he'd been wrong about her and that he was sorry for the things he'd said.

Her chin had gone up, the flash in her eyes warning him that he'd trespassed on ground she had marked as off-limits. Wyatt pride again, maybe. Or perhaps it was just her pride, her determination to carry the burdens alone. Whatever the reason, she clearly wasn't willing to talk to him about her father's—and her—financial problems. And though that was understandable, it bothered him that there were things she couldn't tell him, places in her life that weren't open to him.

He told himself that he'd only come back into her life days ago—and acted like a bastard when he did—so he couldn't expect the path to be a smooth one. But the patience that had always come so easily to him seemed beyond reach now. He *needed,* and the hunger was as much emotional as physical, leaving him more vulnerable than he'd ever been in his life and urging him to hurry, to grab and hold on tight.

Before he lost her again.

He felt a shock and then a strange, cold tightness in his chest. It was fear, and he knew it. A fear of somehow making the same mistake he must have made ten years ago, the mistake that had driven her away from him.

"Here are the papers." She came into the sitting area and dropped a thick manila envelope onto the coffee table, then immediately turned away.

Drew took three long steps and blocked her way out of the room, his hands lifting to rest on her shoulders. "Spencer, I was wrong about you, and I'm sorry. I want you to know that. To believe it."

"All right." She didn't meet his eyes, but looked fixedly at the top button of his shirt. Her voice was a little breathless, and she was very still.

Just thinking about her had his control on the fine edge of impossible; touching her was pushing him over the brink. Even through the thick terry of her robe he could feel warm flesh and delicate bones, feel how petite she was. Her hair smelled like sunshine and her skin looked so silky that he had to touch it. His hand moved before he was even aware of it, sliding beneath the dark curtain of her hair to touch her neck. Her skin was silky, and so fine he could feel her pulse thudding rapidly as he gently pushed her chin up.

"Have I made you hate me?" His voice was strained.

She looked up at him with huge eyes, the smoke gray of them disturbed and nervous. "I don't hate you. But . . . I don't understand you."

His thumb rhythmically stroked the clean line of her jaw, feeling the tension there. Gazing down at her, he was seeing the girl she'd been all those years ago— lovely, sweet, accepting the role of woman with grace and doubt. What had he done to push her away then? He didn't know, couldn't ask, and he wanted her so intensely he could hardly think. The distraction was reflected in his voice when he said, "I'm not so complicated."

"You are." She sounded a little bewildered. "You've changed so much since the night you came to the house. I don't know what to think, what to believe. Who are you? What do you want from me, Drew?"

He didn't have an answer, at least not one he could explain to her—or to himself. Except that he wanted her and was afraid of losing her. That was the only thing he was sure of.

Driven, he lowered his head and covered her slightly parted lips with his own, the hand at her shoulder moving down her back to pull her closer, until he could feel her against him. Hunger jolted through him, so abrupt and potent it was like a blow, and his mouth hardened fiercely on hers as his tongue probed deeply. She trembled, her delicate body molding itself to his and her arms lifting to slide around his waist. She made a soft, muffled sound of pleasure.

Even though desire had been tormenting him, Drew hadn't intended this to get out of hand. He was too aware of her exhaustion and her wariness not to know that the timing wasn't the best. But her response, so instant and total, tested his uncertain control to the limits, and he wasn't at all sure he'd be able to stop. His need for her was almost intolerable, burning and aching through his entire body until he nearly groaned aloud. Her mouth was so sweet and hot under his, and her body felt so good in his arms, against him. It felt so right.

He wanted to carry her into the bedroom and press her back into the softness of the bed, cover her slender body with his. Tortured by the erotic feel of her breasts against his chest, he wanted them naked in his hands, wanted to take her nipples into his mouth and stroke them with his tongue, taste them. He wanted to feel her satiny legs wrap around him as he settled between them, feel her soft heat sheathe his aching flesh.

He wanted her to belong to him.

Suddenly certain that if he didn't stop now he wouldn't be able to, Drew tore his mouth from hers. He held her against him, trying not to hold on too hard and hurt her, while he struggled to regain at least a fingertip grasp on his control. He wasn't at all sure he could do it; his heart was slamming in his chest, every rasping breath was like fire in his aching throat and his muscles were so rigid they quivered from the strain.

It was several long moments before he was able to slide his hands up to her shoulders and ease her trembling body away from him. Her arms fell to her sides as she stared up at him, and her eyes were wide, dazed, her lips a little swollen and reddened from his fervent passion. There was color in her face now, a soft flush of desire, and knowing he'd kindled that heat almost made him forget his good intentions.

But he managed, barely, to stop himself from yanking her back into his arms. "Go to bed, honey," he said in a thick voice. "I'll see you in the morning." He took his hands off her with an effort and moved away, crossing the room to stare once more out into the dark Paris night.

"Drew?" Her voice was husky.

He turned his head, looking at her as she stood hesitantly in the doorway to her bedroom. "Go to bed," he repeated, his voice more normal now.

She swallowed visibly. "Why? I wouldn't have said no." The admission was clearly difficult but honest.

"You wouldn't have said yes."

Spencer shook her head a little, bewildered. "I wouldn't have stopped you."

"I know. But it isn't the same thing." He managed a faint smile. "Get some rest. Tomorrow will probably be a long day."

After a moment she turned away and went into her bedroom, closing the door softly behind her.

Drew glanced toward his own bedroom, but knew without even thinking about it that he wouldn't be able to sleep. Luckily, he really didn't require much sleep, and was able to function quite well for days at a time with very little rest. He looked at the envelope containing copies of Allan Wyatt's notes. At least he could occupy his mind and possibly distract his thoughts from Spencer's presence in the next room.

His entire body ached dully, and when he moved toward the phone it was slowly. He'd managed to contain his desire, but it was like a storm trapped under glass, the fury restrained illusively but not in the least diminished. God, he'd waited twelve years for her and he didn't know how much longer he could stand it. The need he felt intensified by the hour, and his control was wearing away under the force of it.

And he hadn't yet been able to ask the one question that had haunted him for years, the one question that, more than any other, he needed to have answered.

Why? Why had she run away from him to marry another man?

He called room service, requesting that the remains of their meal be removed and ordering a large pot of coffee. He had a long night ahead of him, he knew.

A very long night.

SPENCER HADN'T EXPECTED to sleep well. The brief, passionate interlude between them had left her feverish, aching and more than a little confused. It didn't make sense, *he* didn't make sense, and she didn't know what to think.

In the end, she was too exhausted to think at all. She called home to let Tucker know she'd arrived safely in Paris and to check on her father. Her father was fine, Tucker told her, and seemed at ease because, he'd said several times, Drew was with her.

"He is with me," she reported with more than a little wryness.

"He came to the house," Tucker said in his usual expressionless voice. "Upset, but not angry, I thought. He guessed you'd gone to Paris."

"Umm. He got here before me. The Concorde."

"He can help you," Tucker said.

"It looks like he's going to." Spencer sighed. "Anyway, I'll call you tomorrow, from Austria."

She hung up after saying good-bye, wondering if her father was still lost in the past or merely psychic. She climbed into the big, lonely bed, turned out the lamp on the nightstand and was almost instantly asleep. She slept dreamlessly for more than eight hours, waking to a bright, quiet room that was briefly unfamiliar. Then she remembered. A hotel. She was in a hotel in Paris, and Drew was here, too.

Keeping her mind carefully blank on that point, Spencer slid from the bed, relieved to find that her weariness was gone and that she felt better physically than she had in a long time. She took a quick shower to finish waking up, then dressed as casually as she had the day before in white jeans and a pale blue sweater, putting her hair in a single braid to fall down her back and applying only a bare minimum of makeup.

It was only when she was sitting on her bed putting on her comfortable shoes that she caught herself listening intently for some sound of Drew in the next room. Awareness of what she was doing shattered the careful blankness of her mind, and she sighed a bit raggedly.

In the light of the morning it still didn't make sense. At her house, Drew had been cruel and scathing, promising to take her, to make certain she was in thrall to him. At the farm the next day he'd been cool and calm at first, then a little mocking, then angry, but not like before, not cruelly angry, and he'd talked to her without tearing her to shreds. Then, last night, he had been quiet and watchful, careful, it seemed to her, as if he were trying to guide their relationship in a new direction. He had begun taking care of her. He had even apologized for having misjudged her, and when he'd held her in his arms and kissed her so hungrily, when she'd been totally unable to resist the desire he'd ignited between them, he had pulled away.

Not saying no, he had said, wasn't the same as saying yes.

Spencer stared at the door leading out into the sitting room, wondering which man was out there. Complicated? The man was baffling. *Had* his opinion of her really changed? Or was he still bent on revenge? She didn't know.

And then there was the other matter, the cross. Unless he disagreed with her conclusions and could state flatly that there was no chance of finding it, they'd be searching for the cross together. She had to tell him about the stolen papers. He needed to know that.

Spencer rose to her feet and unconsciously squared her shoulders. There was nothing she could do except just go on, one step at a time, the way she'd learned to these past months. Whatever Drew intended, worrying about it wasn't going to help her a bit, and fretting over the cross wouldn't do her much good, either. She had to keep going, that was all. One step at a time.

She opened her door quietly and went out into the sitting room. The television near the window was on, tuned to a news program with the volume down low, and Drew was on the couch. The copies of her father's papers were spread out on the cushions beside him and on the coffee table, along with a large map of Austria.

He was holding several sheets of paper in his hand, and looked up from them when she came in.

"Good morning," he offered quietly.

"Barely," she conceded, managing a smile. "I didn't mean to sleep so late."

"Do you good." He nodded toward the dining table. "The coffee's still hot, and there's fruit and rolls. If you'd rather have something more substantial—"

"No, that's fine." She went over to the table and sat down, reaching for a cup. While she ate breakfast she watched him covertly. She had the feeling he hadn't gone to bed at all, and a glance into his room showed her a neatly made bed with no signs of having been occupied. His golden hair was still a little damp from a recent shower and he'd changed into jeans and a dark sweater. Like her, he was wearing comfortable running shoes.

He was intent on studying the papers, going through those in his hands slowly and methodically before setting them aside and reaching for more. He made several notes on a legal pad resting on the arm of the couch, and once leaned forward to study the map with a considering gaze.

Spencer couldn't guess what he thought. She finished her breakfast and carried her coffee over to the sitting area, taking the chair at right angles to him. Drew looked up to watch her for a moment, still without expression, then gathered the papers into a neat stack on the coffee table.

"Well?" she said finally, unable to stand it a moment longer.

His cool blue eyes warmed slowly, and a crooked smile curved his lips. "You're your father's daughter," he said softly.

chapter six

SHE FELT A jolt of relief, mixed with an unfamiliar feeling of accomplishment. "You think I'm right?"

"I think you did a hell of a fine job." Drew's tone was very deliberate. "The only reason I found it was that I knew your destination was Innsbruck. I sorted out the references to that area and backtracked. I never would have seen it otherwise. How did you figure it out, Spencer?"

"I didn't for a long time," she said a bit wryly. "I went over those papers every night for more than a month, and all I got was a headache. You've studied them. Because so many experts said it didn't even exist and never had, Dad had done most of his research trying to establish that Maximilian I did have the cross commissioned in

1496 when he arranged the marriage of his son to the daughter of the king of Spain. I decided to assume he was right, and to weed out all the references before 1618, when the cross was supposed to have vanished at the beginning of the Thirty Years' War."

He was listening intently, wondering if she had any idea how assured she sounded—and how expert. She may not have been trying to learn from Allan, but she had obviously absorbed much more than she'd realized. "So then you were left with about a quarter of Allan's original notes."

"Right. I started from the point where the Protestants in Bohemia revolted in 1618. There was one contemporary reference, a report to Rome written by a priest, that mentioned something about how the Protestants had stolen a cross—*the* cross, Dad believed—from the Hapsburgs. That didn't make sense to me. I mean, why would they? They were fighting for their rights, but I didn't see why they would have stolen a cross. It's a Protestant symbol, too.

"So I wondered if maybe somebody had had the bright idea to hide the cross—someplace safe—and claim it was stolen, just for personal gain. Or to fan the flames. It did seem to do that—the Protestants made a number of denials that they'd stolen anything, but the Hapsburgs' vague accusations seemed to carry more weight. Still, the priest was the only one who mentioned what, exactly, was supposed to have been stolen."

As far as Drew remembered, that theory had never

been advanced by any of the so-called experts, and it showed, on Spencer's part, a direct and coolheaded understanding of human nature that was surprising in a woman who had been very sheltered for most of her life. It also caused his opinion of her intelligence, gaining ground rapidly, to take another leap forward. "And you focused on the priest, because his was the only contemporary reference that was specific."

"Yes, and because he'd mentioned the theft in a report to Rome—it was like official notification that things were getting out of hand and something had to be done about it quickly. There was almost an air of smugness in the way he worded it, like he knew something, and I wondered if he did."

Allan Wyatt had never been known for his intuition, but his daughter was showing a definite flair for sensing undercurrents and reading between the lines, Drew thought. He had the feeling that if he commented on it, she'd shrug off any claim to talent and merely say it had been a lucky guess, but Drew knew only too well that inspired guesses came from intuition—and that hers had been inspired.

She went on in a matter-of-fact voice. "I managed to find the rest of the report—Dad didn't have it with his notes, but he had translated it—and saw that it had been sent from Innsbruck. That was a long way from Bohemia, *and* a long way from other areas that had been searched for the cross."

Slowly, Drew said, "Earlier researchers who accepted the existence of the cross also accepted the theft, so they'd searched the areas closer to Bohemia, where the revolt had taken place, and closer to the family seat." He nodded again. "Very good, Spencer. And then?"

She looked momentarily confused, as if the praise had surprised her, then went on. "Well, I doubted the original idea was the priest's, or that he had access to the cross even if he'd wanted to steal it, so there had to be at least one of the Hapsburgs who took it to Innsbruck and hid it. By using the date of the priest's report, and comparing it to the letters and journals that Dad had copied or collected over the years, I found out that one of the Hapsburgs—Kurt—was in Innsbruck visiting his sweetheart during the same time the priest was there. He'd written half a dozen letters to a friend of his, and since the friend was related to at least three royal families his letters turned up around the turn of this century in a Vienna museum, where Dad had found them and made copies. He wanted anything mentioning any of the Hapsburgs, but hadn't connected those particular letters to the cross. Luckily for me, though, he had translated them verbatim, and that's how I found the clues."

Drew glanced at the legal pad beside him and said, "The trips Kurt took into the mountains with a friend."

Spencer nodded. "They were very chatty letters, weren't they? Very descriptive of the scenery. On the surface the details seemed almost casual, but when I studied them with the idea that Kurt and his friend—probably the priest—were searching for a place to hide the cross, they really stood out. Kurt had also asked his friend to keep the letters, which struck me as odd until I wondered if he'd used them to record where he'd hidden the cross on the chance that he might forget."

"If hiding the cross was just meant to be a temporary measure," Drew said, "then why do you think it never turned up again?" His tone wasn't disbelieving, just curious, as if he wanted to hear her opinion.

Spencer had given that a lot of thought, and she'd found an answer that had satisfied her. "I think that Kurt never intended to return it to the rest of the family," she said dryly. "He was from a junior branch of the Hapsburgs, and from his letters I'd say he was awfully ambitious. He'd tried several times to finagle more power within the family, without success. I think he took the cross to Innsbruck, planning to hide it purely for his own future need. He enlisted the priest's help—both in hiding the cross and in reporting the 'theft' to Rome—because it was his idea and because *he,* not the Hapsburgs, wanted somebody to blame. The family wasn't likely to admit that one of their own had stolen it even if they knew. And *if* they knew, it would have been a good reason why they didn't make more of a fuss about a valuable family heirloom being stolen. Anyway, with so much going on just then, if they did know he'd taken it, they probably decided to deal with Kurt when he returned to Vienna."

"But the cross never surfaced again, and there's no mention of it in later letters or journals. Because something happened to him?" Drew said. "It wasn't in the notes."

"I was curious about that, and I found the answer in one of Dad's books about the Hapsburgs. It seems that Kurt's sweetheart fell ill a month or so after that last letter he wrote, and he nursed her. She survived, but he caught the fever and died. The priest, by the way, never made it back to Rome—notice of his death appears in the town records. It seems he had a bad fall shortly after his report to Rome and broke his neck. I'd like to think Kurt had nothing to do with it, but who knows?"

Drew was smiling slightly, and that look was in his eyes again, the warmth that had unsettled her before. "Allan didn't research Innsbruck specifically—how did you find the bit about the priest?"

Spencer wondered what he was thinking. "Well, I was curious, like I said. I called the university in Innsbruck and, luckily, their records were very complete."

After a moment, and in a very deliberate tone, Drew said, "Spencer, I hope I never again hear you question your own intelligence. I know I won't question it."

She had quivered under his insults, and Spencer found that his compliments affected her even more strongly. She didn't know what to say, and had to look away from the warmth of his eyes. Almost at random, she said, "So . . . you think we have a good chance of finding the cross?"

"I would have gone after it knowing a lot less than you've put together," he said. "Unless someone stumbled over it and moved it in the last three hundred years or so, I think you've found it."

Remembering suddenly, Spencer wondered if he would take back his compliment on her intelligence. She cleared her throat and looked at him. "Somebody else could have found it already, or at least be ahead of us."

His eyes sharpened. "What makes you think so?"

"The reason I came over here ahead of schedule and in such a hurry was because someone broke into the house Friday night. It was a very professional job—except that he took a lot of worthless things."

"You believe he was looking for Allan's papers?"

"Do you remember Dad's trick safe? I know he showed it to you."

"I remember. The real safe was behind the clock."

"The thief ignored the trick safe behind the painting, which was empty, but he got the other one open easily enough. I'd made two sets of copies of Dad's papers, and one set was in the real safe. It was taken."

Drew's face was without expression, almost remote, but his eyes were curiously hard. "An ordinary thief wouldn't have bothered with handwritten papers. You're right—he was after the notes."

Spencer realized that he was angry, and it made her a little nervous. "That's not the worst of it," she confessed reluctantly. "My itinerary was lying on the desk.

I had meant to leave it for Tucker, in case he needed to get in touch with me. The thief didn't take it, but if he noticed it . . . You figured out where the cross was in just a few hours, you said, because you knew the area was Innsbruck. If he knows that, too, then he could be ahead of us."

"Why didn't you tell me this sooner, Spencer?" Drew asked very softly.

"It wouldn't have mattered if—if you'd studied the notes and told me I was wrong—"

"No, I meant why didn't you tell me when it happened?" Then an odd laugh escaped him, and he shook his head. "Never mind. It was a stupid question. You wouldn't have come to me if I was the last hope between you and hell."

He was angry at himself, she realized in surprise. Because his behavior that first night had made her staunchly determined not to ask him for help? If she *had* asked him and he'd agreed, they might well have been in Austria by now. It was her limited funds that had brought her to Paris and prevented a more direct route. Was Drew angry because they might have lost the cross partly due to his earlier hostility?

"I'm sorry, Spencer," he said.

She looked at him, wondering what to say to that. "I probably wouldn't have asked you for help no matter what your attitude had been," she said finally, then went on immediately before he could comment on that. "The only thing that makes sense is that some collector or black market dealer somehow found out that I was close—or thought I was—and paid a professional thief to get the papers. We have to assume Dad's notes are in the hands of someone who knows what they're looking for, and how to look for it. Even if they aren't as good or as quick as you, they'll find the clues, given enough time."

Drew took a deep breath. "And if they were prepared to leave at a moment's notice, they may already be in Innsbruck."

"I wish I knew who they were," Spencer murmured, "and how they found out. . . ."

Rising abruptly to his feet, Drew went over to the phone and placed a call. He spoke in French, rapidly, and she had no idea who he was talking to or what he was saying. She glanced at her watch, which she'd reset to local time, and was vaguely surprised to see that it was barely noon. Drew's voice distracted her. He seemed to be arguing, but then his tone turned decisive, and when he hung up he was obviously satisfied.

Looking at Spencer, he said briefly, "Are you ready to leave?"

She nodded. She hadn't unpacked the night before, so all she had to do was pick up her bags and go.

Drew made another call, a short one this time. After cradling the receiver a second time, he said, "A bellman's coming up for the bags."

Spencer nodded again.

"If I read those clues correctly," he said, "the hiding

place for the cross is miles outside Innsbruck in the mountains. Even bypassing Salzburg we won't have time to get started today, but we might be able to find out who our competition is."

"Bypassing Salzburg? I thought there were no direct flights available."

"I've chartered a plane," Drew said.

HE HAD, ACTUALLY, chartered a jet. A Lear jet. Spencer, sitting in the efficiently soundproofed and luxurious cabin, gazed around at plush carpeting and furnishings as they left Paris far behind. Her background was one of wealth and privilege, but she had never before flown in an aircraft like this one. She was less impressed by the luxury than by the convenience, speed and efficiency that were possible when there were no budget considerations.

Drew was still in charge, making arrangements with cool authority so that she hadn't had to even think, and she hadn't objected. She kept telling herself that he was doing this because of the cross and because of her father, not because he wanted to help her. To take care of her. It wasn't personal, she thought. He'd shown no protective impulses all those years ago, had given no sign that accepting a woman's burdens was something he desired or was even prepared to do.

But, then, she hadn't needed him in that way at the time. She wondered, now, what would have happened if she had. Would she have seen a less remote side of Drew, as she was seeing now, if she had turned to him with a problem? Were the changes she saw and sensed less his than her own? She needed his help now, and she knew it, needed his intelligence, his expertise and his knowledge. He'd been right in saying he was the best ally she could have.

Because of that, because his inner qualities were far more obvious and more imperative to her now than the elegant surface of him, she didn't feel so intimidated by his confidence and sophistication. Those traits were only part of him. Since he'd come back into her life, she had begun to understand that he was more complex than she'd known—and certainly not detached. She wasn't seeing him now as a schoolgirl's fairy-tale prince, but as a man a woman could count on for far more than handsomeness, courtesy and social composure.

Was that the difference? Ten years older and wiser, a woman instead of a child, she was more comfortable with both herself and him, less inclined to shy away like a frightened child from the terrors of uncertainty. He still had the power to unnerve her, and she still felt vaguely threatened by him sometimes, but there was less fear in that now, and more . . . excitement. As if the woman she was now had some instinctive knowledge that the girl of ten years ago had lacked, some understanding that losing herself in him would be as exhilarating as it would be terrifying.

"You're very quiet," he said.

As the jet reached its cruising altitude and leveled off, she loosened her seat belt and looked at him. He was sitting across from her, his face still, the way it had been ever since he'd become angry—at himself?—at the hotel. He hadn't said very much and, grappling with her own thoughts, she had said very little to him.

Now she said the first thing she could think of. "The customs official at Orly certainly knew you."

"Most of the customs officials in Europe know me." He unfastened his seat belt and got up, going over to a wet bar placed toward the front of the plane. "Would you like something to drink? I see a variety of fruit juices here."

"Orange juice, please." She watched him, thinking of the laconic response that said a great deal. During the past ten years she had heard or read of dozens of spectacular finds Drew had made, as well as confrontations with black market dealers and transactions with other collectors for various antiquities and art objects. Customs officials all over the world probably knew him by sight and most, judging by the Frenchman's attitude, no doubt both liked and respected him.

Drew returned to hand her a glass, holding one for himself that also contained fruit juice and sitting down beside her this time. The seats in this jet ran lengthwise, more like plush couches than standard airline seating, so there was no armrest separating them. Very conscious of his closeness, she sipped her juice and then clung to what seemed like a casual topic.

"The official at Orly was very friendly. Are they all like that?"

Drew was half turned toward her, one arm along the back of the couch so that his hand was very close to her shoulder. His tone sounded a little absent when he replied, "No, not all of them. Most of them trust me, though, after all these years. They know they can be pretty sure I'm not carrying contraband, or trying to smuggle anything in or out of a country."

He couldn't stop looking at her. She was no longer pale as she'd been last night, her gray eyes clear and steady, and Drew wanted to touch her so badly that it was a constant ache inside him. She seemed to have no awareness of her effect on him and, despite her instant response to him last night, if she felt any urge to cast herself into his arms now she was hiding it well. He wondered again, with an odd blend of wry amusement and acute frustration, if he really was losing his mind. He was having trouble stringing two coherent thoughts together, and she seemed bent on keeping the conversation casual.

"You don't approve of black-market trading, do you?" she asked.

He forced himself to concentrate. "When it comes to antiquities or art objects, no. But some things sold on the black markets of the world, especially where there's no free trade, are beneficial." He smiled suddenly. "I doubt that the invasion of blue jeans and stereos into communist countries had much to do with sparking a few revolutions, but you never know."

Looking at him curiously, she said, "I've heard that you've gone into some pretty rough places searching for antiquities. As much as you travel into and out of countries without free trade, have you ever been tempted to . . . ?"

After a moment Drew said, "I have a good reputation with most officials and border guards, and it isn't wise to abuse something like that. But there have been a few times in the past that I've helped to transport supplies into a country. Medical supplies, usually. Never guns, and never anything that a democratic government would consider contraband."

It didn't surprise Spencer, though she thought it would surprise some people who knew him. She had a feeling that even those who knew him well actually knew little about him and the things he'd done.

Smiling a little, she said, "No nerves to speak of?"

"Plenty of nerves." He returned the smile. "But, hell, what's the fun of trying if you're sure you'll win?" That philosophy applied to most things, he acknowledged silently, but he wasn't sure it applied to them. He felt as if he were walking a high wire without a net, and *fun* wasn't the word he would have chosen for that.

"Fun? Risking being thrown into some dark prison for the remainder of your natural life?" Her voice was still casual, and she appeared faintly amused.

"That possibility has given me a few bad moments," he admitted, still smiling. "But there's a sense of triumph in beating the odds, and even in just trying to.

Think of Allan's search for the cross. A lifetime's work and plenty of disappointment—but you know he wouldn't have missed it for the world."

They were, Spencer realized, slipping out of the casual topic and into something more sensitive, despite her efforts. The cross. Always it came back to the cross. She wondered, had to wonder, if Drew was with her now only because of that.

"I know that," she said, pushing the question aside. "And I suppose if you have the triumph, it's worth it. But what if you fail?"

His smile faded a little, and Drew's eyes were intent on her face. "Failure isn't an ending, Spencer, it's just a place to stop for a while and consider your options. You try again, or try something else."

"Learn from your mistakes, you mean?" she asked lightly, staring at her glass.

"You can do everything right and still fail." In a deliberate tone, he went on. "Take you and the cross, for instance. You've done everything right—more than right, in fact. You found clues that have eluded experts for centuries, and pieced them together to find an answer. It wasn't your fault that someone stole Allan's papers, and it won't be your fault if they get to the cross before you do."

"It certainly won't be yours." She managed to hold on to the light tone. "You're spending a great deal of time and energy—to say nothing of money—to get us there as quickly as possible."

"Does that bother you?" Drew asked.

It had bothered her all along, but she'd managed not to think about it. Now she had no choice. "I don't like being indebted. Even if it's for Dad, I—"

"Spencer, there's no debt." His tone roughened suddenly. "And I won't claim one later, if that's what you think."

She had an almost painful urge to apologize, but couldn't form the words. Instead, still gazing into her glass as if it contained the secrets of the universe, she said, "Then it is for Dad that you're doing this?"

Drew took the glass away from her, setting both hers and his on a low snack table at his end of the couch. Then he reached over and made her look at him, his long-fingered hand gentle but firm against her face. "I want Allan to see the cross." His voice was low, still a little rough; his expression was grave and very intent. "But if you weren't hell-bent to find it, I wouldn't be here."

"You said—"

"I know what I said. I thought you'd fight me if I said I only wanted to help you. Either that or think the worst of my motives. So I said it was for Allan."

Spencer stared into his eyes, doubtful but conscious of her heart beating rapidly and of all her senses coming alive as a pulse of heat throbbed inside her. Something else, she realized, that it always came back to. This. This potent desire between them was never far away. It was difficult to think at all, but she tried, be-

142

cause she had a curiously certain idea that they were at a turning point of some kind. He was saying this was for her, that he wasn't with her because of the cross or her father—and she had to decide whether she believed him.

"Then how can I believe there's no debt?" she whispered. His eyes, she thought, were the color of blue topaz, a shade that wasn't light or dark but somewhere in between. There was heat in them, blue heat that melted something inside her.

"Because I say there's no debt. Spencer, I want to be with you. Is that so hard for you to believe? I just want to be with you."

It was difficult for her to accept, but his insistence and her own silent yearning made it impossible for her to say so. She had to believe him, and if it was a mistake, if she had to pay a price for trust, then she'd pay it.

"I guess I have to believe it," she murmured. "But . . . you're very confusing."

"Am I?" He was smiling again. His hand moved slightly, so that the fingers lay along her neck while his thumb brushed her cheek in a slow, stroking caress.

She'd been very conscious of his hand on her, but that little caress made her want to close her eyes and actually whimper out loud with the pleasure of it. It was increasingly difficult to think, but she tried. "Last night—"

"Last night, you were tired," he murmured. "And

you didn't trust me. I want you to trust me. I want you to believe we'd be good for each other. This time."

His low voice was almost hypnotic, as acutely erotic as his touch, and Spencer wondered vaguely if this was what drowning felt like. She was sinking into something velvety soft and warm, and she had absolutely no urge to save herself. When his mouth touched hers, she was incapable of doing anything except sway toward him, an unconscious purr of pure sensual bliss vibrating in her throat. His tongue slid deeply into her mouth, the small possession so hungrily insistent that her response was instantaneous. The now-familiar but still astonishing burst of desire jolted through her body like an electrical shock, and her arms lifted to wreathe around his neck.

His arms were around her now, holding her as close as possible, but even that wasn't close enough for Spencer. The constriction of her seat belt kept her from turning completely toward him as she wanted to do, and the throbbing emptiness deep inside her was a torment. She could feel his hands burning through her sweater, feel the hardness of his chest flattening her breasts, and his thick hair was like silk under her fingers.

He kissed her as if he were starving for the taste of her, the intensity of his need overwhelming, and that fierce desire ignited an answering passion in her that had never been touched before. Spencer had never even imagined anything like this; the sheer raw power of it was stunning, and if she could have said anything at all she would have said yes, because she wanted him with every throbbing nerve in her body.

He finally pulled back with obvious reluctance, murmuring her name huskily, and she became vaguely aware of a scratchy voice on the jet's PA system announcing that they were nearing Innsbruck. The information sank into her numb brain, but she could only stare up at Drew's taut face with helpless longing.

He kissed her again, quickly this time, and gently pulled her arms from around his neck. He held her hands in both of his, darkened, heated eyes fixed on her face, and his voice was still a little thick when he spoke. "If we weren't twenty thousand feet up in a jet . . . I wouldn't have stopped this time. I've waited twelve years for you. I don't think I can wait much longer."

Twelve years? She was dimly puzzled by that, but it didn't seem important at the moment. Her entire body was filled with a pulsing ache, and she didn't even try to hide what she was feeling because that would have been impossible. "I don't want to wait," she whispered.

His eyes burned hotter, as if banked embers had suddenly burst into flame. "Don't say that unless you mean it." His voice was even thicker, rasping over the words.

Somewhat to her surprise, Spencer was utterly calm and certain about this. Her body was still throbbing, but slowly now, and what she felt most of all was anticipation. She already belonged to him; fighting that was like pitting her strength against a force of nature, a battle she could never win.

"I don't want to wait," she repeated steadily.

Drew leaned over to kiss her, the heat inside him banked again but searing her nonetheless, and muttered as he lifted his head, "Dammit, it'll take hours to find out anything in town, and it has to be done today."

She smiled slowly, understanding that the digression was made with extreme reluctance and not a little strain. "The cross is our priority. You said that."

His mouth twisted. "I may have already cost you the damned thing. I don't want to make another mistake."

"Drew, it won't be your fault if somebody gets there ahead of us. I couldn't have asked you for help—not because of anything you'd said or done, but because of what *I'd* done. Ten years ago."

"You know we're going to have to talk about that," he said, his hands tightening around hers.

Spencer half nodded, then glanced away as the altered sounds of the jet's engines indicated that they'd be landing soon. "Yes, but not now."

He didn't like the way she'd looked away from him, or the sudden wariness in her eyes. She hadn't withdrawn from him exactly, but there was a barrier he hadn't been conscious of only moments ago. It bothered him. He was certain she wanted him now, and both his usual judgment and his peculiar instincts kept assuring him that her words and her responses to him were completely honest. Why did she shy away from telling him her reasons for marrying another man? Were those reasons so painful that, even now, she couldn't bear to remember them?

SPENCER HAD NEVER been to Austria and, knowing that she probably wouldn't have time to do any sightseeing, tried to see as much of Innsbruck as possible from the taxi as it conveyed them from the airport to their hotel. She immediately felt an affinity for the valley city, particularly the older sections with their narrow streets and tall Gothic buildings, and she loved the spectacular view of mountains that ringed the city.

Drew had told the driver where to take them—his German was as fluent as his French—and told Spencer that he'd chosen an inn for them in the section of the city nearest the area of mountains where they hoped to find the cross.

"You've been here before," she noted.

"A few times. I have at least a couple of contacts in the city, so we may be able to get some information."

Spencer looked at him curiously. "Wouldn't whoever's after the cross be cautious? I mean, how could your contacts know anything about it?"

Drew smiled and took one of her hands. He'd been touching her almost constantly since the interlude on the jet, and if the touches seemed casual and undemanding Spencer was still highly aware of them. "People who deal in antiquities," he said, "or even have knowledge of them are very adept at reading signs. They notice certain questions or actions, or an unusual preoccupation, and take note. After all, it could be something they'd be smart to go after themselves."

"Innsbruck is a big city," she commented, still looking at him.

"Yes, but the community of people interested in antiquities is relatively small, even worldwide. Most of us know each other, certainly by name and usually by sight. Aside from that, to find something hidden in the mountains, whoever's after the cross—including us—will need certain supplies and equipment the tourists don't bother with, and that's a signal which an expert would read quite accurately."

Spencer was fascinated "You mean that if I had come here alone and didn't ask a single question of anybody, but just rented a horse and bought supplies—?"

He answered dryly, "At least two people that I know of in Innsbruck would hear of it within an hour. And once your name was known—which would be fairly quickly—there would be a dozen or so people across Europe speculating frantically that you were in search of the cross."

"I hadn't realized so many people knew about Dad's obsession," she mumbled somewhat dazedly.

"He hasn't exactly kept it a secret during the last fifty years," Drew reminded her. "Even the collectors who didn't believe it existed were interested, not only because of intrinsic and historical value, but because there are so few disputed relics left to find. Collectors want one-of-a-kind objects, Spencer, and the more elusive they are, the greater their value."

He should know, she thought, and said, "You're a collector."

"I enjoy the hunt as much as the find," he responded lightly.

Spencer didn't say anything else on the subject, because they arrived at the inn. It was a beautiful old building, Renaissance in style, with such a gracious, Old World atmosphere that Spencer was instantly enchanted. She followed Drew into the lobby, her hand still securely held in his, and stood looking around as the bellman brought their bags in.

"Are you up for a little sightseeing?" Drew asked, gazing down at her.

Knowing that he intended to get in touch with his contacts, she didn't think he meant that literally. She was intensely curious about the procedures involved; her imagination conjured up images of furtive meetings in shadowy alleys, and she had to smile at herself even as she replied to his question.

"Of course I am."

Drew tried to remember what they were talking about. Those slow smiles of hers had a devastating effect on his mind, his pulse and his blood pressure. Granted, it didn't require much to upset his precarious control where she was concerned. After she had said on the jet that she didn't want to wait, he was dimly surprised he'd been able to talk at all. If he hadn't fiercely concentrated on the search for the cross . . .

"Drew?"

He looked at her upturned face and cleared his throat. He could hold on a few more hours. Couldn't he? "I'll get us checked in," he said with only a trace of hoarseness, "and have the bags taken up."

She nodded, then gestured toward a small gift shop tucked discreetly in one corner of the lobby. "I think I'll see if they have a guidebook and a more recent map of the area."

He released her hand with reluctance, conscious once again of a haunting fear that if he didn't keep hold of her she'd somehow vanish out of his life. It was a perfectly understandable and rational fear based on past mistakes and he knew it, but reminding himself of that was an ongoing battle. He was hardly given to flashes of foreboding, and certainly not precognition, but the fear of losing her was so strong inside him that it was almost like a premonition of actual danger.

For a moment, watching her gracefully cross the lobby toward the gift shop, Drew's mind went absolutely clear and cold. A premonition? Or years of experience whispering to him? Someone had broken into Spencer's house and stolen her father's notes. That indicated both haste and a disregard of the law, to say nothing of ruthlessness. What would happen if the search for the cross ended in a confrontation of some kind? Would the strange, elusive history of that relic end, as so many had, in violence and death?

Danger was not only possible, Drew admitted silently to himself, it had to be expected. He hadn't been so successful all these years by ignoring risk, and he knew he had to be prepared for anything.

Anything except losing Spencer.

He turned toward the desk, a last chill thought filtering through his mind even as he automatically went through the procedure of registering for a suite. He was well-known to collectors and black-market dealers alike. Was it a coincidence that the theft had occurred almost immediately after he had reappeared in Spencer's life?

chapter seven

DREW TOOK HER to lunch first, at an outdoor café that provided a splendid view of the Goldenes Dachl, which was the top tourist attraction in Spencer's guidebook and, judging by the crowds, was quite popular today. She knew the history of the beautiful Gothic building, which had been built to commemorate Maximilian's marriage, and could see how its name, "Golden Roof," had originated with the gilded copper tiles that shone brightly in the sunlight. She wished there was more time to just sit and look at it, or to go nearer, but she sensed a certain restlessness in Drew and she didn't protest when he rose as soon as they'd finished eating.

He seemed to be in a peculiar mood, as briskly informative as any tour guide, yet almost imperceptibly distracted, as if his mind were elsewhere. Despite that, though, he held her hand or tucked it into the crook of his arm constantly, making certain she never strayed more than a step away from him.

As they walked through the picturesque quarter, Spencer became so wrapped up in her fascination for the sights it took her some time to realize that Drew was already seeking information about the cross and their competitors for it. He'd been talking to her all along, casually pointing out this or that with far more knowledge than her guidebook displayed, but he'd also spoken to at least half a dozen people in German.

"I thought you had only a couple of contacts in Innsbruck," she said mildly as they stood looking at a museum that had once been a ducal palace.

Answering the implied question readily enough, Drew said, "They referred me to a few other people."

She would have sworn their casual walking had been just that, and was a little amused to realize that Drew had followed a definite but unobtrusive route from contact to contact. Looking up at him, she asked, "What have you found out?"

"Nothing yet. It may be tomorrow morning before the questions I've asked begin to produce answers—if they do."

Somewhat wryly, Spencer said, "I think I've been reading too many intrigue stories. I expected your contacts to look furtive and dangerous. The last man you spoke to looked like an ordinary street vendor to me."

"He is an ordinary street vendor." Drew tucked her hand into the crook of his arm and led her away from the museum. "People who work on the streets of any city tend to know what's going on around them. Besides, that man's brother-in-law happens to own a stable and rents horses for mountain rides."

It was like a network, she realized, a series of connections between people, each possessing a specific kind of information. Drew was obviously plugged in to that network.

"Is this how you work anywhere in the world?" she asked curiously. "Asking questions until they spread out like ripples in a pool?"

"That's a good description," he replied. "It doesn't always work that way, but if I go into a situation with more questions than answers it's an effective way to operate. The people I talk to may not know anything helpful, but the people *they* talk to just might."

"Why do they bother to help? Money?"

"Sometimes, but it's often a question of favors. Having someone owe you a favor may be worth more than money."

Spencer thought about that as they continued to wander almost lazily through Innsbruck. Drew pointed out various sights and she responded appropriately, but she noticed that he spoke to three more people as casually as he had the others. As far as she could tell from her almost nonexistent German, two of those responded with negative answers and one appeared doubtful.

She didn't ask Drew to confirm her impressions. The sense of urgency she'd felt since the thief had stolen her father's papers was still with her, but there was also— though she was reluctant to admit it to him—a very strong feeling of confidence in Drew. She had little doubt that her chances of locating the cross had increased tenfold once he had joined her in the search. And for the first time, she truly felt that her certainty in his abilities did nothing to diminish *her.*

This was his world, his area of expertise, and she could accept that now with no loss of her own hard-won confidence. She no longer felt so inadequate, uncertain, or even in awe of him. She respected his knowledge and abilities, and found both fascinating rather than threatening.

What a difference ten years could make.

There was something else, Spencer admitted silently, which had pushed her urgency regarding the cross out of the forefront of her mind. She had fallen in love with Drew with all the wild desperation of a teenager, had run from him in an equally intense panic two years later, and had realized only when he reappeared in her life days ago that all these years, in some deeply buried part of herself, she had been waiting for him to claim what belonged to him.

Now he was going to. Though she hadn't asked, she was certain that he had chosen a one-bedroom suite for them this time. Since her arrival in Paris he had taken charge with cool authority, and after what she had said on the jet she had little doubt that he expected to be in her bed tonight and that he had arranged the accommodations accordingly.

It was difficult to think of anything but that waiting bedroom, even though she had tried to. A part of her was filled with a sense of expectation she'd never known before—heart thudding unevenly, a vague weakness in her knees and vivid memories of earlier kisses and touches rising up with no warning to catch at her breath. But she was nervous, too, and more than once she glanced up at the tall man by her side and felt a pang of alarm.

Those fleeting sensations of anxiety were the hardest to push away because they came from her own awareness of vulnerability. She knew that whatever Drew's intentions were—to scratch an old itch, to get her out of his system or to begin some kind of new relationship between them—she had committed herself to him. From now on, and particularly after tonight, she would be vulnerable to him as she'd never been before.

If anything had been needed to prove to her that her marriage had been a mistake, that was certainly proof enough. She had never committed herself to Reece or to their marriage; the divorce had brought pain only in her realization that she'd been a fool to marry him. She would never be able to say good-bye to Drew so painlessly, she knew.

"You've gone quiet on me again," Drew said.

"Have I? I'm sorry." She looked around to find that

they were heading back toward the inn, and wondered just how long she'd been silent.

"Tired?"

She glanced up, encountered the warm concern in his eyes and immediately forgot whatever she'd been about to say.

"Don't look at me like that," he murmured. "We're on a public sidewalk."

They were stopped on a public sidewalk, she realized, and tried to think of something to say. It was ridiculously difficult. He was holding her hand now. She liked that. "I'm not tired," she managed finally.

He took a deep breath, looked away from her with an obvious effort and said, "It's getting late. I know a good restaurant just around the corner from the inn. Why don't we have dinner before we go back."

Years before, that nearly toneless voice would have made her believe he was indifferent, and the remoteness of his handsome face would have further unnerved her. Now, what she saw and heard was an almost rigid mask of control over emotions a long way from detached. For the first time, she wondered if that stern self-command would desert him in bed, and the possibility that it would sent a warm shiver through her body.

What kind of a lover would he be? Would he be gentle? Rough and urgent? Impetuous, or slow and deliberate? A considerate lover or a selfish one? She didn't think he'd be selfish. She knew he was skilled. He had to be. From what she'd heard and seen herself, he'd had women chasing him since his teens, and during the past ten years there had been a number of stories circulating in D.C., where he made his home base, about women he was involved with in various corners of the globe.

Spencer hated those women. She hated them with a wave of emotion so sudden and so powerful it shocked her. The feelings were raw and primitive, churning inside her until she could hardly bear it. Jealous. That was it, that was what she was feeling. She was painfully, furiously jealous of every woman he had held in his arms.

He must have felt the intensity of her gaze, because his voice had changed when he murmured her name.

"Spencer . . ."

He wasn't looking at her, and she could hear the strain now, the faint tremor of something stretched so tightly it was in danger of snapping. It was a quality that seemed alien to his deep, low voice, and it was strangely moving.

She cleared her throat in an uncertain little sound and tried to remember what he had said. Dinner, that was it. "Fine," she said huskily. "Dinner's fine."

Dinner was fine, though neither of them had much to say and Spencer, at least, had no idea what she ate. It occurred to her that Drew always seemed to be feeding her, and she wasn't quite sure how she felt about that; no one had ever taken care of her before, not the way Drew did. Her father, though she had no doubt of his love, had always been absentminded when it came to the practicalities of life, and during their short-lived marriage, Reece had been concerned, first and foremost, with himself—his needs, his pleasures, his emotions.

Drew, it seemed, was very different. Some might have called him domineering, but Spencer didn't think that was it. Though she couldn't be sure, she doubted that it was his nature to be autocratic. The feeling she got from his matter-of-fact attitude was that he was just doing everything he could to make this trip easier for her. At the farm in D.C. he had been angry that she refused to take a break and hadn't eaten, and he'd promptly made certain she did both. In Paris she had been conscious of her exhaustion and had probably showed it—he had even commented on it later. Again, he'd made certain she ate something and got enough rest.

Was that why she hadn't felt a desire to fight it when he took charge of all the travel arrangements? Because her instincts told her his motive was concern? Whatever the reason, she decided to stop worrying about her own acquiescence. It hardly seemed important compared to everything else.

They finished eating and left the restaurant, both still relatively silent. She thought Drew seemed a bit tense, and thought she knew why—until he stopped in the lobby of their inn and handed her a room key.

"The suite's on the second floor," he said.

Spencer looked at the key, then at him. "That sounds sort of like 'see you later,' " she noted a bit dryly.

In a voice that held reluctance he said, "Unfortunately, that's what it is. Spencer, there are a couple of men I have to locate, men who might be able to help us, and they won't talk to me unless I'm alone."

"More contacts?" She stared down at the room key in her hand.

"Yes. I should be back within a few hours."

"I see," she murmured.

Drew had released her hand when he'd stopped, and now reached up to brush a strand of shining raven hair away from her cheek. His hand lingered, thumb brushing her cheekbone. "I don't want to leave you," he said a bit roughly.

A little embarrassed by the intensity of her own disappointment, Spencer managed, with an effort, to meet his steady gaze, and was immediately reassured. Her cheeks remained unusually warm, but at least she was able to smile at him. "I see that, too," she said softly.

He bent her head and kissed her swiftly and briefly, then looked at her, a muscle leaping in his tightly held jaw. "When this is over and Allan's seen the cross," he said, "I'm taking you to Wales."

She blinked. "Wales? What's in Wales?"

"A castle. With a moat and a drawbridge. It kept out invaders a few centuries ago. I think it can keep the world at bay long enough for you and I to have a little unhurried time alone." He kissed her again, just as briefly as before. "Do me a favor and stay in the suite while I'm gone, all right?"

"All right," she agreed, a bit dazed. It wasn't until she was in the suite a few minutes later that she wondered why he'd asked her to stay put, and by then she was thinking clearly enough to know the answer.

He had warned her, more than once, that by going after the cross she was entering a dangerous world where the rules were different and the stakes were high enough to spark violence. All afternoon, she realized now, Drew had been unusually alert. That was why she'd sensed a distraction in him—and partly why he'd made certain she never strayed from his side. Despite his almost lazy attitude and the casual questions to his contacts, he had been extremely wary and watchful.

She didn't know if he expected trouble or was merely cautious enough to be vigilant, but it was clear that Drew was readying himself for whatever might come.

Spencer frowned as she pushed herself away from the door she'd been leaning against since coming into the suite and walked slowly into the sitting room, dropping her tote bag absently onto a chair. She wondered about the contacts he was trying to locate now, the ones he'd said wouldn't talk to him unless he was alone. She doubted that was because they were shy. Maybe her imagination hadn't been so far off when she'd envisioned furtive meetings in dangerous places.

"He knows what he's doing," she said, startling herself with the sound of her own voice in the silent room. She blinked and looked around, seeing that she'd been right in thinking he would get a one-bedroom suite. The realization distracted her mind from anxious thoughts that, if not entirely leaving her, at least retreated a bit so that they were shadows in the back of her awareness.

She went into the bedroom, turning on a lamp since it was getting dark outside. The king-size bed had been readied for the night, covers turned back invitingly. It was odd, she thought, the things that got to you: her bags and Drew's had been brought up by a bellman and were now neatly on luggage racks near the bed. The sight of them made her throat ache for some reason.

Before she could ponder that, she looked at the phone on the nightstand and noticed that the message light was blinking, and a pang of fear shot through her. Had Tucker called about her father? Had he—

Then she remembered that she hadn't known where they'd be staying, so Tucker couldn't know, either, or at least it wasn't likely that he could know, and her racing heart slowed. She went over and sat on the bed, then lifted the receiver and called down to the desk. The message turned out to be for Drew, and she wrote it on a notepad she found in the top drawer of the nightstand.

It was a simple message, though it made little sense to Spencer. Someone named Pendleton had called and said that they were in Madrid if Drew needed them. They? Who were they? Friends, or at least allies, from the sound of it. Were they, she wondered, some of the people Drew had gotten in touch with early this morning in Paris? Or had one of his questions today sent a ripple all the way to Spain? The terse message seemed to presuppose that he'd know where in Madrid he could find them. Spencer had no idea if he would, but made a mental note to ask because she was curious.

While she was sitting on the edge of the bed, she called home to let Tucker know where she was staying and to check on her father. Unexpressive as always, Tucker told her that her father seemed to be stronger physically, but that he'd been fretting over her.

"Why?" she asked.

"Unfortunately, he's been muttering in German, a language I've never been comfortable in, but I gather he's saying something about a journal you haven't seen."

Spencer frowned to herself. "I saw all the journals that related to his notes. Didn't I?"

"I thought so." Tucker paused, then continued slowly. "Just before he had the stroke he received a package from a man who had been doing research for him. It could have held a journal."

She knew that her father had hired researchers during the past few years, because his doctors had forbidden him to do any globetrotting, but she wasn't certain what information they'd been instructed to search for. A journal she hadn't seen?

"Tucker . . . without upsetting Dad, try to get him to tell you what he means, all right? If there is a journal, try to find it. I need to at least know who wrote it, especially if Dad thinks it's important."

"He may be rambling, you realize that?"

"Yes. But try, anyway."

"I'll see what I can do."

"Thanks." Tucker was a storehouse of information, especially when it came to the people with whom Allan Wyatt had associated throughout his life, and Spencer wondered . . . She hesitated, feeling a bit foolish, then said, "Tucker? Does Drew have a castle?"

There was a moment of silence and then Tucker's voice carried over the line calmly. "In Wales, I believe."

"Oh." What else was there to say in response to that, she wondered. How would she have reacted at eighteen, discovering that her prince had an honest-to-God castle? For heaven's sake . . . "I was . . . just wondering. I'll try to call tomorrow, but we may be up in the mountains most of the day so don't worry if you don't hear from me."

"Take care."

Her laugh was a little shaky. "Drew's doing that. 'Bye, Tucker."

After hanging up the phone she went into the sitting room to turn on a couple of lamps and the television set, which she tuned to an international news program in English, more for the sound of voices than because there was anything in particular she wanted to know about. Deciding once again not to unpack except what was necessary, she chose a change of clothing for the following day—anticipating a ride into the mountains—and sleepwear.

The last gave her something of a problem. She'd packed for practicality and comfort on this trip, and her bedtime choices consisted of a couple of overlarge sleep shirts. They were dandy for sleeping when one slept alone, but hardly what any self-respecting woman would call sexy. Last night a thick hotel robe had hidden the sight of a football-jersey-type shirt from Drew's gaze.

What about tonight? Spencer wasn't a vain woman, but she was certainly feminine enough to want to look her best tonight of all nights. After debating with herself briefly, she left the sleep shirts packed, got her room key and tote bag and left the suite. She'd told Drew she would stay in the suite, but surely going down to that little shop off the lobby wouldn't hurt.

Luckily, it didn't. Spencer was able to get down there and back in fifteen minutes without incident. She didn't know whether to be amused or distressed by the pride that had sent her in search of a nightgown. Here she was, in Innsbruck, Austria, engaged in a kind of treasure hunt for a centuries-old cross, with possible enemies lurking about, and the goal uppermost in her mind had been to buy a sexy nightgown.

In the end, she had to laugh at herself, and that wry amusement turned out to be a blessing. Without it she probably would have been forced to cope with ragged nerves much sooner.

It wasn't so bad at first. She took a long shower, washed and dried her hair, then put on the shimmering lavender nightgown and negligee. She ordered some fruit juice to be sent up before room service closed down for the night—the inn didn't keep chain-hotel hours—and sipped a glass of that as she watched the coverage of a competition at the Olympic Ice Stadium on television.

Sometime around nine she found herself staring at her hands, vaguely bothered. Her nails were still long and perfectly polished. She kept them that way, requiring a conscious effort considering her rough work with horses, because her mother had had beautiful hands. But Drew had said something that first night, she remembered now. Something about hands that had never done any work.

Frowning, she dug out her travel manicure set, stripped off the pale polish and ruthlessly filed her nails down to neat, short ovals. She told herself it was because they'd probably have to do some digging or the like tomorrow and long nails would only get in her way. It wasn't, of course, because of anything Drew had said.

As time passed, things began nagging at her. All kinds of things. Where was Drew? Was he all right? That journal . . . A journal her father thought she hadn't read, and why was it important? She'd run from Drew ten years ago—what made her think she could handle him now? Furtive meetings in dangerous places. She was asking for heartache, just *asking* for it, and he'd been so angry that first night, a man couldn't change that much in such a short time. Could he? Was he all right? He was the threat to their competitors for the cross, not her, so he'd be the target if someone wanted to . . . Reece had been the glitter; was Drew the gold? He'd been gone a long time, but surely he knew what he was doing. Surely. Would she please him as a lover? She felt so nervous about that. She lost control when he kissed her, touched her, and maybe . . . The intensity of her response to him was something she'd never felt before, something overwhelming . . . Was that wrong?

The jumble of questions and thoughts went on and on, becoming more tangled as the minutes ticked past. A small, rational voice in her head told her it was just nerves, that she was worried about Drew, about them and what they might be after tonight, about her father and the cross, but the whisper of reason didn't help. Uncertainties were chasing her like tiny, snapping demons, and her earlier confidence began to desert her. There was too much she couldn't control, and she'd fought so hard for at least the illusion of control in the past months.

An illusion. That's what it was. Or a delusion. Yes, she was deluding herself. Falling in love with him all over again despite the mess she'd made of things the first time—

The realization had barely risen in her mind when the sound of a key in the door cut through the silence. She had turned off the television and had been pacing. When she heard the door being unlocked she stopped near the bedroom door and swung around to face the short hallway.

When Drew stepped inside and closed the door, what he saw made him forget everything except her. She had obviously just turned toward him, the full skirts of her long nightgown and negligee sweeping out around her, and the silky material shimmered with the movement. Her black hair tumbled around her shoulders, and wide gray eyes met his with a disturbed intensity he could feel as well as see.

He came slowly into the room, shrugging out of his jacket, and dropping it carelessly onto a chair. He stopped a few feet away from her, trying and failing to read the emotions stirring in her eyes. The light was too dim or she was too wary—he didn't know which. Wary himself, he said, "I'm sorry—I didn't mean to startle you."

She took a quick breath, almost as if she'd forgotten to breathe for a moment, and when she spoke her voice was husky. "Did you find out anything?"

"No, but there's a good chance we'll know something by morning."

Spencer moved away from the bedroom doorway and away from him, toward a window. "I called home. Tucker says Dad's fretting. Something about a journal I haven't seen." Her voice sounded nervous to her own ears, and she tried to steady it. "I don't even know if it's important, but Tucker's promised to try and get Dad to explain. If he can. Sometimes Dad gets an idea into his head and just won't let go, even if it doesn't make sense to anyone else. It may not mean anything—"

"Spencer."

She felt herself tense even more, and a sudden wave of panic swept over her. No, it was a mistake, another mistake. She wasn't ready for this, she couldn't handle him, he was too much and she'd be lost in him. She swung around to voice the wild protest, but it tangled in her throat when she found him too close. He'd crossed the space between them in silence, and she couldn't back away because there was nowhere for her to go.

Drew didn't give her a chance to try to move, or to say anything at all. He pulled her stiff body into his arms, bent his head and covered her parted lips with his. He kissed her with a hunger so intense it seared through her like a brand, his mouth hard and greedy, his tongue sliding into her mouth with the certain intimacy of a lover.

Her rigidity melted away instantly, her body molding itself pliantly to his. She lifted her arms to slide them around his lean waist, holding on to him, her panic replaced by a wave of sharp pleasure and urgent need every bit as uncontrollable. As always, she was his the moment he touched her, doubts and questions scattered to the winds, the familiar desire spreading through her like wildfire.

She murmured a faint, wordless protest when his mouth left hers, opening her eyes reluctantly. She wondered with only vague interest why she had wanted to protest this. She belonged here, in his arms. She belonged to him.

"I left you alone too long," he said thickly, one hand sliding down her back to press her even closer. The blue heat in his eyes intensified when she caught her breath, and a muscle leaped in his taut jaw. "Maybe that was the mistake I made before."

"Mistake?" She felt so dazed and feverish that she could hardly think.

"I should have ignored the rules." His lips feathered along her jaw, and when her head fell back helplessly he explored the vulnerable flesh of her throat. "I shouldn't have given you time enough to think."

Spencer didn't want to think now—she only wanted to feel. Her whole body was hot and aching, her heart was racing and she couldn't seem to breathe. Her body moved against his, instinctively seeking, and the instant response of his hard body sent a shudder of need rippling through her.

Drew made a low, rough sound and kissed her again, the intensity of his desire already so much greater that it was as if he touched her with a live wire. She moaned into his mouth, her fingers digging into his back, and all the strength drained out of her in a rush.

Still kissing her urgently, he gently broke the death grip of her arms and swept her up, carrying her into the bedroom. She was dimly aware of the movement, conscious of a feeling of lightness in his arms as if she were floating. Then she was on her feet again, beside the bed and still enveloped in his heat. The negligee was tugged from her shoulders, and her hands blindly pushed his sweater up until he paused long enough to yank it off and throw it aside.

He hadn't worn a shirt under the sweater, and when her hands encountered his bare skin she made an unconscious sound of pleasure. The hard muscles of his back rippled under her seeking fingers, his flesh smooth and heated, and she loved the way he felt beneath her touch. And the way his touch felt. She could feel his mouth moving down her throat, feel the hot darts of his tongue touching her skin. His elegant, powerful hands cupped her buttocks, moving sensuously as the silk of her nightgown provided a slippery friction, and he began drawing the long skirt up slowly as his fingers caressed her.

"You feel so good," he muttered hoarsely, strong fingers kneading her firm flesh and slowly, very slowly, gathering the material of her skirt into his hands as he pulled it up.

Spencer got her own hands between them and touched his hard stomach that was ridged with muscle, then moved higher to explore the hair-roughened expanse of his chest. Unlike most blond men, Drew possessed a literal pelt of golden hair covering his chest, so soft and thick to the touch that she wanted to purr at the erotic feel of it. Her breasts seemed to swell, her nipples tighten in anticipation, and she was suddenly wild to press herself against him.

Then she felt his hands on her bare bottom, the skin of his palms a little rough, and a jolt of pleasure caught at her breath, "Drew," she whispered, unconsciously pleading, her short nails digging into his chest. She couldn't bear much more; the intensity of sensation was so sharp it was a bittersweet pain.

He raised his head and looked down at her, his hands still moving over her silky flesh. He was so hungry for her that the slow caresses were torture, but it was a torture he had to endure. For ten years she had haunted his dreams, thoughts and memories of her shut up in his subconscious because his waking mind had been too bitter to accept them, and touching her now was as necessary to him as every beat of his heart.

She was here, in his arms, her smoke-gray eyes dazed and lovely face soft with wanting him, reality instead of a dream, and he wanted to prolong the loving no matter what it cost him. He wanted to explore all the textures of her body, touch and taste and sate himself in her. Even more, he wanted to please her, and needed to forge a bond between them that would leave them connected when morning and all its potential problems intruded.

"I want you so much," he said in a thickened, rasping voice, merging all the wants and needs into a single, overwhelmingly simple statement.

"Yes," she murmured, her eyes fixed on his face. "Yes, please."

He kissed her parted lips again and again, feeling

her hands moving restlessly against his chest, and when she kissed him back wildly the threads of his self-control began snapping. What his mind wanted and his body could stand were two different things. Desire spiraled inside him, hot and greedy, and a ragged sound escaped him.

He pulled the nightgown up and off her, tossing it aside, then lifted her in almost the same motion and bent to lay her on the bed. Reluctant to stop touching her even for a moment, he swiftly discarded the remainder of his clothing, unable to take his eyes off her. She was beautiful, slender and perfectly formed, her breasts surprisingly round and firm, her waist tiny and hips curved gently. He'd always thought her beautiful clothed, but naked she was magnificent. Her black hair spread out on the pillow in a cloud of gleaming darkness around her face, and she was looking at him with gray eyes so bottomless he knew he could lose himself in them.

Naked, he eased down beside her, moving slowly because he was fighting to control himself. His need for her had grown so intense it edged into savagery, and the delicacy of her slight body was a vivid reminder of how easily he could hurt her. He kissed her deeply, exploring the warm sweetness of her mouth, and her arms lifted around his neck.

She made a little sound when his lips left hers, and he concentrated fiercely to hold on to his threadbare control. That sound . . . It was a soft, throaty purr of pleasure, and it drove his desire impossibly higher. He braced himself on an elbow beside her, brushing his lips over the warm, satiny skin of her face, her throat, then drifting lower to her breastbone. He slid a hand slowly up over her narrow rib cage and surrounded one swollen breast, his thumb circling the nipple rhythmically as his mouth closed over the other one.

Spencer caught her breath and jerked slightly, his hand and mouth on her breasts affecting her like nothing she'd ever felt before. She had thought she'd reached the absolute limits of what she could bear, but the hot, sweet tension coiled even more tightly inside her, tormenting her, as he caressed her breasts. When his hand moved down her quivering belly and his fingers probed gently between her thighs, she jerked again and moaned. The most exquisitely sensitive nerves in her body throbbed wildly at his touch, and she felt a strange, panicky sensation well up inside her.

"Drew . . . don't . . . I can't—"

He lifted his head, burning eyes fixed on her face. His expression was so fierce, so utterly male and primitive that it made her pounding heart skip a beat, and in that flashing instant she realized with utter clarity that Drew was capable of depths of emotion she had never suspected.

"Please," she whispered, and some part of her knew that it wasn't just an end to the physical torment she pleaded for, but something far more elusive.

He kissed her hungrily, shifting his weight until he

rose above her and between her trembling thighs. His powerful body was so much larger than hers, so much harder and more forceful, and the feverish need in him was a primal male demand that called out commandingly to everything in her that was female. She could have refused him nothing. Her eyes locked with his and the breath caught in her throat as her body slowly accepted him.

It had been a long time for her and he was a big man; she could feel the taut stretching of her flesh and the brief, instinctively shocked feminine awareness of an intruder. But then, in a curious melding she'd never known before, he seemed to become part of her, filling an emptiness she hadn't been conscious of and making her feel, for the first time in her life, complete.

A single tear slid from the corner of her eye and a shuddering breath left her as he settled fully into the cradle of her thighs. She could feel him pulsing deep inside her, and the hovering tension of desire began winding tightly again. His eyes were burning down at her and his mouth was hard as it covered hers. He was heavy, wonderfully heavy. Then he began moving.

I love you. She didn't say the words aloud, at least she didn't think she did, but Spencer heard them echoing in her mind even as her body went totally out of her control. She had few clear memories of that first joining, except for sensations and the certain, dimly shocking realization that her need for him was so overwhelming that nothing else mattered.

She was virtually untaught in the art of giving or receiving pleasure, but with Drew either her instincts or her love for him made knowledge unimportant. Her body knew how to respond to him, and she was incapable of controlling or even tempering her acute desire. Even as he claimed what belonged to him, his own urgent hunger had, in some way, set her free.

She barely heard the sounds she made, or realized how wildly her body writhed beneath his. All she was conscious of was the maddening tension, the frantic straining and striving to reach something just beyond her grasp. She wasn't aware of crying, of clinging to him desperately and pleading with him in a voice she would never have recognized as her own.

Until, finally, the pressure increased beyond bearing and snapped with a shock that was waves and waves of burning, pulsing ecstasy. The heat washed over her, consumed her, and she held him with all the strength left to her when it consumed him, too.

chapter eight

"YOU CRIED," HE said.

Spencer had felt him lift his head and ease the weight of his upper body onto his elbows, but she'd kept her eyes closed. Her arms were still around his neck, her legs coiled limply with his. She felt utterly drained, almost boneless, and she didn't know if she could look him in the eye. She'd gone crazy in his arms, and her own lack of control embarrassed her. In fact, it appalled her. That had never happened to her before, and she was half afraid that it was somehow wrong. Even though he hadn't seemed to notice anything to complain about, and even though it had certainly *felt* amazingly wonderful—

"Sweetheart, did I hurt you?"

She looked at him then, startled by the question as much as the troubled undertone in his low voice. She hadn't known his mouth could curve so tenderly or that his eyes could hold such a glow. Her heart turned over with a lurch, and she had to clear her throat before she could say huskily, "No, you didn't hurt me."

He brushed a strand of hair back from her temple, his thumb stroking the soft skin there as if he could feel the wetness of her tears. "You cried," he said again.

That wasn't all she'd done, Spencer thought. How many times had she pleaded with him? She didn't remember, but heat rose in her face and her eyes skittered away from his. "I didn't know I could feel that way." She had to admit it, if only to ease his concern. "I guess that was why."

Drew seemed to hesitate, a brief look of indecision on his face, then kissed her gently. "I knew you were having second thoughts when I came back, but I couldn't wait. I'd waited so long for you already. Even now . . . I don't want to leave you. Am I too heavy?"

"No." She focused her gaze on his chin, still unable to meet his eyes except fleetingly. She hadn't realized that the lamplight was so bright, but it was, and they were lying on top of the covers, naked bodies still entwined. Still joined. So close and starkly intimate. He wasn't too heavy, she wasn't physically uncomfortable, but . . . His weight and much greater size held her easily beneath him in an unnervingly primitive way, and with memories of her wild pleas and frantic, passionate sounds becoming more and more vivid in her mind, her embarrassment was intensifying rapidly.

Her wanton behavior was all the more shocking to her because it was so vastly different from the way she'd been with Reece. He'd been obsessed with her during the first short months of their marriage, so much so that he'd been gentle with her and concerned about her pleasure—even if his own had come first. But she had never lost control with Reece, and she'd never felt anything more than mild pleasure in their bed.

With Drew, what she'd felt had been so acute it was a kind of sensual madness, so utterly overwhelming that she'd had no hope of controlling it—or herself. She had given herself to him as if some ancient instinct had demanded it, with passionate intensity and total abandon. One difference, of course, was that she loved Drew as she'd never come close to loving Reece. She belonged to Drew in a way that was basic and primitive, touching all her deepest emotions. But knowledge of that didn't help ease her anxiety now. She was so vulnerable to him, and her mindless abandonment with him made her feel even more defenseless.

His hands surrounded her face warmly, and he moved subtly against her and inside her. She caught her breath and looked into his eyes helplessly.

They were a little narrowed as he gazed down at her, veiled so that she couldn't guess what he was thinking. And when he spoke his voice was lower, rougher, something implacable in the words. "You're trying to hide from me. I won't let you do that, Spencer. What is it? What's wrong?"

She didn't want to answer, but refusing him anything was still beyond her, and she couldn't look away now because his eyes held her trapped. "I couldn't . . . control myself," she whispered.

Drew brushed one thumb across a delicate cheekbone, feeling the heat of embarrassment burning in her skin. He could see it in her smoky eyes as well, along with anxiety and uncertainty. Was that why she seemed so far away from him now despite their physical closeness, because she was worried about the intensity of her response?

He thought that was it, and it gave him a strong sense of both pleasure and triumph to know that no other man had felt the fire of her passion, but he had no intention of allowing her to try to temper that response in any way. He wanted her to be certain that nothing she felt in his arms, nothing she said or did, could ever be wrong.

He kissed one corner of her trembling lips and then the other, his lower body moving again subtly so that she could feel his renewing desire. "Do you know what you do to me?" he murmured against her soft skin. "You make me so crazy I can't even think, so hot with need that nothing else matters. I love the way you feel, soft and warm against me, the way your body fits mine so perfectly. I love the passion in you, the wild, sweet way you respond when I touch you."

Spencer felt his mouth on her throat, the slight vibrations of his words an added caress, and she closed her eyes as dizzying pleasure began welling up inside her. He was moving just enough to make her aware of it, and her breathing quickened as her body responded wildly to the erotic sensations. She felt feverish, and exhaustion was forgotten as her legs lifted to wrap around his hips and her hands wandered restlessly over the taut muscles of his back and shoulders.

He lifted his head to gaze down at her. "Look at me," he murmured, and when her eyes flickered open dazedly he held them with his own. His voice grew rougher and more strained, the slow, deliberate movements against her combined with the tight heat of her flesh sheathing his so erotically charged that every nerve in his body was screaming with pleasure.

"That night at your house . . . you looked so cool, so distant. Untouchable. It drove me mad. I wanted to see you like this, naked and burning for me." She made a tiny sound and he kissed her deeply, taking it into his mouth. "I wanted to make you go crazy, just the way I go crazy when my hands are on you. You feel so good, so tight and silky. . . ."

Spencer whimpered a little, her body beginning to move instinctively beneath him. She couldn't be still, because he was torturing her and she couldn't bear it. Her short nails dug into his back, the hot, sweet tension coiling, stealing her breath. She couldn't control herself, just like before, her body writhing, desperate pleas and wordless sounds winging free of her.

He held her securely, his hands stroking her heated flesh as his body seduced hers. His voice encouraged her to let herself feel, to let herself go completely, as he hoarsely muttered bluntly sexual words of passionate need. Until finally Spencer's restless shifting beneath him became the lithe, graceful undulations of essential female desire, an imperative hunger that could no longer be denied or resisted.

Drew groaned and tangled his fingers in her thick hair, kissing her urgently, and his subtle movements abruptly became deep thrusts as his control shattered. He knew he was going to explode, the pressure building so violently that he was conscious of nothing but the torturing fire of that and the woman who cradled his straining body, urging him on with her own frantic need. He drove into her again and again, barely hearing her soft moans and cries or his own hoarse sounds, the primitive drive toward completion so overwhelming that if he had known release meant death, he wouldn't—couldn't—have stopped.

He was deep inside her when the hot, rhythmic contractions of her pleasure caught him in an unbelievably sensual caress, and her gasping cry was trapped in his mouth as he kissed her with an unconscious, ancient possessiveness. She was crying again—he could taste the salt of her tears—and his own release shuddered through him with a force so intense it bordered on agony, leaving him drained.

Spencer didn't think at all during the following

hours. She slept for a while, held warmly in his arms, not even aware when he got them under the covers and turned out the lamp. She woke once in the darkness, his hands and mouth bringing her body vividly alive again, the pleasure so acute that she lost herself in it without even trying to resist. Lost herself in him. And it was still terrifying and exhilarating and something she had no will to withstand. Even if his words and his own intense passion hadn't reassured her, she couldn't have held back, couldn't have tempered her response to him. If she didn't cry out her love it was only because she was convinced he wouldn't want it.

IT WAS THE chill of being alone that woke Spencer the second time, and even before she opened her eyes she knew that if he'd left her without a word she wouldn't be able to bear it. As soon as she opened her eyes she saw him, standing by the window. Moonlight spilled through the panes to show her a stark profile that was too beautiful to belong to a man and yet was utterly masculine. She lay there for a moment watching him, vaguely conscious that her body felt different but far more aware of him than of herself.

His body was in shadow, the darkness hiding his nakedness, and the expression on his face was remote. Knowing him better now, Spencer recognized that remoteness and understood that it was his mask of control. He was disturbed about something, his disquiet strong enough to have driven him from their bed in the cold, lonely hours before dawn.

With a vivid memory of the lover he had been in this bed stamped deeply in her mind and body, Spencer felt a chill touch of fear. Demons of uncertainty snapping at her heels. He'd said he would teach her what it felt like to be in thrall to someone else; now she knew. Had that been his goal all along, to have the satisfaction of knowing that her desire for him was like an addiction, a craving in her blood?

If he wanted to hurt her, there would never be a better time. A few cutting words or merely a cool good-bye, and she'd be devastated. She wanted to close her eyes and pretend she hadn't awakened, pretend that nothing was wrong. Morning was soon enough, she thought painfully, to face whatever he'd say.

She couldn't pretend. There had already been too much pretense in her life. Feeling so vulnerable that it was terrifying, she sat up slowly in the bed and wrapped her arms around her upraised knees.

He didn't turn his head to look at her, but obviously knew she was awake. His voice was soft when he spoke. "Why, Spencer?"

She waited, not sure what he was questioning.

"Why did you marry him?"

Not an easy question to answer, but at least it wasn't—yet—good-bye. She drew a breath and held her voice steady. "Because I was afraid."

He did turn his head then, his eyes sharply probing

the dimness of the room. "Afraid of me?" His surprise was obvious, and there was more, something she couldn't identify.

Spencer managed the ghost of a laugh. "You. Me. So many things. It was nothing you'd done. I was just afraid. I think I knew even then—"

"What?"

She hesitated, but just couldn't bring herself to say, *I knew I was lost even then, knew I belonged to you.* Instead, she explained another part of the truth. "I knew that I could never measure up. That I was . . . inadequate."

"What are you talking about?" He left the window and crossed the room to the bed, sitting down on the edge. When he reached toward the lamp on the nightstand, she spoke quickly.

"We don't really need the light, do we?"

Drew hesitated, but then allowed his arm to relax. The room wasn't totally dark, so they were vaguely visible to each other. Blurred features and the colorless dark shine of eyes. "Do we need the dark?" he asked finally, quietly.

She was silent, and after a moment he seemed to accept the tacit reply. "Spencer, why did you think you were inadequate? In what way inadequate?"

"I was pretending." Her voice was so low it was only a murmur of sound, but perfectly clear and audible in the hushed room. "Pretending that I was someone else. Being . . . assured and confident, and always in control.

As if that was the real me, as if I belonged. But I didn't. It was all a sham. I was just pretending. And there you were, the real thing."

"Spencer—"

She cut him off, going on in the same soft, deliberate tone, almost without expression. "That first time you came to the house, when I was sixteen, I knew who you were. I'd heard Dad and other people talk about you. About all the things you'd done—and you were barely out of college. The way they talked, about summer digs and trips to dangerous, exotic places, about your uncanny instincts and how brilliant you were, it made me picture you as something larger than life.

"Then I—I looked up that night and saw you." Spencer was lost in memories, the night she had first seen him so vivid in her mind that the clarity of the image was almost painful. "You came through the door, and maybe it was the light falling a certain way or—or something, but whatever it was, you seemed to be . . . all gold. Something so bright it made my eyes hurt and stole my breath. People made way for you, as if they knew it, too, as if they knew you were apart from the rest."

She blinked, looked at him. She was unable to read his expression in the dimness, but was grateful that he said nothing. It gave her the chance to get hold of herself, so that she was able to manage an almost impersonal voice. "Larger than life. Not only that, but you were everything I wanted to be. Elegant. Sophisticated. Confident and assured. Always calm and in control. I had . . . polished up myself, and the gloss fooled just about everybody. But you were the genuine article. Something I could never be."

Still unmoving, he said in an odd voice, "That was why you ran? Because I made you feel inadequate?"

Spencer was too honest to say yes and let it go at that. "It was partly that. I didn't know what you saw in me, but I knew I was pretending. I felt like a phony." A humorless breath of a laugh escaped, and she shrugged a little. "I was afraid. Confused. I didn't understand you or myself, and both of us scared me. Drew, I was eighteen, and not a very mature eighteen at that, not inside. If I was thinking clearly at all, the only thing I was sure of was that there was . . . too much of you and not enough of me. I was afraid of getting lost. That was the most terrifying thing of all. So I ran."

"To Cabot." Drew's voice had an edge now, a curiously ragged edge. "Why him, Spencer? Why did you run to him?"

She shook her head slightly, almost helplessly. "It seemed so clear then. The only answer. Now . . . I don't know. Because he was uncomplicated, I guess. Because he was brash instead of controlled. Because he wasn't larger than life. Everything that he was lay on the surface of him, easily seen and touched and understood. He had no secrets or shadows, no complexities, and I thought he was—safer. I'd known him for years, and for years he'd been saying he was going to marry me. Even after I got engaged to you, he sent me flowers and called me, and he kept saying he was going to marry me."

"You didn't love him." It wasn't a question, and yet there was a question in it.

Spencer hesitated, then shook her head again. "No. But I thought I could learn to love him. He—he didn't expect anything of me, Drew, ask anything except that I *be*. I didn't feel as if there was something I had to live up to with him, some image of myself that wasn't real. I didn't know what you wanted of me, but I was afraid that whatever you wanted I didn't have. He just wanted to love me, I thought, and I believed it would be better to be loved—without complications."

Drew was silent for a moment, still motionless, then said flatly, "What happened?"

This time her soft laugh was wry. "If I'd been older or wiser maybe I would have realized that any love with no depth couldn't possibly last, any more than a man with no depth could feel anything except fleetingly. Reece was like a child with a bright, shiny new toy. Intense, passionate, almost obsessed. Until the next toy caught his attention. Once I was no longer out of his reach I became less . . . desirable, I think. He couldn't love me forever. He couldn't even love me for long."

"Who asked for the divorce?"

She wondered at the question, but answered it honestly. "I did. I wasn't as hurt as I probably deserved to be when I realized Reece was habitually unfaithful, but

I was more than a little humiliated by my own stupidity. There were no big fights between us, I just said I was leaving."

"He didn't contest the divorce?"

Spencer's voice held real, if rueful, amusement. "He barely noticed it. He had a new toy he was trying to entice away from her husband, and that was occupying all of his attention." Then her amusement faded, and she said, "His family didn't like it. I think they were afraid I'd drag all the dirty linen through the courts. Before I could file the papers, their lawyer did. So, officially, Reece divorced me on the grounds of irreconcilable differences. I didn't care. I just wanted out."

She drew a deep breath and held her voice steady. "I wish I could make it all sound more dramatic somehow, or at least more compelling. I wish I could make my motives sound less vague and selfish. But I can't. I can't, Drew. I never meant to hurt anyone. I was just afraid."

There was a long silence, and then he said, "You were so afraid of me you couldn't tell me any of this."

Anxious that he had misunderstood, she said, "I wasn't afraid you'd hurt me or—or anything like that. I was just—oh, in awe of you, I guess. I didn't feel close to you, or understand you at all."

"Then why in God's name did you say yes when I asked you to marry me?" he demanded with suppressed violence.

Spencer wanted badly to reach out and touch him,

wanted to crawl into his arms and hold on to him with all the desperate love churning inside her. But she held herself still and kept her voice quiet and steady. "Because I was in love with you."

"What? Spencer—"

"Drew, I don't expect you to understand. I don't understand myself. Everything I felt then was so damn confusing. When you asked me to marry you, I'd been mooning over you like a silly little girl for two years, building fantasies around you. I had no idea you wanted to marry me until you said so. Then I didn't know *why* you wanted me."

"I told you I loved you," he said roughly.

"Yes, but . . . I didn't believe that. I couldn't, even though I wanted to. You were always so calm and you never seemed to feel very much except amusement. You were polite and kind, and sometimes I saw you watching me, but you seemed detached. What I felt was so— wild, and I never saw anything like that in you."

He was silent.

Spencer took a deep breath. "I said yes because it was like a dream falling into my lap, and it was only later that I started wondering if there was anything real in the dream. I was sure you wanted a wife as assured and sophisticated as you were—and I *wasn't*. I thought you'd been fooled by me like everyone else, and it was terrifying for me to imagine what you'd think when you discovered the truth."

"What truth?" Drew demanded almost harshly. "What is it you think you were hiding?"

"Me." She felt very tired now, and the room seemed colder than it had been only minutes before. "The real me. Always uneasy and unsure and frightened. I wasn't woman enough for a man like you, and I knew it."

When he moved suddenly it caught her off guard, and before she could say a word she found herself lying back on the bed with Drew leaning over her. "Just for the record," he said in a taut voice, "I'm not made of gold, Spencer. I'm not a schoolgirl's fairy-tale prince and I'm sure as hell not larger than life. I'm just a man, like any other."

"Drew—"

"You were the one who was fooled," he continued in the same taut, relentless voice. "About me and about yourself. The mask you wore was almost transparent— everyone saw through it, including me. We could see the shyness and uncertainty and sweetness, even the fear sometimes. But there was something so . . . graceful about the way you tried, so gentle and gallant. We all saw that, too. Spencer, why do you think I handled you so carefully? Why I was such a bloody gentleman instead of carrying you off over my shoulder as I wanted to? If I'd believed you were the assured, confident woman you tried so hard to be I'd have married you out of the schoolroom instead of waiting for more than two long years to even ask you."

Staring up at him, all she could think of to say was, "I didn't know you wanted to marry me then."

"I made up my mind to marry you that first night," he said, his voice still tight. "But you were too young, and I knew it. So I waited. I knew you were wary, nervous of me, that you were more comfortable with all the damned polite social rules and I tried to be patient and not overwhelm you. You were like a shy little bird, so beautiful and sweet, and so fragile I was almost afraid to touch you."

She lifted a hand to his face almost unconsciously, feeling the hard tension there, and her heart was pounding, aching. If he had felt so much then, and she hadn't hurt him too badly, then maybe there was a chance. . . . But he went on speaking before she could complete that thought, and hope died a silent, agonizing death inside her.

"When Allan called me to the house, I knew there was something wrong," he said, his voice as hard as his face now. "I'd never seen him so upset. He didn't know much, he said. He didn't know why. All he knew was that you'd gone, and you'd eloped with Reece Cabot. He gave me the ring, the one I'd given you, and I wanted to throw the damned thing across the room. I wanted to go after you, tear you away from Cabot and carry you off somewhere."

He laughed suddenly, a strange, harsh sound. "Of course, I didn't do that. It wouldn't have been civilized. I told Allan very quietly that I hoped you'd be happy, and I left. I left the country, getting as far away as I could, because I knew if I saw you with his ring on your finger, I wouldn't be able to be civilized about it. I didn't come back until I thought I could. When was that, Spencer, when did we see each other again?"

She swallowed with difficulty, and whispered, "More than two years."

"Twenty-six months, almost to the day. It was at the opening of a gallery. You were divorced by then. You were with Allan, and he was the one who spoke to me first. All three of us were polite and civilized."

Spencer was biting her bottom lip so hard that she tasted blood, staring up at him. Her hand fell away from him, because she couldn't bear to go on feeling the granite stillness of his face. "I'm sorry," she said almost inaudibly.

"Do you think that helps?" His voice was suddenly quieter, not so harsh as before.

She drew a ragged breath. "Nothing I can say is going to help. It's too late for that."

"Is it?" He bent his head, his mouth brushing hers very lightly, almost absently, again and again. "This helps. Knowing I can make you want me. Knowing he never found the fire in you. Knowing you belong to me now. You do belong to me, don't you, sweetheart?"

She would have denied it if she could have, but he had to know by now. And what did it matter, after all? She'd already given him all she was; admitting it aloud wouldn't change anything, and keeping it to herself wouldn't protect her from hurt. There was still nothing she could deny him, nothing at all.

"Yes," she admitted softly.

His arms gathered her closer, pushing the covers away, and his mouth hardened slowly with desire as he kissed her. Spencer clung to him, and even as her body responded wildly to his passion she was filled with the painful knowledge that she had given her heart and soul to a man who could never love her again—because he had loved her once.

A long time later, as she lay close to his side almost too pleasantly exhausted to think, she murmured, "Drew?"

"Hmm?"

"You said I'd been fooled by you. What did you mean?"

His arms tightened around her. "We all wear masks. Some of us have just had more experience at it than others. Go to sleep, honey. We have to be up in a few hours."

Spencer closed her eyes, but it was a long time before she drifted off to sleep. Where would they go from here? She no longer feared that Drew would be cruel to her, even though she had a better understanding now of just how badly she'd hurt him, but it was clear to her that all he wanted from her was passion. He'd as good as said it himself. She belonged to him now, and that in some way helped ease his bitterness.

Maybe she owed him that, no matter what it cost her.

In any case, it wouldn't be her who walked—or ran—away this time. She loved him too much to end this even if she could summon the strength and will to do it, and she didn't know what she would do when he ended it. All she could do now was to go on a step at a time. A day at a time.

She slept deeply and dreamlessly, waking to the delightful, drowsily sensual feeling of warm kisses. She opened her eyes and smiled when she saw him sitting on the edge of the bed. Her embarrassment of the night was forgotten. He'd been convincing when he'd said he loved her passionate response to him, and since the heat of their desire was a tie between them—the only possible tie—she couldn't feel it was in any way wrong.

"Good morning," he said, smiling just a little.

Spencer realized that he must have been up a while. He was dressed in jeans and a sweater, was freshly shaved and his golden hair was still damp from the shower. "Good morning," she murmured, stretching slightly and wincing at a few twinges.

Drew's intent gaze never missed much, and his smile faded. "Was I too rough?"

She pushed herself into a sitting position and absently held the covers to her breasts as she looked at him. "No, of course not. I'm just not used to . . ." She felt a touch of heat in her face, and shrugged a bit defensively.

He looked at her a moment longer with probing eyes, then cupped her warm cheek with one hand and leaned over to kiss her slowly and thoroughly. When he straightened, she was a little breathless and he was smiling again.

"Why don't you take a hot shower while I order breakfast," he said. "That should help."

Spencer felt self-conscious about getting out of the bed naked even though, heaven knew, she had no secrets from him, but she pushed the covers back and slid from the bed when he stood up, telling herself not to be an idiot. She was so intent on not being embarrassed that she was startled when Drew's hand grasped her wrist with a sudden hard strength that wasn't quite painful.

She had taken a step toward a chair where she'd left fresh clothing the night before, but was stopped abruptly by his grip. Before she could say anything he turned her around and his free hand lifted to touch her back.

"What the hell is this?"

Spencer couldn't see his face, but his voice was so harsh that for a moment she couldn't think and had no idea what he was talking about. Then, as his fingers very gently touched her, she remembered. It had been a few days since her tumble off the horse, and she'd more or less forgotten about it. Unfortunately, she bruised very easily, and though she hadn't bothered to examine herself, she realized that the mark of the wooden jump pole was probably a multicolored band across her back by now.

"When I hit the jump Friday," she explained, trying to look back over her shoulder at him but still unable to see his face. "It doesn't hurt. I just bruise easily."

His touch brushed across her skin, halfway between her shoulder blades and the small of her back. The grip on her wrist finally relaxed and he bent his head to kiss her bare shoulder as he released her. "Go take your shower," he said in an odd, gruff voice.

Before she could turn toward him or respond, he had gone quickly from the bedroom and into the sitting room. Spencer stood there for a moment staring after him, then gathered her clothing and went into the bathroom. She put her tumbled hair up carelessly, and before getting into the shower paused a moment to look at her back in the big mirror over the vanity.

It looked as if someone had been beating her. The mark of the pole she'd hit was most obvious, a solid line of bluish yellow from one side of her back to the other and more than two inches thick. But there was another, fainter bruise running diagonally across her back—the second pole, she supposed, although she didn't remember feeling it hit her—and a number of lavender splotches of various sizes. From rocks on the ground where she'd landed, presumably.

A bit ruefully, Spencer realized now why she'd been so uncomfortable on the plane from D.C. No wonder Drew had been so startled to see the marks on her. They looked vicious. But they really weren't painful now, and she didn't think any more about them as she got into the shower.

Drew heard the water running, and though it distracted him from the note he'd just found pushed underneath the door, his thoughts this time were less sensual than worried. The bruises on her back had been another reminder of how fragile she was, how susceptible to hurt. He'd been vividly conscious of how delicate her slender body was as she lay beneath him in their bed, and even though he knew she was both stronger and tougher than she looked, she seemed to him terrifyingly defenseless.

All she had to shield her was a steely core of will, and though that had brought her through the past difficult months he was worried that more pressure would shatter her. She'd already endured so much stress and she doubted her own strength, her own ability to cope. He knew that—he'd seen the moments of uncertainty in her eyes.

She was very vulnerable right now, risking a great deal of herself in the attempt to find her father's dream and put it into his hands. Failure might destroy her; even a setback or a delay could be too much for her. Drew tapped the note against one hand, staring at the message he didn't have to read again. What would this do to her?

And what would it do to her if he forced her to stop, if he ended it here and now? It was something he would have done in an instant if he hadn't been so certain that the action might well do her more harm than going on.

But the haunting fear of losing her was cold and tight inside him now, because there was a very real danger. If she went on. If she got anywhere near the man who had beaten them to the cross.

He could stop it now, he knew, by refusing to go any farther. Spencer lacked the experience necessary to find elusive information in this dangerous game, and when he told her their competitor had already beaten them to the cross, she would be unable to follow the trail without his help. But she would try, he knew, unless he could somehow stop her, and that kind of failure would surely mark her. The cross meant more than a last gift to her father; right or wrong, consciously or unconsciously, to Spencer it represented a vital test of her own self-confidence.

She wouldn't be willing to call off the hunt; she wouldn't stay put here or return to the States without a fight. And even if she trusted him now, he didn't think she'd let him continue alone.

What she had told him in the dark hours of the night had stunned him in more ways than one, but what he remembered most clearly was the pain in her soft voice when she had talked of her feelings of inadequacy. She seemed to see herself in a distorted mirror, where the reflection was always lacking. He thought she had a great deal more quiet confidence now than she'd had ten years ago, but it was a fragile assurance she had little faith in.

If she failed in her quest for the cross, it could damage that shaky confidence beyond repair, and if he forced her to go home so that he could search alone it would be even worse.

Drew hesitated a moment, checked his watch briefly, then sat on the couch and reached for the phone. He'd seen the message on the nightstand when he'd gotten up, and though it took him a moment's consideration, he did indeed know where in Madrid to call. He was a little impatient as he waited for the connections to be made, because he didn't want Spencer learning his news by listening to him tell someone else. He heard the shower cut off just as a very irritated voice in Spain demanded to know what the hell he wanted.

"Help," Drew responded mildly.

"Oh, it's you." Kane Pendleton's aggravated tone smoothed somewhat, though he still sounded rather like a bear that had been prodded with a sharp stick a few times too many. "You don't happen to know a crazy sheik with a suicide wish and a lust for redheads, do you?"

"I can think of one or two," Drew murmured, amused despite the dark thoughts and emotions churning inside him. "Are you ready to trade her in so soon?"

"Trade, hell, I'm ready to give her away."

Since at least one sheik Drew knew of had already attempted to steal the lady in question years before and had barely escaped with his life when Kane got a bit upset about it, Drew didn't make the mistake of believing the threat. And since he could hear Tyler laughing in the background, it was clear that she didn't believe it, either.

They had an interesting relationship, those two. Both fierce, temperamental and passionate, they'd fought for years as violently as two cats tied up in a bag. They'd fought as bitter rivals, as enemies, as unwilling partners and finally as lovers. Like the two of them—separately and, especially, together—their fights were rather magnificent, and had earned them a worldwide reputation among the community of people interested in antiquities. They were also well-known for their abilities and knowledge when it came to antiquities, and for their solid integrity and honor.

Drew knew them very well, despite the fact that he'd met them face-to-face less than a year before. He trusted both of them implicitly—and he couldn't say that about many.

Now, rightly guessing the reason for Kane's temper with his spirited wife, Drew said, "Are you in Spain because of Tyler's doing?"

Kane grunted, sounding as annoyed as a man could when he absolutely adored the woman he wanted to strangle. "We were *supposed* to be going back to Montana, but then that asinine curator in London had to mention a rumor he'd heard about a jeweled dagger. And here we are. Tangling with crooks, as usual. Ty just had a run-in with a smuggler who would have killed her as soon as spit, and she just won't—"

He broke off, there was an unidentifiable sound or two and then Tyler's cheerful voice came over the line.

"Hi, Drew. Pay no attention to Kane, he's just grouchy because a donkey kicked him yesterday."

Since Drew could hear an exasperated sigh, he gathered that Kane was on an extension. "I thought he got along with donkeys," he commented.

"I should," Kane growled. "I married one."

Not at all offended, Tyler merely said, "This one—I mean *that* one—was possessed of a fiend. Anyway, we found the dagger and handed it over to a museum here in Madrid, so we're pretty much at loose ends."

"What about Montana?" Drew questioned, knowing that Tyler had just endorsed Kane's earlier offer of help.

"The world's round," Kane replied, his temper fading. "Any news on the cross?"

If Drew had believed that Kane really was hell-bent to get back home to Montana, he wouldn't have asked them for help. But he knew very well that even though Tyler's frequent close brushes with danger shook Kane so much that he invariably stated his determination to take her home where she'd be safe, he could no more resist the lure of elusive antiquities than she could.

"Yeah, there's news," Drew said. "Bad news. One of my sources just confirmed that Lon Stanton went up into the mountains before dawn yesterday. He was back within hours, and he didn't waste any time leaving Innsbruck."

chapter nine

"STANTON?" KANE MUTTERED something about Mr. Stanton's ancestry, which that individual would have found more than a little offensive.

"If he was that quick," Tyler said, obviously thinking along more practical lines, "he must have found the cross."

"Even worse," Kane said. "He must know you're no more than a step behind him."

"I have to assume that, even though my being after the cross is a very recent development," Drew said, looking at the note in his hand and certain that it was more than an assumption. Stanton knew. Drew had no doubt now that it had been his own sudden presence in Spencer's life that had caused Stanton to steal Allan

Wyatt's notes and then race to Austria with no loss of time. Stanton would expect to be followed.

Some enemies knew you more intimately than a best friend ever could.

Holding his voice steady and quiet, Drew said, "The problem is that I can't afford the time for him to relax his guard. I have to go on the offensive, and that means finding him before he's crossed too many borders."

"Okay, then," Kane said briskly, "we'll start getting in touch with our contacts and see what we can turn up. The bastard isn't invisible—he has to show up somewhere."

"Will you be on the move right away?" Tyler asked. "Or stay in Innsbruck?"

"We'll be here at least long enough to go up into the mountains and make sure he did find it."

Tyler didn't question the plural. "All right, then. We'll call you by tonight, one way or the other."

When Drew cradled the receiver, a sudden awareness made him look toward the doorway to the bedroom Spencer was standing there, one small hand gripping the doorjamb tightly, and she was very pale.

"It's all right," he said involuntarily, dropping the note on the coffee table and rising to his feet.

She was looking at him in an odd, probing way, as if she were puzzled but didn't know why. "Is it?"

Before he could answer, a knock at the door signaled the arrival of breakfast, and Drew had to deal with that. By the time the waiter had gone, Spencer had obviously gotten herself under control. She wasn't as pale, and she even managed a small smile when he went to her.

"Even though I knew someone else was after the cross," she murmured, "I kept thinking it would be there, waiting. Pretty stupid, huh?"

He put his hands gently on her shoulders, unable to resist kissing her, then led her to her chair at the table. He was still worried about her, still trying to decide how to handle the situation without risking her in any way, and made his voice matter-of-fact as he responded to what she'd said. "No, not stupid. There was every reason to suppose we could get to it first. I'm just sorry you had to hear about it like that."

She poured coffee for them both and then sipped hers as she looked at him gravely. "I don't think I heard it all. You know who did get there first? His name, I mean?"

Drew told her about the note he'd gotten, just mentioning Stanton's name without description, and about whom he'd been talking to on the phone and why. He explained that Kane and Tyler Pendleton not only were expert hunters with good instincts and solid contacts, but also were unusually quick when it came to finding information.

"Quicker than you?" she asked, surprised by that.

"We've never had a contest," he replied, pleased when that brought a smile. He loved her slow smiles, and they were still rare enough that they speeded up his heartbeat. Or maybe, he thought, it wasn't because they were rare. Maybe it was just because he loved her smiles.

"So they're going to help?"

"If they can. Stanton has an edge if he knows he's being hunted. He'll avoid the obvious routes and keep out of sight, and that won't make it easy for us. But he has to get the cross out of Europe and back to the States, so he has to move, and he can't afford to risk too many cute tricks. He'll want to move fast at least out of Austria, because he has to assume the first thing we'll do is sound the alarm, and that means every border guard will be on the alert and half of Interpol will be sniffing out his trail."

"Will we sound the alarm?"

Drew sipped his coffee as he considered that, still trying to decide. "I have a few friends in Interpol who'd take my word for it that Stanton got his hands on the cross, but they couldn't move against him without proof. He doesn't panic easily, but too much attention could make him go to ground, and we don't have time to wait him out. I think we should find out which way he's gone and then decide."

Frowning a little, Drew went on. "If he's following his usual methods, he's over here with his own passport, big as life, with a hired gun in case there's trouble. He isn't likely to move the cross via one of the airlines, at least unless he's willing to risk it crossing the Atlantic, because of customs and because even checked luggage is X-rayed. He could charter a plane, but not out of

Innsbruck because too few are available and that's a sign anyone on his trail would be able to read."

Spencer was so fascinated she'd forgotten to continue eating as she listened.

"He won't go to Vienna," Drew said slowly, obviously working it out in his mind. "Trying to get out of the capital city with an Austrian treasure would be a bit too reckless, and heading east just makes the route home longer. Germany to the north—there's a lot going on there right now, and I wouldn't risk it. Switzerland to the west—maybe, but doubtful unless you're trying to move or safeguard cash. The safest bet would be to go overland and head south, through Italy to the Mediterranean. The border wouldn't be too risky, and once he reached the coast there are any number of vessels he could book passage on without having to go through customs. Once he's at sea he can pick a nice, safe, out-of-the-way port where smugglers will take him anywhere he wants for the right price."

Spencer had the feeling her mouth was open. She reached for her coffee hastily and took a sip, then murmured, "God help the world if you take to crime."

Drew looked at her, smiling slightly. "You can learn a lot about your enemies—and their methods—in ten years," he said dryly.

"He is an enemy, isn't he? Stanton, I mean. The way you talk about him, you must know him very well."

A part of Drew's mind had been occupied by that very certain knowledge even as he'd mentally traced

Stanton's possible route, and now, as he looked at Spencer, the coldness he was becoming familiar with was heavy in his chest. "I know him," he said.

Spencer frowned a little at the tone, which was curiously bleak and hard. "Is he . . . dangerous?" she asked slowly.

So dangerous that I don't want you anywhere near him. Drew pushed his plate away, his appetite gone. "Spencer . . . would you consider going back to the States—or waiting here—and letting me find the cross for you?" He saw the instant flash of some strong emotion in her eyes, but forced himself to hold her gaze steadily.

"No," she said.

Very softly, he said, "I don't want you to get hurt."

She hesitated, but even though it was almost painful to refuse him anything, she had to, and shook her head in response. It wasn't only because she still felt driven to find the cross for her father. There was something else now, something she'd been aware of ever since she'd walked into the room and heard Drew talking on the phone. Maybe it was just because she loved him, but she had the strongest, strangest feeling that if she didn't go with him, if she didn't stay as close to him as possible, something terrible would happen to him.

In a way, it was absurd to believe that her presence would keep him safe; she certainly couldn't protect him physically and he'd proven himself adept at surviving dangerous situations in the past. But what she felt was a conviction too deep to be questioned or ignored, and she had to accept it even if she didn't understand why.

"No," she said quietly. "I have to go with you."

"Because you don't trust me?" His voice was taut now, his face very still.

"I trust you." It was the truth, and one she had to admit. "I know you'd get the cross and bring it back to me if you could. It's just . . ." She couldn't tell him that, it sounded too senseless. "I have to go with you. Please, Drew, it's very important to me."

They both knew that he could keep her from going with him, by trickery or by force if there was no other way. But after a long moment Drew muttered an oath and looked away from her, and she knew she'd won. She wasn't sure why she'd won, and she was too relieved to ask. Instead, she asked another question.

"Why is Stanton so dangerous?"

Flatly, Drew said, "Because he cares about nothing on this earth except his collection, and his only emotion about that is cold, ruthless greed. He has plenty of money, but the things he wants money can't buy, so he just takes them. It doesn't matter who they belong to, and it doesn't matter what he has to do to get them. He doesn't give a damn about anything but his own gluttony, and he's completely soulless." Drew hesitated, then added in a voice that was stony with control, "I once saw him cut a woman's throat."

Spencer was so shocked that for a long moment she couldn't say anything at all. She had no experience of violence, no understanding of how any human could commit such an act. A wave of nausea passed over her and she had to swallow hard before she could speak. "He—he wasn't punished for that?"

"Not the way he deserved to be."

Something about that grim reply made Spencer's heart turn over with a lurch. What other unbearable things had Drew seen? And what kind of strength did it require of him to show a composed face to the world with memories like that haunting him?

"What happened?" she asked.

Drew half shrugged, his gaze fixed on something only he could see. "It was in Central America years ago in the middle of some cockeyed revolution. Stanton had gone down there after a gold idol that had been stolen from a museum. I was—I was just there. Our paths crossed by accident. I was too far away to see all of what happened, but I found out later that the thief wasn't willing to part with the idol even though Stanton had paid him to steal it. Stanton grabbed the thief's wife and held a knife to her throat. The man immediately handed the idol over—but Stanton killed her anyway.

"There was fighting going on all around. Stanton was shot, wounded, but not fatally. He managed to get away. There was no government to speak of, and if the thief reported his wife's murder, no one cared."

Spencer thought that someone had cared. Someone still remembered the brutal, senseless waste of a life.

But she couldn't say anything because her throat was aching so badly.

Drew looked at her, focused on her face. His eyes were very dark, and his voice was so low it seemed to come from deep inside his chest. "The cross isn't worth a life, Spencer. Allan would be the first to say so."

She swallowed hard. "I know."

"We'll track Stanton if we can, but we won't get close. As soon as we have something solid, we'll alert the Austrian authorities and Interpol, and let them handle it."

Spencer nodded. "Yes. All right."

He reached over and grasped one of her hands. "It could take more time than Allan has," he warned quietly. "Once the authorities are involved in investigating the theft of a national treasure, things will get complicated in a hurry. You may not be able to take the cross back to the States for months."

She turned her hand so that her fingers twined with his, and smiled. "I know that. But it seems to be the only way."

Drew sighed a bit roughly, almost as if he'd been holding his breath, and squeezed her hand before releasing it. "Okay. I need to make a few calls, and then we should ride up into the mountains and make sure Stanton got what he came for."

Spencer agreed to that, and while he made his calls she finished her cool coffee and thought about everything he had told her. Now she knew why she had to stay with him. It was because she loved him, but it was also because her presence did have the power to keep him safe.

When she had come into the room and heard him on the phone, something in his voice had touched an alarm bell deep in her subconscious. Though she hadn't understood it then, she did now. Alone, Drew would have gone after Lon Stanton without hesitation, not just for the cross but for that cruelly murdered woman—and perhaps even others he hadn't told her about. He would have hunted Stanton, and finding him wouldn't have been enough, turning him over to the authorities wouldn't have been enough.

What Spencer had heard in Drew's voice had been the soft echo of an emotion so primitive only her deepest instincts had recognized it for what it was: the utter loathing of a man of conscience for something evil.

Alone, Drew would have confronted that evil, risking his life without a second thought. But he wouldn't risk her life. She knew that. As long as she was with him, he would take care of her. He would keep his distance from Stanton to protect her, and that would keep him safe.

THEY FOUND THE cave midway through the afternoon. Miles from Innsbruck, and carved into a cliff face so steep they'd had to leave the horses below and climb, it had been hidden from sight by a cunning arrangement of boulders that looked natural. Or at least had looked natural before Stanton had found it. Now, two of the huge rocks were scarred by marks of pickaxes and a third had been broken into pieces, leaving a thin opening that gaped darkly in the sunlight.

Drew helped her up the last couple of feet so they were standing on a narrow ledge and, glancing back down the way they'd come, he said almost idly, "How much mountain climbing have you done?"

Spencer, who was carefully not looking down, replied with the truth. "None. Why?"

He smiled slightly. "Do you know what courage is, Spencer?"

Puzzled by the seemingly oblique question, she frowned up at him. "The dictionary's definition?"

"No, the true definition. Courage is doing what you have to do, even if it scares you silly." He leaned over and kissed her, so deeply and thoroughly that she was shaking when he finally raised his head.

She was glad he was holding her hand, because she was so dizzy she might easily have tumbled off the ledge. Blinking up at him as the dizziness cleared, and wondering why he'd said that about courage, she said, "Um—shouldn't we go into the cave?"

Drew turned his head to study the opening with a considering gaze. "You stay put a minute, all right?"

She nodded as he unclipped the big flashlight he carried from his belt. She could still feel the warmth of his mouth on hers, and though a night of intense passion had left her feeling wonderfully sated, she was conscious of desire stirring deep inside her now as she looked at him.

The sunlight gleamed in his golden hair and made his blue eyes seem even brighter than usual. The sweater he wore set off his broad shoulders, just as the snug jeans complemented lean hips and long, powerful legs. He'd been graceful on horseback and now, as he went toward the cave opening, she admired the lithe, catlike suppleness of his movements. She felt amazingly primitive when she looked at him, her body heated, her emotions fierce, and it was a struggle to contain that.

But she managed to. Barely. She didn't know why he wanted her to wait outside the opening, but remained there and watched as he disappeared into the darkness of the cave. It was only when he came back out less than five minutes later that his absent comment told her why.

"I didn't think he'd had time to rig anything, but it never hurts to be sure," Drew murmured, taking her hand and leading her to the opening.

"Rig—you mean a booby trap?" As soon as the words were out, Spencer reminded herself yet again that he'd warned her from the beginning how dangerous this could be. Still, she was shaken—and not only by the threat of that. She had stood there, wrapped in sensual thoughts and feeling absolutely no sense of danger, and had calmly watched Drew walk into what might very well have been a deadly trap.

Before he could answer her question, she snapped, "Don't do that again, dammit."

Drew looked down at her in surprise. "Do what?"

"Just—just walk in when you know it could be a trap. What if it had been?"

"Worried about my hide?" he murmured, smiling a little.

Spencer felt herself flush, but met his eyes very steadily. "Yes."

He looked at her for a long moment, his face curiously still, then smiled again. "Sweetheart, I've been doing this kind of thing for half my life. I've probably studied every kind of device ever used to defend anything of value, from the state-of-the-art technology smugglers use to guard their shipments to the traps the pharaohs' engineers designed to protect their tombs. And I'm never careless."

It reassured her—but only a little. Yes, he did know what he was doing; she didn't doubt that. But she had sensed the depth of his loathing for Stanton, and she had a very strong feeling that the hatred was a mutual one. Enemies could be vicious. If Stanton knew who was tracking him . . .

Abruptly, she said, "Does he know? Does Stanton know it's you who's after him?"

Drew hesitated, then said, "Probably." His hand squeezed hers gently and he pointed his flashlight ahead to show them the way as he led her into the cave.

As they went in and the thick stillness of immense

weight above their heads closed about them, Spencer told herself with steely determination that she'd be alert to possible danger from now on and not just meekly expect Drew to do everything. Unlike him, she hadn't been exposed to the kinds of danger that would have sharpened her instincts, but fear for him was a very strong and primitive spur to learn what she had to in a hurry.

The passage they walked through was wide enough for them to go side by side, with smooth stone curving above them several inches higher than the top of Drew's head, and turned gently in a slow arc to the west of the point where they'd entered. Beneath them the floor was stone with a thin, grainy top coat. The air was heavy and very dry, with no circulation at all.

In a low voice that nonetheless echoed softly, Drew said, "Only one opening to the outside, and that was blocked off. This place was airtight until Stanton broke in. With no oxygen or moisture, it was a perfect place to hide something valuable. Spencer, if you start to feel dizzy, tell me. There hasn't been time for much fresh air to get in here."

"All right." She kept her eyes fixed on the circle of his flashlight ahead of them, aware of the thickness of the air but not troubled by it. Not yet, at least. "I wonder how long Kurt searched before he found this place? When he sent those letters to his friend, I think he'd been in Innsbruck for a couple of months already."

"I'll bet it took him that long, at least," Drew said.

Spencer opened her mouth to say something else, but whatever it was remained unsaid. The passage had taken a sharp left-hand turn and abruptly dead-ended, and in the glow of Drew's flashlight a life-size figure of a man stood squarely before them with his back against the wall. He stood as if at attention, straight and proud, with both hands held out together at his waist, palms up. Lying on his hands was a lidless box made of the same grayish material he was constructed of, and it was empty.

Standing beside Drew in silence, Spencer watched him reach out and touch the statue, rubbing a thumb consideringly along the edge of the empty box. "A kind of plaster," he said. "Heavy enough so it wouldn't be easily moved. And it definitely dates from the early sixteen hundreds."

"The box is the right size to hold the cross," she said softly. "The Hapsburgs supposedly kept it in a carved wooden box a little smaller than that plaster one. All Stanton had to do was pry the wooden box out and carry it away."

"Funny," Drew mused, "that Kurt went to all this trouble when he intended to get the cross later. He could have just left the box on the floor here—why the statue?"

Spencer, who had been studying the face of the statue, was frowning to herself, and answered absently. "Maybe it was vanity. That's him, Drew. It's Kurt. In that book about the Hapsburgs, there was a painting of him, and the face of this statue looks just like . . ." Her voice trailed off.

"What?" Drew asked, looking at her in the dim back-wash of light from his flashlight.

She was concentrating so hard on trying to figure out what was bothering her about the plaster face that Spencer was hardly aware of how difficult breathing had become. "I don't know. It looks like Kurt Hapsburg, even to the little scar bisecting his left eyebrow, but it isn't quite right."

"Portraiture isn't an exact art," Drew reminded her. "Different artists interpret subjects in different ways."

The comment seemed to ring in Spencer's ears, and she thought with total clarity, *That's it.* But she didn't know why she thought that, or what it meant, and she had no idea why a little voice in her head kept insisting in an annoyingly repetitive way that there was some-thing important she knew if she could only remember what it was.

"Spencer?" Drew reached out to her quickly, then swore softly and lifted her into his arms. He turned away from the statue and carried her back along the pas-sageway, not pausing until be slipped through the nar-row opening and out onto the sunny ledge.

She blinked at the bright light, vaguely surprised to find herself sitting on the ledge. Drew was supporting her as he knelt beside her, and as the dizziness began to recede she felt like an absolute fool. A lot of help she'd be in case of danger—she couldn't even stay alert enough to know when she was running out of oxygen!

"Take deep breaths," he urged.

Spencer obeyed, breathing slowly and deeply until the scenery stopped dancing, then looked up at him. "I'm sorry, I should have realized."

"It usually creeps up on you the first couple of times," he said in a reassuring tone, though his eyes remained watchful. "After that you learn to be wary. Better now?"

"Much better, thanks."

Drew eased back onto his heels, but one hand remained on her thigh as he turned off the flashlight and clipped it to his belt. "Something was bothering you about the statue."

She frowned. "Yes, but I can't remember what it was."

He half nodded. "You probably will eventually. If we have time, we can come back up here later on. Once the wind shifts, it should clear out all the bad air in the cave. In any case, it's a pretty good bet the statue will end up in a museum as soon as the authorities know about it."

The little voice Spencer had been hearing was only a whisper now, maddeningly indistinct, and she felt frustrated because she was sure there was something . . . She glanced down at Drew's hand on her leg, and all thoughts of the statue faded away.

His hand, elegant and powerful, lay over her upper thigh in a light, casually possessive gesture. It was a very simple thing, but intimate as well, the unthinking, familiar touch of a lover. Vivid memories rose in her mind with suddenness that stole her breath, memories of how those strong hands had touched and caressed her, how they had held her beneath him. Her body responded to the mental images so instantly that she felt overwhelmed, and she could only look up at him in helpless longing.

Drew went very still, blue heat flaring in his topaz eyes. His hand tightened, then began to slowly stroke her thigh as if obeying a compulsion. "One of these days," he said a bit thickly, "you're going to look at me like that, and I won't give a damn if we're on a public sidewalk—or a narrow ledge on the side of a mountain."

"I can't help it," she murmured, his rough voice sending an even stronger wave of desire through her.

He leaned over to kiss her with a hard brevity that made strained control obvious, then rose to his feet and grasped her hands to pull her gently up. "Just hold the thought long enough for us to get off this bloody mountain," he told her.

Spencer followed him to the rim of the ledge, her hand held firmly in his, and she didn't even look back at the cave. Nor did she hesitate to start down the cliff despite her fear of heights. All her attention, all her awareness, was focused on Drew. Everything else in her world had shrunk to a dim, distant unimportance.

Drew went first, staying close behind her as they picked their way slowly down the cliff face. It wasn't a particularly dangerous climb since there were numerous solid handholds and sturdy granite outcroppings, but he'd seen the flicker of nervousness in her eyes before they'd gone up and knew that the trip down would test her courage even more.

It was a test he knew she would pass with flying colors. She had guts—and she didn't even know it. She also had a trick of looking at him in a way that was so intensely erotic it sent a jolt of urgent, almost primal need through him.

If he had ever really believed that possessing her would be enough, he knew now he'd been wrong. He wanted her even more fiercely, despite a night of passion so incredibly fiery and satisfying he'd felt raw with the pleasure of it. The pleasure of her. Yet desire was like a tide inside him, ebbing with completion and then almost immediately surging again. She had only to look at him in that intimate way, her eyes soft and dreamy, lips slightly parted, and he could hardly think for wanting her.

He had been able to concentrate for a while today, his mind grappling with the potential danger of Stanton, his own determination to get the cross for Spencer and the surprising and unsettling things she'd told him in the night. But his concentration was shaky at best where she was concerned, and more than anything else he wished it could be just the two of them with no outside pressures.

Drew wanted time with Spencer. He'd hated leaving her in bed alone this morning. What he'd wanted was to keep her in bed, to wake her by making love to her slowly, to watch her body come alive under his touch, her eyes glow with desire. Looking down at her as she lay curled on her side sleeping, he had felt fascination and desire and an aching in his chest. She was such a delicate thing to hold so many varied emotions, from the muted pain of self-doubt to the astonishing force of her passion. She was so beautiful, and she'd worked her way under his skin a second time until he could barely think of anything but her.

He had wondered then if she loved him, because her response in bed was so sweetly wild and giving, and because she had softly agreed that she belonged to him. Belonged to him . . . What did that mean? She had loved him once—he believed that—and yet had run from him in a panic to marry a man she *hadn't* loved, a man with whom she'd felt safer. That had been ten years ago, yes; she'd been a schoolgirl frightened of trying to live up to the image of him she'd fixed in her mind, and the image of herself she believed was in his mind. It was different now. Her self-confidence was tenuous, but she was no schoolgirl dreaming of princes and she wasn't wary or nervous of him as she'd been then.

But love? She hadn't said it, and he thought that if she had loved him she would have said it last night. It had been a night of honesty, after all, and she hadn't flinched from showing him her vulnerability. He wondered if, between them, he and Reece Cabot had cured her of the desire to love anyone. One man had hidden his feelings so completely that she'd thought him remote, while the other had run off with her in a violent tempest of emotion that had barely outlasted the honeymoon.

Perhaps this time Spencer had opted for uncomplicated passion.

As for his own feelings, Drew avoided defining them. She was under his skin, yes, and his hunger for her seemed stronger with every passing hour, but he couldn't forget what he'd felt when Allan had handed him the ring and told him Spencer had eloped with another man, even though it had been ten years ago. It had been like a hot knife in his gut, the pain so bad it had taken him months to stop hurting. He never wanted to feel that again, never wanted to be so vulnerable to someone else that the loss of them was devastating.

He wanted her, though, with a desire he couldn't control. He needed her. In his bed, her mouth lifting for his kisses, her silky heat sheathing him. He wanted more of her slow smiles, her sensual gazes, her sweet passion.

Now, one hand on her hip guiding her as they climbed slowly down the cliff face, he watched her supple movements and every muscle in his body slowly tightened. He'd never have believed that climbing down a rocky cliff could be erotic, but he was coming apart just watching her, his attention so fixed on her that it must have been blind instinct that kept him from putting a foot wrong and falling. That look of hers before they'd started down had inflamed his senses, but he'd thought he could keep his hands off her at least until they returned to Innsbruck.

It would take a couple of hours, less time than had been needed to find the cave—but more time than he could stand. His control was splintering even now, his heart pounding, breath rasping in his throat, his body heavy with an ache that would only grow and grow until it became unbearable, until he had to lose himself in her or go mad.

Drew felt solid ground beneath his feet not a moment too soon, and put both his hands on Spencer's hips to guide her the rest of the way. She took a step away from him, but he immediately pulled her back against him.

"The horses—" she began, then broke off with a gasp when she felt him behind her. "Drew?"

He wrapped his arms around her, his mouth nuzzling her hair aside to seek the warmth of her neck. "I want you," he muttered in a thick, rasping voice.

Spencer went weak, all the strength draining out of her legs as if a dam had burst. Even through the barrier of their jeans she could feel the pulsing hardness of his arousal, and the hands that closed over her breasts were shaking a little, almost rough, urgent with need.

When he'd told her to hold the thought until they got off the mountain, she'd assumed he meant back to Innsbruck. He'd seemed perfectly in control, and though her own desire had been feverish it hadn't occurred to her to suggest anything else. Even if she'd considered what making love out under the open sky with him would be like—which she hadn't—her imagination would have balked at the idea of a man as calm and elegant as Drew so overcome by desire that he was unwilling to wait for the comfort of a bed or the privacy of a locked door. She would have shied away from the idea herself if she'd been given a moment to think.

He didn't give her a moment. His hands and mouth seduced her, the hunger in him so strong and immediate that it kindled an instant, answering fire in her. She was trembling, breathless, aching with a desire so imperative she didn't care where they were or anything else. She was barely aware of being turned and lifted into his arms, of being carried, because his mouth was hard and fierce on hers, and if he'd put her down on solid rock she wouldn't have murmured a protest.

They were in a kind of valley, a relatively small area where several mountains shouldered against one another in a series of tumbling hills. Clumps of tall trees gave way to rocky outcroppings and patches of thick green grass. Drew put her down on one of the grassy places and immediately began stripping her clothing off.

If she'd been thinking at all by that point, she would have expected him to remove only as much as necessary, because his face was a primitive mask of passion and the look in his burning eyes was almost wild. But Drew wanted them both naked, and their clothing was flung aside carelessly.

Spencer wasn't aware of the faint chill of the mountain air. The summer sun warmed the ground beneath her and when his body covered hers she was conscious of nothing else. She was as frantic as he was, so desperate to feel him inside her that she was writhing and whimpering beneath him, her arms tight around his neck and her legs lifting to wrap around his hips. Wildfire was racing through her veins, searing her senses, and she moaned into his mouth when she felt the burning hardness of him sink deeply into her body.

Whether it was the primitive influence of the musty earth beneath them and the wide sky above or something equally ancient in them, this time they mated. It was hasty and a little rough, their bodies straining together in an almost silent conflict as old as the mountains that cradled them.

SPENCER WAS SO drained she didn't want to move. The ground beneath her was hard, but surprisingly cushioned by the thick grass. Drew was heavy, but her body seemed perfectly designed to bear his weight without strain or discomfort, and this time the starkly intimate sensations caused her no shyness or embarrassment at all. She didn't even think about the fact that they were lying naked on a sunny patch of grass in an area where the odd tourist might well ride or hike through.

She felt his mouth moving against her neck, and then he raised his head to gaze down at her. His forearms were under her shoulders, his fingers tangled in her hair, and there was an expression in his darkened eyes she'd never seen before, almost a look of awe.

"Spencer," he murmured, and kissed her very gently.

Spencer felt blissfully happy. She wasn't thinking beyond this moment, and for this moment there were no problems or doubts or questions. She nuzzled her face into his warm throat briefly, then smiled up at him. "We'd better move," she said, "or you're going to get sunburned in a very painful place."

chapter ten

ALL THE WAY back to Innsbruck Spencer could feel herself smiling. She couldn't seem to help herself, and whenever her glance caught and held Drew's he smiled as well. They were able to ride abreast occasionally as they made their way toward the city, and each time he reached for her hand as if touching her was a compulsion.

She felt oddly serene, the frantic, primitive mating having given her something she couldn't even define. All she was certain of was that, for the first time in her life, she felt entirely comfortable with herself. Comfortable enough to tease Drew, predicting that he would indeed be sunburned, and laughing when he reminded her that, as easily as she bruised, she'd probably have a black-and-blue rear end by morning.

"Then we'll both sit on pillows," she said, unworried by the prospect.

He glanced at her again, unable to stop looking at her. She had laughed a moment ago, the sound as clear and sweet as the mountain breeze, and it was only when he felt the shock of it that he realized he'd never heard her laugh. Not really, not like that, her lovely face alight with amusement, her eyes bright with simple enjoyment.

For the first time, she was utterly tranquil in his company, the little smile curving her lips so secret and feminine, her glances warm with an intimacy that was without obvious sensuality and yet held the glowing embers of passion. The promise of what he'd seen in her all those years ago was realized now: beauty, grace, intelligence, humor, an inner poise, strength she had no awareness of—and a depth of passion he had never expected to find.

He reached for her hand as they came abreast again, and as her fingers twined with his, his curious instinct for detecting the genuine sounded inside him. Over the past days, the tone of that inner intuition had grown clearer and clearer with each touch, and now the single note was so perfect in its distinct, sweet sound that it was haunting.

The real thing.

This was Spencer. This was the woman she was meant to be.

His instinct only confirmed what other feelings had

told him, and after that compulsive joining on a patch of sunny grass he could no longer avoid facing another truth. He loved her. He had loved her since she was sixteen years old.

He should have known from the moment he came back into her life, because it had been the uneasy suspicion that she was in trouble that had drawn him back to her. Even then, even believing he no longer felt anything for her, he had acted almost instinctively by going to her despite everything that had happened between them. The shock of realizing he still wanted her had collided with all the gnawing, unresolved emotions he'd thought long dead—and that was when he'd begun reaching for excuses, for rationalizations, even for lies he could tell himself, to avoid the truth.

Not love, lust. That was all it was, he'd told himself. He couldn't love her—she was a greedy little gold digger. He just wanted her, that was all, wanted to purge himself of the bitter desire. He'd be a fool to trust her, a fool to let her get to him a second time, he'd reminded himself harshly. Besides that, he couldn't love her again, it wasn't even possible; he'd learned his lesson too well, and would never again leave himself so vulnerable to her that she could destroy him.

Lies. All lies. It was love, and it had always been love. He had been able to lie to himself about it only because it was possible to grow accustomed to anything, even pain, until it was so familiar it went almost without notice. But now she was here, with him, tranquil by his side, eager in his arms, and what he felt for her was an emotion so vast it filled his entire being. This time the roots of love were sunk so deeply inside him that tearing them out would cost him his soul.

It was terrifying to love so much, to know without doubt or question that his life would be hollow and unbearable without her. He wasn't a man who had known much uncertainty in his life, but it was tormenting him now. She had loved him once, but that had been a girl in awe of a man she saw as something larger than life. She knew better now. She'd seen him at his worst, knew how anger and bitter hostility could make him cruel, how scornful and cutting and implacable he could be.

Could she love that very human and flawed man? He was afraid to ask. They'd been together for such a short time and so much had happened. Though she seemed happy now, he couldn't forget the stresses and strains she had withstood during the past months, and he was afraid that her peace was a fragile thing. He couldn't put more pressure on her, demand a commitment when she'd barely had time to think. All he could do was love her and try to be patient, try not to hold on to her too hard out of his own terror of losing her.

"Drew?"

He looked at her, his throat aching, knowing that his patience was threadbare with anxiety, and that he wouldn't be able to be civilized about it if she left him again. Not this time. This time he'd kill any man who dared try to take her away from him. And if there was no other man, if she just left him, he'd go after her and he'd spend the rest of his life trying to convince her that they belonged together.

"Are you all right?" she asked, reining her horse a bit closer and studying him with a slight frown.

It was easy to smile at her even though what he felt was savage. It was even easy to find a mild, wry voice when he answered her, because he would have cut his throat rather than disturb her happy serenity. "Sunburned and exhausted, but otherwise flourishing."

She lifted an eyebrow at him in a quizzical expression that was adorable. "Exhausted? I haven't noticed you having problems with energy so far."

"You may notice tonight," he murmured, knowing she wouldn't but enjoying the way her eyes widened slightly and her secret little feminine smile returned.

"Are we going to stay in Innsbruck tonight?" The question was casual, and Drew answered in the same tone.

"That depends on Stanton." He wished it didn't, wished that very dangerous man was on the other side of the world or, better yet, in hell where he belonged. Where he would have been, Drew thought viciously, if only his own aim had been better.

She glanced at him again, not upset by his return to silence but wondering at the cause. She thought it was Stanton, thought that the man's very name had the power to disturb Drew. She acknowledged that, thought about it, but it didn't break her serene mood. She felt incredibly optimistic about everything. As long as she stayed with Drew he was safe, and she had faith that they'd get the cross eventually. She was also certain that it would be in time, that her father would wait for them.

Still casual, she said, "I wish I could figure out what bothered me about the statue. It's the most peculiar feeling, like hearing a song and *knowing* the words are in your head somewhere."

"It'll come to you."

"I guess." She pushed the question out of her mind, knowing that if she tried to remember it would only be more elusive. They reached the outskirts of Innsbruck about then, anyway, and by the time they'd returned the horses to the stable and taken a taxi back to the inn she'd forgotten the matter completely.

They were crossing the lobby when Spencer became aware of a great deal of noise coming from the veranda at the rear of the building. It sounded like a roar from a wounded bear, followed immediately by other, less identifiable sounds a bit lower in volume but still impressive.

"What on earth?" she murmured, halting when Drew did.

He cocked his head to one side briefly, then smiled and squeezed her hand. "I had a feeling they'd be showing up."

"Who?"

"Kane and Tyler Pendleton."

Spencer glanced up at him as they headed toward the

wide hallway that led to the veranda. "Your friends from Madrid? They sound as if they're about to murder each other."

"They've sounded that way for years," he explained a bit dryly. "In countless places all over the world. I've seen them fight with each other when most people would have been making peace with their Creator."

She felt a spurt of amusement, and the feeling grew when they stepped out onto the veranda. The wide, tiled porch boasted a splendid view of the Alps, with scattered groupings of chairs and tables placed so that guests could take advantage of the scenery. All the chairs tended to be occupied at this time in the late afternoon but, even as Spencer watched, one couple retreated into the inn and another opted for the relative peace of the garden off to one side.

Only a lone man, casually dressed and seemingly either tired or just a little sleepy, remained near the combatants. He was slouched back in his chair with a drink on the table before him, watching them with an air of lazy interest.

Spencer heard Drew chuckle softly, but most of her fascinated attention was fixed on the man and woman who stood a few feet away near the low balustrade.

The man was about Drew's height, but he was heavier through the shoulders and a great deal more rugged looking, especially wearing jeans and a black sweatshirt that emphasized the sheer, raw strength of his large body. He had shaggy black hair and vivid green eyes that were almost literally shooting sparks at the woman who was confronting him. She was a tall and strikingly beautiful redhead with a figure, Spencer noted enviously, that no doubt caused traffic jams whenever she walked down the street and that was obvious even beneath the khaki slacks and loose blouse she wore. Her voice was as fiery as his, and since they were both yelling at the same time it was impossible to understand what the blistering argument was even about.

Drew led her over to the watching man, who immediately climbed to his feet with a faint grin of welcome on his thin face. "Don't mind them," he said over the roar of battle. "They should be winding down any minute now."

Spencer was introduced to Burke Corbett and found herself sitting at the table between him and Drew, still conscious of amusement. "Interpol?" she asked, questioning that part of the introduction.

"For my sins, yes." He smiled at her, and Spencer acknowledged to herself that she'd never seen a more exotically handsome man. He had eyes of a peculiarly vivid and unusual shade of gray, so pale they looked almost silver, with perfectly shaped bat-wing brows flying above them. His thick black hair grew in a widow's peak atop his high forehead, his smile was singularly charming and his voice was low and pleasant.

"Did you just happen to be in Austria," Drew asked, "or did you tail along with those two?"

"I came with them," Burke answered. "I was working on a case involving a smuggling ring in Madrid when they crashed the party. After the dust settled they told me about the cross, and since my usual bailiwick is Italy, Kane thought I might be of some use to you here."

Drew lifted an eyebrow. "Did he get confirmation that Stanton crossed the border into Italy?"

"No, not yet." Burke shrugged. "He just thinks—like you do, I imagine—that Stanton will aim for the Med and pick the shortest route."

Spencer was so interested in the conversation that she only then noticed the abrupt cessation of noise. She turned her head to see the Pendletons glaring at each other in total silence. Then the redhead grinned suddenly and stood on tiptoe to kiss her scowling husband. His fierce expression didn't change very much, but it was easy to see he kissed her back even as one big hand lifted to gently encircle her throat.

"One of these days," he growled warningly.

"You and what army?" she retorted, grasping his hand and holding it in her own as she turned toward their audience.

Neither of them was at all self-conscious as more introductions were made and they took their seats at the table. Both seemed to recognize Spencer's name, or at least appeared to know who she was, either because Drew had mentioned her to them or else because of her father's reputation.

Tyler was cheerful, Kane somewhat morose, and only Burke had the temerity to ask dryly, "Who won?"

"I did, of course," Tyler said cheerfully.

"She makes me crazy," Kane grumbled.

Her amber eyes laughed at him, and after a moment Kane's scowl faded and he grinned. "Drew, keep the name of that sheik in mind, will you? Maybe I could get a tasseled saddle or a couple of camels for her."

Spencer had realized quickly that the Pendletons were quite deeply and securely in love—it was as openly obvious and without constraint as one of their fights—so she wasn't very surprised when Tyler's only response to that was a soft chuckle.

Drew obviously knew it as well, since he ignored Kane's request and said, "I expected you to turn up here sooner or later, but not this soon. Why the rush?"

"Madrid was very hot," Tyler said solemnly. "And Kane wanted to hunt down that poor donkey."

Kane gave her a look, then answered Drew's question. "We didn't expect any word from our contacts until tonight anyway, and since Innsbruck was closer to the action we decided to come ahead."

"I hope there won't be any action," Drew told them. "Not the violent kind, anyway."

Burke was looking at Drew very steadily, and his voice was quiet when he said, "In the past five years you haven't missed a chance to go after Stanton, and the three times that I know of when you caught up with him, you cost him plenty. Do you expect it to be different this time?"

Somewhat grimly, Drew said, "I thought you were

just a bit too casual about why you were here. Come to keep an eye on me, Burke?"

"I'm just on my way back to Milan," Burke replied in an unruffled tone. "Stopped by to see an old friend. Are you going to answer the question, or aren't you?"

"It's not Stanton I'm after," Drew replied. "Not this time. Just the cross."

Spencer, listening silently, was very much alert as she looked between the two men, and a glance showed her that Kane and Tyler were also deadly serious now. There were undercurrents, ripples of meaning in what was being said, and she listened even more intently as she tried to figure it out.

"How can he know that?" Burke asked, his voice becoming flat and hard. "You've always gone after him before. The last time he ventured out of the States you were on his trail within days, and he was damn near killed before he got away."

Drew's expressionless eyes met Spencer's briefly, then returned to Burke's face. "Past history."

"History he hasn't forgotten. Drew, I was there, remember? I saw his face. Hate's a mild word for what he feels for you, and you can't expect—" The Interpol agent's voice broke off abruptly as a waiter approached and spoke briefly to Drew in German.

Drew nodded in acknowledgment to the waiter, then looked at Spencer. "I have a call—it might be news about the cross."

"I'll wait here," she said quietly. She said nothing

more until he left, then looked at Burke. "Why does Stanton hate Drew so much?"

Burke was frowning a little, and it was Tyler who said softly, "I think she has a right to know, Burke."

"Then he should tell her," the agent snapped.

"He won't. You know that."

Spencer kept her clear, steady gaze on Burke. "Drew's after the cross because of me," she said, and there was a world of emotion in that statement.

After a long moment Burke sighed explosively. "A few years ago we got word that a gold idol stolen from a museum in Mexico was about to change hands in Central America. Drew was in Colombia on business of his own, but we got in touch and unofficially requested that he try and find out who the buyer was."

"Why Drew?" Spencer asked, guessing the answer but wanting it confirmed.

"Because he knows most of the world like the back of his hand and can get into and out of places where we wouldn't stand a chance. It wasn't the first time we'd asked a favor. He's done work for us off and on since he was in college."

She nodded. "I see. So—he went to Central America?" Drew, she thought, hadn't told her why he was there. She wondered what else he'd left out of his brief retelling.

"Yeah, he went. It was hell down there. The country was in the middle of a revolution, and foreigners were considered fair targets by both sides." Burke's pleasant

.voice became impersonal in the way that some men learn to speak, in order to save their sanity, when they've seen too many unendurable things in their lives. "We'd heard rumors about a rabid collector, but we didn't have a name then. That was all we wanted, just a name. Drew knew that. His instructions were to try and observe the exchange if he could, to try and identify the buyer.

"He managed to locate the meeting, God knows how. He had to stay well back, out of sight. When Stanton got there the thief decided he wanted more money, or the idol. Stanton grabbed a woman who was there, the thief's wife, and held a knife to her throat. The thief gave in without hesitating, but Stanton killed his wife. She was several months pregnant."

Spencer caught her breath and half closed her eyes briefly. He hadn't told her that part, she thought, and she wondered suddenly if it had occurred to Drew that she might well have conceived his child. He had said nothing about birth control, and they hadn't used any kind of protection despite the fact that both of them had had the time to consider that and decide. She had said nothing because, she realized only now, she wanted his baby. But his silence seemed uncharacteristic to her, given his responsible nature, and she wondered about that.

They'd been lovers so briefly, and so much else was going on around them—perhaps he just hadn't thought about it. She hadn't, not until now. And there wasn't time to consider, to untangle what she was feeling; she had to push the disturbing emotions aside and concentrate on what Burke was saying.

He had hesitated for a moment, bothered by the fleeting intensity of emotion on her face, then went on in the same remote tone. "Drew didn't know Stanton then, and he couldn't believe the man would actually murder that woman. When it happened he blamed himself, because he could probably have taken Stanton out if he hadn't hesitated. Stanton ran almost immediately and Drew got off one shot. Considering the terrain and the distance, it was remarkable that he hit his target. Unfortunately, it wasn't a fatal wound. Drew tracked him as far as possible, but in the chaos down there he lost him within a couple of days."

Clearing her throat, Spencer said, "So that's why Stanton hates Drew? Because Drew shot him?"

"He didn't know who was after him then," Burke said. "But since then, whenever Stanton left the safety of the States—where he's a taxpaying, law-abiding citizen—Drew was on his trail. We couldn't touch the man legally, because we've never been able to get any solid proof against him, and Drew isn't a man who could kill in cold blood, although God knows he wanted to kill Stanton. So he kept pushing. If Stanton was after something, Drew got there first. If there was a corner, Drew backed him into it. If there was a chance in hell he could ruin Stanton's plans, he did it. He alerted everyone he could, made it so hot for Stanton that the man could hardly maneuver outside the States—and by then he knew who to blame for it.

"A few months ago things finally came to a head. Working with us, Drew helped arrange a setup to nail Stanton. We still don't know what went wrong. There was a mix-up, somebody jumped the gun, I don't know. Stanton got away again, but this time the man was . . . disfigured. He blamed Drew, of course. The last thing we heard him say was that he'd make Drew suffer."

Fiercely, Spencer said, "You can't get him for that? You can't stop him?"

"Threats aren't against the law," Burke replied stonily. "And as far as the international police are concerned, Stanton hasn't done a thing to be arrested for. We have no proof. The only witness we have to an illegal act is Drew, and what he saw took place in a country that was coming apart at the seams."

Spencer stared at him for a moment, then said, "I'm sorry."

The strange silvery eyes lost their metallic sheen and he smiled faintly. "So am I."

Tyler looked at both of them, then said mildy, "As soon as Drew told us it was Stanton, we grabbed Burke and hustled him on a plane. He'd told us the story a while ago—Burke, not Drew—and we figured there could be trouble. But it looks like Drew means to stay back this time."

There was a tacit question in the words, and Spencer looked at the redhead, half nodding. "Because of me. I won't let him go without me and—and he doesn't want me near Stanton."

Tyler smiled at her. "Sounds like a good reason to me."

"And me," Burke said definitely. "As a matter of fact, I'd already made up my mind that if Drew tried to cross the border into Italy—assuming Stanton went that route—I'd throw him in jail the moment he set foot on Italian soil."

Sliding into his chair beside Spencer, Drew said calmly, "I'd like to see you try."

Burke looked at him with very steady eyes. "Watch me."

After a moment Drew smiled. "No need. Not this time." He spread open a map on the table, studied it for a moment, then indicated a spot along the Austrian-Italian border. "According to a border guard who's always been straight with me, Stanton crossed over into Italy right here, at about noon today."

Kane frowned over the map. "He isn't making very good time."

"No, he isn't," Drew agreed. "I would have expected him to be halfway to Milan by noon."

Burke looked at Drew from under his flying brows. "I don't suppose it occurred to you to alert us as soon as you knew it was Stanton so we could catch him at the border?"

"It occurred to me," Drew replied, meeting the stare squarely. "But unless he left Austria with the cross, there wouldn't be much of a charge you could hang on him. This way, he's transported a stolen national treasure into another country. With any luck at all, you can nail him this time."

"If we can catch him before he reaches the Med."

"You'd better get busy," Drew suggested, pushing the map toward him.

Spencer could almost feel Burke relax suddenly, and she realized that until that moment he hadn't been entirely certain that Drew really intended to leave the matter of Stanton's capture to the authorities.

"I've been busy all day," the Interpol agent said. "I have half a dozen men stationed between the Austrian border and Milan, and a few more making certain we have the coast covered. Every police agency in Italy has been quietly alerted, as well as the relevant Austrian authorities—who are, by the way, biting their nails and going nuts."

Drew looked at him. "You do realize that we have absolutely no proof that Stanton stole the cross? Or even that he found it if it comes to that. Spencer and I located what we both believe was the hiding place for the cross, and an empty box seems to indicate the cross was stolen, but everything else is based on hearsay."

"Yeah, I know. Sometimes I scare myself." Burke shrugged with a faint grin. "But since your hearsay seems to be on par with other people's facts, I'll risk embarrassment and disgrace, to say nothing of the loss of my pension."

"If you wind up needing a job," Kane said, "I could

use another hand at the ranch. Mucking out stalls or something."

"I'll keep that in mind," Burke told him politely.

LATE THAT NIGHT, cuddled close to Drew's side in their bed and feeling utterly sated in the peaceful aftermath of lovemaking, yet oddly wide awake, Spencer murmured, "You didn't protest when Kane and Tyler decided to fly to Milan first thing in the morning. I thought you would."

He rubbed his chin in her soft hair. "I don't think Stanton will risk going through Milan, and I don't think Kane believes it, either. He just wanted to distract Tyler before she got impatient and decided to try and track down the cross herself."

"Would she?"

"Sure she would. And could. Kane calls her a lightning rod for trouble, and he's right. Of course, he's just the same."

"But he doesn't want to go after the cross?"

"The cross, yes. Stanton, no. He's encountered Stanton at least once that I know of, and he doesn't want Tyler anywhere near the man. Like you, she wouldn't let him go alone." Drew was silent for a moment, then said quietly, "Burke told you, didn't he?"

"Yes." She could feel the steady beat of his heart beneath the hand resting on his chest, and a chill of fear went through her as she thought of how quickly and ruthlessly a life could be snuffed out. "Why didn't you tell me?"

His arms tightened around her. "Because I didn't want you to look at me and know how easily I could kill."

Without hesitation Spencer said, "You could never kill easily, I know that."

"I could kill Stanton."

"Yes. But not easily. Not without it costing you."

Drew was vividly aware of the silk of her skin touching his, the warm aliveness of her body pressed against him, and thought that if Stanton in any way threatened her, killing him would be a very easy thing. He wondered if Spencer had yet realized that his mask of civilization—that any man's—was only a thin veneer of polish over savage instincts that two million years of evolution had failed to tame.

No man was civilized when he loved a woman. Once her brand marked his heart—once her unique scent and taste filled his senses, her eyes looked at him in passion and her body accepted his—all the instincts of the cave were reborn in him. She was his, to be protected and cherished, and he belonged to her body and soul.

Drew wanted to tell her that, wanted to tell her that he loved her. Talking about Stanton had reminded him again of how vulnerable he was to her. Like that thief who had instantly handed over a gold idol and had begged for the lives of his wife and unborn child, Drew knew that if a knife was held to Spencer's throat, he'd do anything. Anything.

Patience was wearing away under the strain of uncertainty. He wanted—needed—to bind her to him with all the words a man could utter, all the hopes and promises and dreams, all the tenderness and potential pain that came with love and need, and life.

She moved against him just then, snuggling closer, and he felt the softness of her belly pressed against his hip. Life, he thought, and a strange sensation that was both yearning and alarm welled up inside him. His child growing inside her delicate body . . . It was possible, he knew. They might already be connected in the most basic and primitive way possible, their very cells merged to form a new life.

Drew made a rough sound, shifting on the bed so that he could kiss her. She responded to his tenderness as instantly as she did to his passion, her lips clinging softly to his, her hands lifting to stroke his face gently. His heart was hammering and he knew his voice was too harsh when he spoke, but he couldn't rein in the surging emotions that forced the words out of him.

"I just realized . . . you could be pregnant."

Spencer went utterly still, her hands motionless against his cheeks, and in the dimness of the room the dark shine of her eyes told him nothing. But she didn't flinch from the abrupt words and harsh tone, and her reply was very soft.

"Yes, I could be." She drew a quick breath, not quite

nervously but a little wary, and added even more softly, "As a matter of fact, I think the timing is right. Or wrong, depending on—on how you feel about it. So much has been happening so fast, and— It wasn't deliberate, Drew."

He lowered his head and kissed her deeply, until her hands slid to his neck and the tension drained from her body. Even then he couldn't stop kissing her, brushing his lips over her face, her throat, and his voice was still rough when he muttered, "We're getting married as soon as we get back to D.C."

She tensed again and whispered, "Because I might be pregnant?"

"No," he said against her throat, and raised his head to look down at her with burning eyes. "Because we belong together. Because I love you so much I'm half out of my mind with it." His own body was rigid, and he went through silent agony in the few seconds it took her to respond.

Spencer made a choked little sound and lifted her head from the pillow, kissing him with warm, trembling lips. "I was afraid to hope you could love me again after what I did to you, and I didn't think you'd want me to love you . . . but I do. I love you, Drew, I love you. . . ."

The relief was staggering, and fierce satisfaction filled him. He held her tightly against him, burying his face in the soft curve of her neck. "I kept telling myself I wasn't going to push you any more than I already had," he said huskily. "You'd been through so much, and I was such a bastard at first that I couldn't expect you to trust me. But I needed to hold on to you because I was so terrified of losing you again. God, sweetheart, I've loved you for twelve years."

She'd been right, Spencer thought in a daze of happiness as his hungry mouth and urgent hands brought her body alive. Losing herself in him was exhilarating when he gave of himself as well. And he did. She had no doubts, now, about what he was feeling. There was nothing coolly detached about him, nothing dispassionate or remote.

He loved her as if this would be his one and only chance, so fiercely tender it made her throat ache. His powerful body trembled with the force of his desire, and the heat of it burned in his eyes even in the darkness. He touched her as if she were infinitely precious and desperately needed, his hands shaking, and his voice was choked with intense emotion when he murmured words of love against her skin.

As always, it was frantic and almost wild, but this time openly expressed love made it even more profound, and the hot, sweet tension that built inside their straining bodies was so acute in its power that when it finally snapped they were hurled into a shattering culmination.

She refused to let him leave her afterward, her arms and legs clinging with what strength was left to them. She was so blissfully happy, so gloriously content that she never wanted to move again. It seemed to her a miracle that he could love her, and she almost held her breath for fear of having imagined it.

Drew brushed his lips tenderly across her closed eyelids and, catching the faint trace of salt at the corners, murmured deeply, "You always cry."

Spencer opened her eyes slowly and smiled up at him. "I can't seem to control that," she admitted. "Does it bother you?"

"It's a little unnerving. Scared the hell out of me the first time. I thought I'd hurt you."

Softly, she said, "I feel so much when you love me that it's almost frightening."

"You aren't alone in that," he said, kissing her. "I love you so much, Spencer. I made the mistake of hiding that before, but I never will again."

She didn't doubt that. Curled up at his side as sleep finally claimed them, she didn't doubt anything at all.

But she had peculiar dreams. Unsettling dreams. In them, Drew was holding her hand and telling her how much he loved her while another voice, a distant voice, kept saying, *"The painting and the statue—I did them both, don't you remember? But years later, when I was old and he was gone. You have to remember, it's very important. And I was English, not Austrian. That's important, too."*

Something had her other hand, pulling it as if trying to get her away from Drew, and she was staring at the face of a clock with huge, crooked numbers and wildly spinning hands. She wanted to look at the clock and think about it, because she had the feeling there was something she should have remembered about it. But that other thing was tugging hard, trying to pull her away from Drew, and the grip of it was cold and cruel.

Then her father's voice, strong and clear as it had been before the stroke, said, *"Behind the clock, Princess. Look behind the clock."*

Spencer pulled her hand free of the cruel grip and turned to Drew, wanting to tell him that she knew now, that she remembered everything, but he kissed her with so much warm tenderness that she forgot again. . . .

chapter eleven

SPENCER MURMURED DROWSILY and opened her eyes with definite reluctance. The room was bright with morning, and Drew was leaning over her.

"Go back to sleep, sweetheart," he said. "It's early."

She looked at him, waking up instantly and feeling her heart turn over with so much emotion that all she could say was, "I love you."

He kissed her again, his face so transformed by tenderness that it moved her almost unbearably. "I love you, too." His voice was husky, topaz eyes glowing.

She had heard the love in his voice in the night, had felt it in his touch, but now she saw it in the light of day and it was a naked thing. She had a curious certainty that Drew's mask of detachment was gone forever now, shattered by the power of the feelings between them. He would never again hide what he felt from her, and he would never again be able to hide what he felt from others.

When he straightened, smiling down at her, she tried to think of something casual to say and found it when she realized he'd been up for some time. "You're dressed."

His mouth twisted slightly. "Not because I want to be. I wouldn't leave you willingly, believe me. Burke called, damn him. He wants me to meet him for coffee downstairs."

Uneasiness stirred in her, a reminder of problems even in happiness. "Trouble?"

Drew shook his head. "He's expecting his men to check in with him in the next hour or so. I should be there, so we'll know what's happening."

"I didn't hear the phone," she commented, and glanced at the clock on the nightstand as she sat up, absently holding the covers to her breasts. "I might as well get up, too."

"What you should do is rest," he told her.

"I don't feel at all tired. Besides, I want to have breakfast with you." She smiled at him. "Why don't you meet Burke, and I'll join you when I've had a shower."

He hated leaving her so much that the thought of spending even a couple of hours out of her presence was almost unbearable, but he was also determined to never again see the painful white exhaustion her delicate face had held in Paris. He'd thought a few extra hours of sleep would be good for her, and it hadn't been his intention to wake her at all. But she was glowing, contentment and love shining in her eyes, and it would have taken a much harder heart and far stronger will than his to refuse her anything.

"All right." He rose to his feet. "We'll be on the terrace. Take your time. Burke needs at least half a pot of coffee before he's reasonably human."

Her soft chuckle followed him out of the room, and he was smiling to himself quite unconsciously as he left the suite and went downstairs. He'd been awake since dawn, just lying there watching her sleep and feeling incredibly lucky. God knew the path had been a rocky one, but they'd made it, and there was a sense of wonder in that. He'd thought of all the future mornings and waking up beside her, feeling her warm body against his, and he was so damned grateful.

He walked through the early-morning quiet of the lobby and went out into the terrace, thinking absently that if the chill in the air was still present when Spencer joined them, they'd go inside for breakfast.

Burke, seated at one of the tables with a pot of coffee and a phone, looked up with a scowl and said sourly, "I hate people who're cheerful at the crack of dawn."

Drew sat down and poured a cup of coffee for himself. "Dawn cracked a couple of hours ago, friend. Are you sitting out here in the cold to stay awake?"

"More or less," Burke admitted, smothering a huge yawn with one hand.

Knowing that the agent tended to go weeks at a time short on sleep and that he'd had little chance to rest since completing the investigation in Madrid, Drew merely said, "If that was your first cup of coffee, drink another one. You're still half asleep."

"Three-quarters," Burke muttered, pouring more coffee. "But awake enough. I got two calls during the night," he added abruptly.

Drew felt tension steal over him. "You didn't tell me that. Trouble?"

"Hell, I don't know." Slouched in his chair, the collar of his black leather jacket standing up to frame a hard jaw and his flying brows drawn together in a frown, Burke looked more like a ruffian than a cop in an international police agency. "One of my guys knows the border as well as his own face, and he got antsy. Said the place Stanton supposedly crossed over into Italy was all wrong, too obvious, nobody on the run would pick it if there was an easier way—and there is, a few miles east. I told him to go check it out if he wasn't happy."

"Did he?"

"He went. I haven't heard from him yet."

"What about the second call?"

"From a cop on this side of the border. He said he wasn't sure he should be calling me at such an ungodly hour, but something had been bothering him. He stopped a car for speeding yesterday—before the bulletin on Stanton went out—and gave the driver a ticket. He didn't think any more about it until he heard the bulletin, and realized from the description that Stanton had been his racing driver."

"So?" Drew stared at his friend. "Stanton was in a hurry."

"Yeah," Burke said softly. "An almighty hurry, according to the cop. But he wasn't making tracks for the border. He was heading for Innsbruck."

Drew frowned. "The cop must have been mistaken."

"Don't think so. I recognized the type even though I was barely awake. Very painstaking and thorough, and he's been patrolling those roads a lot of years. He also described Stanton perfectly, right down to the scars on his face."

"What time yesterday?" Drew asked slowly.

"Eleven-thirty," Burke answered. "The cop gave me the precise location, and I checked it on the map. There's no way Stanton could have crossed the border at noon, at least not where your informant said he crossed. Could your man have been bribed to lie about it?"

"I don't think so—but I don't know for sure."

"In that case, we'd better assume the cop was right. Stanton was still in Austria at eleven-thirty yesterday morning, and he was heading toward Innsbruck."

"That doesn't make sense," Drew objected. "He might want to lie low for a while, but not in Austria."

"Maybe he meant to get out and had some kind of trouble. Or maybe he just meant for us to think he'd gotten out."

After a moment Drew said, "He usually has a hired gun. I suppose he could have sent him over the border, looking the part, in the hope that we'd follow a false trail. But to head back toward Innsbruck . . . Why would he?"

"I can think of one reason," Burke said flatly.

Drew immediately shook his head. "He didn't come back to get me, not with the cross in his hands."

"Are you sure about that?"

"Burke, if there's anything I know, it's that Stanton would never risk something as valuable to him as the cross for the sake of revenge. No matter how much he hates me. And he wouldn't trust a flunky to carry it over the border for him. That means he still has the cross."

Burke looked at him for a long moment, then sighed. "That was my reading. So—the question is, what's the bastard up to?"

Drew was silent, conscious of an itchy sensation between his shoulder blades. It was a feeling he recognized. If you could pinpoint an enemy's location, or at least his direction, you could make certain he wasn't coming up behind to blindside you. Stanton could be anywhere.

Absently, he said, "Kane and Tyler get off all right?"

"Yeah, they left about an hour ago. One of their contacts checked in around midnight, after you and

Spencer had gone to your room, but he didn't have anything."

"So we wait," Drew said.

BITS AND PIECES of her dream came back to Spencer as she stood under the shower, but she could make no sense of them. Something about the statue and a painting and a clock. The images wouldn't come clear in her mind.

Shrugging to herself, she decided to forget about it for the moment. She dried off and got dressed, thinking instead about the night before. In a way, she didn't regret the twelve years behind her and Drew. She *had* been too young for him then, too immature to understand him, too timid to love him as she'd longed to do. If he had married her then, she might never have found any certainty in herself, and he might well have ended up with a woman who was too blinded by the gloss of gold to notice the enduring strength of the metal itself.

Now everything was right between them. In a few short days, it seemed that her entire life had changed. Even with the worries about her father, she had never been happier, and the future looked wonderful.

She was smiling to herself as she went into the bedroom to put her shoes on, humming a little. But when she stepped into the sitting room, a cold shock like nothing she'd ever felt before stopped her in her tracks, and a gasp left her lips.

"Don't do anything stupid," he said softly.

He might, at one time, have been a fairly ordinary-looking man. He was a little above medium height, with exceptionally wide shoulders and a light way of standing that suggested both grace and agility. He was dressed casually. But all semblance of normality ended at his neck. From the collar of his plaid shirt, ugly, angry scars twisted upward, puckering the flesh and virtually covering the right side of his face all the way up to his hairline. A dull black patch angled over his missing right eye, and the left eye that was fixed on her face was as colorless as a glacier and just as icy.

"I once saw him cut a woman's throat."

Spencer swallowed hard, tearing her gaze from his ruined face to look at the gun in his hand. It was pointed squarely between her breasts. She had never imagined anything like the primitive terror that held her immobile as she looked at that deadly weapon, and knew without a shadow of a doubt that the man holding it was entirely capable of killing her as easily and unfeelingly as he'd swat a fly.

"What do you want?" she whispered.

His head cocked to one side and an empty little smile curved his lips. "You know who I am?"

"Yes. You—you're Stanton."

He half bowed in a mockery of courtesy, but the gun never wavered. His voice was utterly without inflection. "I suppose that bastard Haviland told you. Well, no matter. I want what I came here for, Miss Wyatt. The cross."

That surprised her so much that fear was overlaid with confusion. "The cross? But you got to it first."

Stanton laughed shortly. The free hand that had been behind his back moved, and he held up a cross. "I got this."

Spencer looked at it blindly for a moment, seeing only a cross shape roughly twelve by eight inches in size. Then she focused on it, saw that it looked like gold and was encrusted with drab, colored stones. *That's wrong. There are too many stones and the ruby's off center.* The thought came from nowhere, and she accepted it numbly. This wasn't the Hapsburg Cross, not the one her father had described.

"I was in such a hurry I barely looked at it," Stanton said flatly. "For a while. Then I looked. It's a damned fake, and not a very good one at that." With a sudden, vicious fury, he flung it across the room, and it thudded against the wall before dropping to the floor. "I want the real one—and you're going to take me to it."

She'd flinched when he threw the cross, and stared at him in total bewilderment as his demand sunk into her brain. "Take you to it? I thought it was in the cave. That's all I knew, to find the cave. I don't know where the cross is."

"You must know," he said, his tone reasonable now. "You still have Wyatt's original notes. What I had were copies. You kept something to yourself, didn't you? Something about why there was a fake cross instead of the real one. You know how to find the real cross, don't you?"

"No, I . . ." Her voice trailed off as the softly insistent voice in her head said that there *was* something she knew, something she just couldn't remember. Her face must have given her away, because Stanton's empty, colorless eye narrowed.

"I thought so." He cocked the pistol and very matter-of-factly said, "Tell me, or I'll kill you."

Whatever she knew was still elusively trapped in her memory, but Spencer was certain of one thing. Stanton would kill her whether or not she gave him an answer. He'd killed that other woman when he no longer needed her, without hesitation or mercy, and he'd probably killed others as well.

The only hope she had was to stall for time, to keep herself alive long enough to try to escape him, or long enough for Drew to realize something was wrong—

No. No, she didn't want Drew coming after them. He'd said he was never careless, but this would make him careless, she knew. Careless of his own life. He'd do whatever it took to get her away from Stanton safely, and if that meant offering himself as a target the other man wouldn't be able to resist, then that's what he'd do.

She couldn't bear the thought of that. The memory of Stanton killing another woman years ago still haunted Drew; what would it do to him to see it happen all over again, this time to the woman he loved—and perhaps the seed of life inside her?

Spencer looked at Stanton, and though the terror was still cold in her mind, another emotion overpowered it. She wouldn't let this animal hurt Drew like that. She wouldn't. And she wouldn't be another helpless victim sacrificed to his greed. There had to be a way, there *would* be a way to defeat him.

"Tell me!" Stanton barked harshly.

Only seconds had passed, she realized, and her mind worked with the clarity of desperation. Time, she needed time. Clearing her throat, she said, "I don't know where the cross is, but I might be able to figure it out. Something about the statue bothered me when—when I looked at it. I don't know what it was, but I think if I could see the statue again, I might remember."

"You're lying." His finger tightened on the trigger.

Spencer held her voice steady with an effort. "Don't you think if I'd found the cross—or knew for sure where it was—I'd have gotten it and gone back home right away? It's for my father that I came after it, and he's dying. I don't have much time."

A frown made his face even more hideous as he considered her words. "Was there something in the notes I didn't see, or are you just stalling?" he demanded.

She swallowed hard. "Dad got a journal. Just recently. And there were some books I found on my own. There's something about the statue I can't remember. I need to see it."

It would take at least two hours and probably three to

reach the cave, she thought. They'd have to go by horseback, and one horse could never carry them both—
they'd have to take two. That would put at least some
distance between them. She didn't know what advantage it would give her, but she was determined to think
of something.

"All right," Stanton said, smiling in a way that made
nausea rise in her throat. "We'll go up to the cave, just
the two of us. I don't want company. So you're going to
write a note to your lover in case he realizes you're
gone. Tell him something he'll believe."

The phone in there was on the end table beside the
couch and there was a notepad and pen beside it.
Spencer glanced at it, then looked back at Stanton a little helplessly. She couldn't think of a single reason she
would have left the inn without Drew, even though she
tried to.

Impatiently, Stanton said, "Tell him you went off to
buy a gift for your father. And be convincing about it."

She moved slowly and carefully as she got the
notepad and wrote a brief message, very conscious of
the gun trained unwaveringly on her. Stanton told her to
put the pad on the coffee table when she was through,
then ordered her to step back and went over to read the
note himself.

"Touching," he mocked.

She'd had to tell Drew she loved him, though she
kept it simple and without undue emphasis. Looking at
Stanton, she understood at least a part of what Drew felt

for the man, because she was conscious of utter loathing for the first time in her life. It was a horrible feeling.

"Listen carefully," Stanton said in a flat, hard voice. "We're going down the back stairs, and out the side door to the street. I have a car waiting there, which you will drive to the stable. If you say a word, or indicate to anyone at all that you might be in trouble, I'll kill you. Understand?"

"Yes."

She didn't remember the fake cross lying on the floor until they were well on their way, and by then there was nothing she could do about it.

THE PHONE RANG, and Burke picked it up with a quickness that belied his air of sleepy exhaustion. They'd been sitting there, more or less silent, for nearly an hour, drinking coffee and waiting for some word of what was going on. Both men were accustomed to such waits and neither was given to restless gestures or movements; anyone watching would have assumed they were merely contemplating the view, with nothing on their minds more serious than idle interest in the scenery.

Burke just said hello into the receiver and then listened, his narrowing eyes fixed on Drew's face. The silvery sheen of them was unreadable at first, then slowly took on the cold gray of polished steel. When he hung up a few moments later, he was scowling.

"Well?" Drew's voice was very calm, almost unnaturally so.

"We just picked up the man who presumably crossed the border yesterday," Burke reported flatly. "Got him near Milan. He still had the fake scars on his face, and an eye patch stuffed in his pocket. Name's Roger Clay. The computer has a rap sheet on him half a mile long from the States. Mostly small stuff, burglary and forgery."

Drew waited a beat, then said softly, "What else?"

Burke cursed roughly, the words angry and a little baffled. "Clay talked—not willingly, but he talked. Said that he and Stanton were halfway to the border before Stanton took a good look at the cross—and went berserk."

"Why?"

"It was a fake, according to Stanton. He seemed pretty damned sure about it."

Drew stared at his friend, his mind moving with a peculiar sluggishness. A fake? That didn't make sense. Unless someone had found the cave long ago and stolen the real cross. But why go to the trouble of substituting a fake cross after the real one had been taken?

"I don't get it," Burke was saying. "There's no reason why anyone would want to *hide* a fake, especially as carefully and securely as you say this one was hidden."

"I know." Coldness was spreading through Drew's body slowly as a more important realization hit him, and his voice sounded hollow to his own ears when he said, "But that does explain why Stanton would come back here. He'd know it wasn't a trap for him—we couldn't have gotten into that cave before him without leaving evidence that we'd been there. He found a fake cross where the real one should have been, hidden hundreds of years ago. If I were him, I'd suspect that the real cross could still be there, somewhere."

Burke half nodded, frowning. "So, obsessed bastard that he is, he sent his hired thug across the border to buy him some time, and comes tearing back here to look again. But he must figure you're here by now—" Breaking off abruptly, Burke saw Drew's still face drain of blood as if a savage wound had opened up his veins.

"Not me," Drew said. "I didn't grow up listening to Allan Wyatt's stories."

Even as Burke was shoving back his chair and following Drew into the building, he was drawing his gun from the shoulder holster and swearing softly in a bitter monotone. They'd missed it, both of them. Drew had said Stanton wouldn't have come back to Innsbruck with the cross in his hand, but he had come back and that should have warned them to be more alert. It should have told them something was wrong. Once his mind was set on possessing something, Stanton would risk anything, even an attempt to slip past his worst enemy, with his soulless gaze fixed on the one person who might have heard more than she realized about the whereabouts of the cross.

They went up the stairs to the second floor, reaching the suite no more than a couple of minutes after they'd left the veranda. Drew used his key and shoved the door open, calling her name hoarsely. There was no reply. When he stepped into the bedroom, the bed was empty, the covers tumbled. A faint moisture in the air and the scent of Spencer's perfume hinted that she'd had time to shower. Drew checked the bathroom and found it as empty as the rest of the suite.

"Drew?"

He went quickly back into the sitting room, fear winding so tightly in his chest that it felt as if it were crushing him to death. Burke held out a notepad to him and Drew took it, reading the short message. His heart clenched at the final three words, remembering her soft voice speaking them.

"What do you think?" Burke asked.

"No. She wouldn't have left—on her own." Drew looked at him. "He's got her."

Burke had to look away from those suffering eyes. He'd known Drew Haviland a long time, had seen him in brutal situations and dangerous ones. He'd seen him amused, furious, charming, exhausted, deadly quiet, and remote with the iron control that was always a mask over unusually powerful instincts and emotions. Until now, he'd never seen his naked soul, or the clawing terror that only a man who loved a woman could ever feel.

Lon Stanton was a dead man. He'd done the one

thing capable of shattering Drew's reluctance to kill. Burke had no doubt of that at all.

He looked around the room, trying to think. The cave, of course, and from Drew's description it was a bitch of a place for any kind of confrontation. His eyes sharpened, focused on a dull object lying on the floor, and he swiftly crossed over to pick it up. "Drew, look at this."

In a moment Drew was turning the cross in his hands. His hands were rock steady, and when he spoke it was mildly. "A fake, all right."

Burke studied his friend worriedly, fully aware that the quiet voice and seeming calm came, not from control, but from the paralyzing grip of emotions too violent to be mastered. It was just a matter of time before they blew, a matter of time before Drew exploded with a force that would leave everything between him and the man he wanted to kill in a shambles.

God, let her be alive, Burke thought.

He made his own voice even. "They're less than an hour ahead of us. Think, Drew. Is there any way we can get up there before them? There's no time to get a helicopter, even if we could find a spot to land it near the cave. Is horseback the only way?"

Drew nodded slowly, then set the cross on a table near the window and started for the door. "The only way," he murmured. "But I know a faster way."

That didn't make much sense to Burke then, but within an hour he understood. They'd gotten horses—

and a rifle, handed to Drew instantly upon request from the stable owner—and made straight for the mountains. Drew rode fast and Burke, less experienced on horseback, clung to his own mount grimly as he kept up. He thought he was doing pretty well, too. Until the horse ahead of his own turned suddenly to begin a suicidal climb up a jagged, rock-strewn ridge.

Burke realized then what Drew intended to do, and though it appalled him he didn't waste breath or energy trying to dissuade his friend. He was too busy just hanging on.

There was only one way to the cave, a winding route among the high peaks and narrow valleys. No sane man would have attempted any other path. But Drew wasn't sane at the moment, and he wasn't attempting—he was doing.

AS SOON AS they left Innsbruck behind, Spencer knew what her edge was. She just wasn't sure how to use it.

Stanton was a lousy rider. He made her ride ahead of him and kept the gun trained on her constantly, but she'd seen enough to know that he was, at best, a Sunday rider. Experienced enough to be able to stay in the saddle under normal conditions, he swayed unsteadily on the uneven terrain and muttered curses to himself as they began the winding climb up into the mountains.

Spencer had never been more grateful for her own

skills, allowing her body to relax into the horse's movements automatically while her mind worked desperately. The gun he held was no longer cocked. At some point he must have eased the hammer down though she hadn't seen him do it. She didn't know very much about guns, but she thought that might give her an extra fraction of a second before he could shoot her.

Little enough.

Could she spook his horse? The instinct of an inexperienced rider was to hold on tight at any sudden movement; would he drop the gun, or at least grab for the saddle horn, wasting a few precious seconds? If he was unable to control his mount, the horse would behave as startled horses tended to and quite likely bolt. Firing a gun accurately from a racing horse looked easy in the old cowboy movies, but in real life it would be sheer luck if he hit anything.

Like her.

She chewed on her bottom lip as they wound deeper into the mountains, closer and closer to the cave. She kept her shoulders a little hunched, trying her best to convey a beaten, submissive posture that might cause his guard to drop a bit. She tried not to think about Drew, because it hurt so badly to think she might never see him again.

The cave. She had to act before they reached the cave. Once Stanton was on his feet, her chances of getting away from him were virtually nil, and the thought of going into that dark, close place with him at her back was terrifying. In all likelihood she would be walking into her own grave.

Don't think about that, either.

A plan, she needed a plan. She could spook his horse easily enough, and she trusted her ability to control her own mount. But she needed to be able to put distance as well as obstacles between herself and him very quickly. Very, very quickly. Looking around without turning her head, she tried to remember if this was the way she and Drew had come yesterday. It seemed to be.

There was, she remembered, a short, level stretch just before they'd reach the cave. Lots of obstacles all around, between the huge boulders and clumps of trees, and if Stanton could even stay on a bolting horse in that kind of terrain he certainly wouldn't be able to fire a gun accurately.

She hoped.

LYING FLAT ON a rocky knoll, Drew sighted down the barrel of the rifle, scanning from the mouth of the cave above and to his right where he expected to see the riders. His mind was focused totally on the crucial need to hit his target precisely. This time. He wasn't even aware of the man beside him, except with some tiny part of his attention.

"You won't get a second chance," Burke said.

Drew barely heard him, but responded anyway. "I know."

"His track record with hostages . . ." Burke didn't complete that thought, just added in a very grim voice, "Don't let him get his hands on her."

"No," Drew said in a chillingly mild tone, "I won't let him do that."

Burke had just gotten his breathing under control. Going up the side of a mountain had been bad enough; coming down the other side was something that was going to give him nightmares for years to come. He wasn't just surprised they'd survived, he was utterly incredulous.

Drew must have infected both horses with his fury, because they'd bounded down inclines so steep they'd been practically sliding on their rumps, skidding on rock and loose gravel, snorting and grunting with the effort of remaining upright—or some reasonable facsimile of it. There'd been a couple of times Burke could have sworn his own horse had actually been airborne, and he knew there'd been daylight showing between him and the saddle on more than one occasion.

By the time they'd made it down, the horses had been covered with lathered sweat and looked both exhausted and wild-eyed, which wasn't, Burke thought, all that surprising.

Drew's attention had appeared to be fixed only on getting here in time, but as soon as he'd dismounted he had thrust his horse's reins into Burke's hands and said, "Walk them."

Burke walked them. He wasn't a man who took orders easily, but he wouldn't have protested that one even if he'd had the breath to do so. He cooled the horses, muttering to himself and to them, glancing up occasionally to make certain Drew was still there, still waiting on the knoll.

When the horses were reasonably cool and a little calmer, Burke tied them in a small grove of trees as far from the cave as he dared to go, and joined Drew in waiting.

"Any sign of them?" he ventured, not even sure Drew would respond to the question, because the other man's tension was building visibly.

"Not yet." Drew's voice was strained now, and the blue eyes that scanned the area below were like windows to hell.

Burke knew all too well that he had no business letting Drew do this. Aside from the legalities, the man was quite simply in no shape to make reasoning decisions right now. But there were some decisions that would always be made with the heart and the instincts, not the mind. Burke knew that, too.

Besides, Drew was a much better shot.

"There." The strain had intensified in his voice, but there was relief as well, because Spencer was alive.

She was riding ahead of Stanton, Burke saw. They were too far away to allow any reading of their expressions, but she was slumped a bit and appeared both very small and utterly defenseless in the saddle. Any man with half a soul would be angry seeing her like that; it must have gone through Drew like a knife.

He tensed even more, and Burke glanced aside to see one long finger curl over the trigger of his rifle and tighten gently. Because of the winding path the riders were taking, Stanton didn't present a solid target. More often than not, Spencer's body shielded his.

Very softly, Burke said, "First clear shot you have— take him."

Drew didn't respond. He was completely motionless and didn't appear to be breathing at all, his unblinking eyes fixed on the riders coming toward them.

Several things happened very quickly then. In a violent movement, Spencer's horse whirled around on his haunches, half rearing so that his forelegs jarred Stanton's horse—which immediately shied away in an equally violent movement. Stanton didn't drop the pistol he held, but he used the same hand to grab for the saddle horn as his other hand hauled at the reins in an attempt to control his mount.

Without hesitation Spencer reined her horse around hard so that he turned full circle, and dug her heels into the surprised animal's flanks. The horse leaped forward, coming straight toward the knoll at a dead run far too dangerous for the uneven terrain. She was crouched low over his neck, obviously trying to make the smallest possible target of herself as she attempted to reach the nearest stand of trees.

It might have worked, except that Stanton's fury was as great as Spencer's need to escape. With raw strength instead of finesse he held his sidling horse under control, and the hand gripping the pistol raised it with almost blinding speed.

The crack of a rifle preceded the more hollow sound of the pistol by less than a heartbeat.

chapter twelve

SPENCER WAS DIMLY conscious of a crack of sound ahead of her and above, but the blast of the pistol behind her was closer and louder, and she knew she hadn't gotten far enough away to be safe. Something tugged at her sweater and she instinctively flinched to one side, but before she could think about what must have happened, her horse somehow got both front hooves into a ridiculously narrow little rut that he should have taken in stride.

Sometimes, Spencer thought in the instant granted to her, there was just no fairness in the world.

With a squeal, her big gelding pitched forward. There was no possible way to remain on a cartwheeling horse, and it would have been suicidal to try. Spencer's feet kicked free of the stirrups, her hands released the reins and she automatically allowed the horse's momentum to throw her as far away as possible so that he wouldn't fall on top of her. Astonishingly, she landed on her feet.

It had all happened so fast that the echoes of gunfire had barely died, and all Spencer's instincts were screaming at her to run. Still, she couldn't help glancing back over her shoulder, and what she saw surprised her so much that she froze.

Stanton's riderless horse was trotting back the way they'd come, reins trailing. The scarred man was draped over a big boulder, limp and motionless, his gun on the ground.

She stared, vaguely aware of her horse climbing to his feet with a snort. She barely had time to wonder what on earth had happened when a sound jerked her head back around, and she instantly forgot about Stanton. Drew was coming toward her, racing down a rocky slope in reckless haste, a rifle held in one hand. She ran to meet him.

Drew didn't realize that he dropped the rifle as soon as he reached her. All he was conscious of was the warmth and life of her in his arms. He lifted her completely off her feet, both his arms wrapped tightly around her, his face buried in her soft neck. In a hoarse, ragged voice, he murmured her name over and over.

Spencer could barely breathe, but it didn't seem important. She held on to him just as tightly, her arms around his neck, feeling too much to be able to say anything at all. His big, powerful body was shaking as he held her, and she could feel the wetness of his tears on her skin.

"I love you," she said, finally able to speak and saying the only thing that mattered.

"God, Spencer, I thought I'd lost you," he groaned, holding her even tighter. "I was terrified when I realized he had you."

He must have shot Stanton, she realized vaguely. He'd gotten here ahead of them—how had he done that?—and had lain in wait at the top of the knoll. She remembered, now, the sound she'd heard when Stanton had fired his gun—that must have been Drew's shot. She had no doubt that the scarred man was dead, and the only thing she felt about that was relief.

"I love you," Drew whispered, lifting his head to kiss her almost roughly.

She kissed him back, her response fervent, and when she could she said, "He thought I could take him to the cross, and all I could think of to do was stall and hope I could get away from him. I didn't know you'd be here—"

He kissed her again, then eased her down until her feet touched the ground. A faint smile curved his mouth, though he was still pale and strained. "You did a good job of shaking him up long enough for me to get a clear shot."

"I wasn't going to let him win if I could help it," she said intensely. "He'd already hurt you too much."

"If he'd hurt you . . ." Drew held her for a moment longer, still so shaken by how nearly he'd come to losing her that he knew he wouldn't be able to let her out of his sight for a long time to come. He had thought losing her ten years ago had been hell, but that was nothing compared to the mind-shattering terror of knowing she was in the hands of a man who would have killed her.

Of the two of them, it was Spencer who'd come through the past few hours in the best shape. She was smiling up at him, a little pale but calm. God, she'd taken a hellish chance by trying to escape Stanton, but the attempt had shown both courage and steely determination. She was far from being a helpless woman despite her slight delicacy, not waiting to be rescued by anyone or anything except her own skills.

And when she loved, it was clear that she loved with everything inside her. In her resolve to protect *him* from further hurt, she'd apparently thought little about her own safety.

Drew kept an arm around her as Burke approached them realizing that the other man had picked up the rifle and gone to check on Stanton. The slight nod he gave was a definite answer to Drew's inquiring look.

"How did you get here ahead of us?" Spencer asked, both her arms around Drew's waist as she gazed up at him.

Burke snorted before Drew could reply. "Remind me to answer that—in great detail—when you've got a few hours to listen. Doesn't matter when—that's one trip I won't forget if I live to be a hundred."

"What do you mean?" she asked, puzzled.

Burke glanced at Drew, who was frowning a little, then said a bit dryly, "We came over the mountain." He went to get his and Drew's horses, muttering to himself.

"Over—" Spencer stared after him, then looked up at Drew. "You came over the mountain. *That* mountain?"

"I guess we did," Drew said, not looking around at the mountain in question. He honestly didn't remember getting here.

"You could have been killed!"

"No," he said. "I had to get to you."

Spencer gazed up at him for a long moment, then buried her face against his chest. Her throat was aching, and in her mind was a kind of numb wonder. She held on to him tightly, feeling his arms close around her and his cheek rub gently against her temple. She wanted to say, *You can't love me that much!* but she knew that he did, and the miracle of that held her speechless.

Burke returned to find them standing just that way, motionless, and even though he was a sympathetic man he was also trying to think of how he was going to explain all this to his superiors, so his voice was a bit wry when he spoke.

"Since Stanton's horse ran off and we can't double up going back to Innsbruck, I vote we leave now so I can send somebody back up here before dark."

Spencer turned her head toward him a little blindly.

"I should look at the statue," she murmured. "Something about it is still bothering me, and since he didn't get the real cross—"

Drew shook his head. "We can come back up here tomorrow if you want."

She agreed to that, partly because she couldn't face the thought of climbing up the cliff after everything that had happened today. Reaction was setting in. She felt shaky and, more than anything else, just wanted to spend quiet time with Drew.

Her horse turned out to be uninjured from the fall, and since the other two horses were weary they rode slowly back down from the mountain to Innsbruck. The stable owner—whose other horse had come home some time before—accepted Burke's brief statement that the rifle, which he was holding, would be returned to him later. It wasn't until then that Spencer considered the possible legal problems of what had happened in the mountains.

It was Drew who mentioned the subject as they entered the inn. "Are you going to have trouble because of this?" he asked Burke quietly.

The Interpol agent smiled. "Nothing I won't be able to handle. Of course, it would have been easier if we'd been able to get our hands on the real cross."

Spencer looked at him steadily. "Will there be any charges against Drew?"

"No. I'm a witness to the fact that Stanton was trying to kill you. Don't worry, nobody's going to waste any pity on the likes of him." He looked back at Drew. "I'll take care of the questions, at least for today."

"I'd appreciate that," Drew said. "I'm taking Spencer up to the suite, and if anybody other than room service knocks on the door before tomorrow morning, they'd better have a damned good reason."

His voice had been quite mild, but Burke thought as he went looking for a phone that he'd make certain he didn't disturb them, at least. He wasn't a fool.

Drew wanted to take care of Spencer. It was early afternoon; she hadn't eaten today, and even though she was still calm he knew that everything was catching up with her. He wanted to baby her, to keep her close and fuss over her, and just delight in cherishing her. So when he led her into their suite, that's what his mind was fixed on. Taking care of her.

"Why don't you change into something comfortable, while I order some food?" he suggested.

She stood on tiptoe to kiss his chin, smiling. "I think I'll take a shower, too. Wash away the dirt."

A sudden thought made Drew's fingers tighten around hers. She didn't look as if she'd been hurt and there were no marks on her that he could see, but he was too familiar with Stanton's ruthless methods to rule out the possibility.

"Sweetheart, he didn't hurt you, did he?"

"No, he never even touched me. I'm fine, Drew, really." She squeezed his hand and then released it, going into the bedroom to undress for her shower.

He went and got the room-service menu, but because she was out of his sight and he couldn't bear it, he went to the doorway of the bedroom thinking that he'd ask her what she felt like eating. He stopped there, a shock jolting through him.

Spencer was standing by the bed, neatly made now since housekeeping had been and gone hours before. She'd pulled her sweater off and was holding it in her hands, looking down at it in faint surprise. As he watched she slowly put one slender finger through a ragged bullet hole.

"My God," Drew breathed.

She looked up quickly and started to cover the hole with her hand as if to hide it from him. Then, in a voice that was trying hard to be light, she said, "He missed, after all. Close only counts in horseshoes."

Drew threw the menu aside and went to her, pulling her into his arms frantically. She was *here,* he told himself, safe and unharmed, but the visible evidence of how terribly close that bullet had come to hitting her was like a knife inside him. He had to hold and touch her, to feel the reality of her warm body against his and the fiery, astonishing strength of her passion. As always, she was instantly responsive, her mouth lifting for his, arms wreathing around his neck as she pressed herself even closer.

The bullet-torn sweater fell to the floor and was soon hidden from sight beneath the jumble of clothing that followed it.

*   *   *

"I'M GOING TO get fat if you keep feeding me like this," Spencer remarked nearly two hours later as she finished the very belated lunch Drew had ordered.

"You barely eat enough to keep a bird alive," he retorted, smiling at her.

She chuckled, but pushed herself back from the table and wandered over to pick up the fake cross. He turned his chair to watch her, knowing that, despite her contentment with him, the loss of the cross was a painful disappointment. She hadn't said anything about it, but he knew her well enough by now to be able to read her smoky eyes.

Right now, they were distracted.

"Something's bothering you about that cross," he said.

"Yes. And, like the statue, I don't know what. I keep thinking there's something I should remember." She paused, turning the cross slowly in her hands, then said, "Why would anyone hide a fake?"

"They wouldn't. It doesn't make sense." Drew might have said more, but the phone rang and he went to answer it. He spoke absently in German, watching her, then switched to English and said, "She's right here, Tucker. Is everything all right?"

Spencer went to him quickly, reassured by his smile as he listened to whatever Tucker had to say. He handed her the phone a moment later, and her relief in-

tensified when she heard that her father was fine—
stronger, in fact—and that his doctor was cautiously
optimistic.

"Your father hasn't said anything more about it, but
I found the journal, Miss Spencer," Tucker said.

"I suppose it's in German," she said dryly.

"No. English."

She felt tension steal over her. "Whose journal is it,
Tucker?"

"A lady by the name of Theresa Garland. The entries
cover the years from 1648 to 1650. I've had no chance
to read it yet, but I can tell you that she lived in Innsbruck, at least during those years."

Garland. Theresa Garland. It sounded familiar.
"Oh—she was Kurt's sweetheart. And she—" Staring at
Drew, Spencer suddenly remembered. "She did that
painting of him. Tucker, when you get a moment, start
reading the journal, would you, please?"

"What am I looking for?" Tucker asked.

"Anything about the cross. She knew about it, knew
Kurt had taken it. She had to. Let me know if you find
anything."

"I will."

Spencer hung up the phone and then sat down on the
couch, frowning. She put the fake cross on the coffee
table before her and stared at it. When Drew came to sit
beside her, she told him what Tucker had found, repeat-
ing her realization that Theresa Garland had been Kurt's
portraitist.

"I've never heard of a female artist during that era," Drew commented slowly.

"I hadn't, either. I guess that was why it stuck in my mind. She painted his portrait—and she sculpted that statue."

"Are you sure?"

"That's what was bothering me. When we were in the cave you said something about different artists interpreting subjects in different ways. What I'd been thinking was that the statue was the image of that painting I'd seen—and it is. Two different artists working in different mediums could never have gotten the statue and painting so precisely alike."

Drew nodded. "Okay, you've sold me. What does it mean?"

Spencer laughed a little. "I was hoping you could tell me." She thought about it. "Theresa painted the portrait sometime around 1650. The journal Tucker found covers 1648 to 1650. But that was years after Kurt died."

"And after the Thirty Years' War," Drew noted. "Didn't it end around 1648?"

"Yes." Spencer brooded, frowning at the fake cross lying before her.

Trying to help her, Drew said, "You thought the journal might be important because Allan seemed to be fretting about it. But Tucker didn't understand him because he was speaking German."

Absently, Spencer said, "Yes, and if you talk in your sleep it'll probably drive me crazy. If Dad's any example, multilingual people run the gamut of their languages whenever their conscious mind isn't in control."

"I don't talk in my sleep."

She sent him a glance that was a little amused. "We'll see, won't we?"

"Never mind," Drew murmured, hoping his subconscious could keep its mouth shut. "The point is that Allan must have read the journal. So what could he have found in Theresa Garland's writings to tell him something about the cross?"

Spencer went very still suddenly. "Wait a minute. Before I left home Dad said something I didn't understand. I thought he was rambling, so I didn't really pay attention."

"What did he say?"

She closed her eyes, concentrating. "It was so disjointed. Something about . . . the cross not being what I thought. Something about them hiding it—like the clock." Her eyes snapped open, and she looked at Drew.

"The clock? What clock?"

Spencer had the strangest feeling. It was like that song she couldn't remember, only now the tune was getting louder, and the words were falling gently into place. "That's what he meant," she murmured. "Drew, he knew we'd find a fake. He knew it was a deception— just like his trick safe."

"The real thing was behind the clock," Drew said, realizing. "A little sleight of hand, to fool would-be thieves. But why would Kurt have gone to all that trouble? The cave alone would have kept the cross secure, certainly long enough for him to go back and retrieve it later."

"Yes, but . . . what was bothering Dad must have been written in that journal thirty years after Kurt died." Her mind was working rapidly now, considering possibilities. "Suppose that Kurt did just put the box holding the real cross in the cave, and told Theresa where he'd hidden it."

"That makes more sense," Drew agreed, watching her. "Since he planned to get it later, he wouldn't have bothered with anything fancy."

"Right. But then the priest was killed, and Kurt died after nursing Theresa. She was the only one left who knew where the cross was hidden."

Drew nodded slowly. "It wouldn't have been wise to go and get it since it was stolen property."

"And she might not have wanted anyone else to know for sure that Kurt had stolen it. Whatever else he was, it seems clear he was devoted to her. She certainly loved him—that comes across in the painting. So she has this worrying knowledge of the cross, just lying there in the cave. It belongs to the Hapsburgs, and it should get back to them—eventually, at least. But she can't bear to brand Kurt a thief, not while she's alive and able to see it happen, anyway."

Drew, who had discovered many such tragic stories while unearthing antiquities over the years, didn't find it at all far-fetched. He did find it fascinating, and even more so to watch Spencer work it all out. "I wonder who helped her get the statue up there?" he mused. "Allan did say 'they' had hidden it, didn't he?"

Spencer nodded. "I remember that distinctly. It had to be someone she trusted. I'm not sure why she would have thought up the trick, though. To keep casual thieves from getting the cross if they found the cave?"

"That sounds likely. Maybe her journal will tell us."

It hit Spencer then. The cross. The elusive relic her father had spent his life in pursuit of—and they'd found it. Together, her father, Drew and herself, each of them supplying bits and pieces of fact and intuition, had located a priceless object nearly five hundred years old.

She held her hands out before her as if holding something on her palms, and murmured, "Behind the clock. Behind the deception." Slowly, one of her hands turned, and a finger pointed at her middle.

"In the statue," Drew said softly.

Spencer laughed unsteadily and looked at him with glowing eyes. "We found it. Drew, we found it!"

"You found it," he said, drawing her into his arms. "You and Allan." He had no doubt that the cross would be there, where it had waited for centuries.

"Dad did most of the work, but you—if you hadn't been with me, it never would have happened." Her delicate face changed, and one hand lifted to touch his cheek. "So much never would have happened. I love you."

"I love you, too, sweetheart," he said, holding her next to his heart where she belonged.

*   *   *

THE AUSTRIAN AUTHORITIES were delighted the following afternoon when Spencer and Drew returned from a final trip into the mountains with a solid-gold cross studded with rubies and diamonds. The Hapsburg Cross.

Since Spencer already had permission to take the cross to the States for her father to see, and since she and Drew asked nothing more than that, they were able to leave Innsbruck the next day. The authorities had decided not to announce the find publicly just yet, so that Spencer and Drew could transport the cross quietly without being bothered by collectors or the media.

One week to the day after Spencer had flown away from D.C. strained, miserable, lonely and afraid, she quietly entered her father's bedroom. Drew was behind her, and in her hands she carried a heavy wooden box.

"Daddy?" she said softly. "We have something to show you."

SHE LEANED AGAINST the parapet and looked out on the lush green Welsh countryside, taking advantage of the bright sunlight and still-warm breeze. The weather could change, Drew had warned her, and probably would since it was early fall. They'd feel the chill of stone walls then, he had said wryly.

Spencer was rather looking forward to that, even

though unobtrusive central heating would no doubt pre-
serve only the illusion of the hardships of an earlier age.
In any case, her surroundings suited her very well.

It had been two months since she and Drew had left
Innsbruck, and six weeks since their quiet wedding. Her
father had been present—in a wheelchair. Holding his
dream in his hands had done more for his health than
any amount of medical care, and though he was still
frail, his doctors were confident.

So was Spencer. Allan Wyatt had stood off the
grim reaper long enough to see the cross, and he'd
continue to battle, she believed, in order to hold his
first grandchild. In fact, if she had anything to say
about it, he might well hang on a good many years
yet, if only to see how many grandchildren he eventually ended up with.

Spencer wanted four children, at least. Drew had
suggested two and Allan, chuckling, had advised them
to split the difference. But Spencer was determined. She
had discovered just how determined she could be—and
so had Drew. Not that he appeared to mind her stub-
bornness.

Strong arms closed around her from behind, and
warm lips briefly kissed the nape of her neck. "Here
you are," Drew said in a chiding tone. "I've been looking for you nearly an hour."

She leaned back against him, smiling. "You should
have tried here first," she told him.

"I should have—especially since I specifically told

you not to come here alone because half these stones are crumbling."

"I was careful," she said serenely. "Besides, I needed some fresh air."

Drew hugged her, then slid one hand down over her still-flat belly. "How's she doing?"

Though morning sickness hadn't troubled Spencer very much, there were occasional bouts of nausea—and a tendency to get sleepy, which was another reason Drew worried about her being up here alone.

Spencer tilted her head back and looked up at him, amused. "She? You're convinced this one's a girl, aren't you?"

"Absolutely positive," he said.

"What makes you so sure?"

He smiled. "Just a feeling."

"Umm. Well, then, *she* is doing just fine. In fact, she's very impressed at being in a real castle. With a real moat and drawbridge. She's already spoiled rotten."

Drew laughed.

"I'm serious," Spencer said severely, trying not to laugh. "How on earth is any other man ever going to be able to live up to her father? Talk about a Cinderella complex!"

"Princess?" Drew was still smiling. "I thought I'd cured you of that nonsense, sweetheart."

She turned in his arms and reached up to touch his face, her eyes suddenly tender. "It isn't nonsense. The problem is that girls get silly ideas of what a prince is.

But if they're lucky—very, very lucky—they grow up and find the real thing."

Drew kissed her, then kept an arm around her as he led her back into the castle. He wasn't a prince, but he no longer minded if Spencer thought he was. With a woman like her by his side, loving and loved, being a man was all that counted.

author's note

TO MY KNOWLEDGE, there exists no Hapsburg Cross. All historical characters mentioned in connection with this mythical object are either figments of my imagination or else—like Maximilian I—merely recognizable names with which I wove the threads of my story.